BACK IN YOUR ARMS

Sandra Kitt
Deirdre Savoy
Celeste O. Norfleet

BET Publications, LLC
http://www.bet.com
http://www.arabesquebooks.com

ARABESQUE BOOKS are published by

BET Publications, LLC
c/o BET BOOKS
One BET Plaza
1900 W Place NE
Washington, DC 20018-1211

All Kensington Titles, Imprints, and Distributed Lines are available at special quantity discounts for bulk purchases for sales promotions, premiums, fundraising, and educational or institutional use. Special book excerpts or customized printings can also be created to fit specific needs. For details, write or phone the office of the Kensington special sales manager: Kensington Publishing Corp., 850 Third Avenue, New York, NY 10022, attn: Special Sales Department, Phone: 1-800-221-2647.

Library of Congress Control Number: 200593142
ISBN: 1-58314-689-X

First Printing: January 2006

10 9 8 7 6 5 4 3 2 1

Printed in the United States of America

Contents

Love Changes Everything

Sandra Kitt

Prologue

"We're taking off, Bro."

Carter Morrison, who'd been quietly observing the poised woman in conversation on the other side of the room, turned at the announcement to find two men and a woman waiting to say good-bye. He'd met them before, years earlier, and knew them by name. They were colleagues of his best friend, Benson Haley.

"Gotta get back to work," the second man said apologetically.

"Hey, glad you could make it. Sorry we had to meet up again under these circumstances," Carter said, shaking the hands offered him by the two men.

"This is rough, but Grace seems to be holding up," the first man observed.

"She'll be fine," Carter said confidently.

"Benson was a great guy," the second man added. "I didn't know what to say. Wished her well. You know."

"I still can't believe he's gone," said the woman, shaking her head in disbelief. "One minute he's making all kinds of plans for the mayor this fall, and then he just—"

"It's a tough thing to say, but the mayor is going to fill Benson's spot and move right on," Carter cut in quietly, not wanting to hear again the blunt way in which his friend's sudden death was being described.

Benson Haley had dropped dead at the feet of three reporters while making a statement on behalf of his boss, the mayor.

"I know you're right, my man, but it's not going to be so easy for Grace. She's got two young kids, a house, a mother-in-law. Damn," the first man muttered and then looked shame-faced at his blasphemy. "They haven't been married all that long, right?"

"Eight years," Carter replied.

"Well, at least they had that. Hardly anyone stays together that long anymore," the woman commented. She then caught the gaze of one of her companions, who silently signaled not to go there.

Carter didn't have to watch the exchange to know where the remark was coming from. The innuendo was not unreasonable, but it was off base. He'd heard some of the rumors that the deceased had stepped out once or twice on his wife but didn't know if they were true or not. Nonetheless, the thought caused Carter to shift his attention and covertly scan the room. He spotted the object of their discussion, Benson's widow, Grace, standing near an occasional table that was top heavy with an extravagant floral arrangement from the mayor himself. Appearing serene, if a bit tired, she was listening and smiling benignly at the emotional testimony of her late husband's assistant.

"Benson said something recently about you moving back to New York from . . ."

"Chicago," Carter responded, bringing his gaze around to the trio, watching as they searched for and found the tickets to retrieve their coats on their way out of the midtown club. "Not just yet. I'm doing some important work there, for the moment."

The first man chortled. "Chicago? Too damn cold," he said, once again catching his irreverence too late.

"Maybe he has family there," the woman suggested to her companion.

"I don't," Carter corrected. "I just can't make a move right now."

"Give me a call when you come back," said the woman, smiling at Carter coyly. "Let's get together."

"Yeah, let's do that," one of the men added.

Carter watched until all three had left the salon before turning to look for Grace once more, Benson's former friends immediately forgotten.

She was shaking the hand of a relative from Benson's side of the family and kissing another, who was also preparing to leave. Then a couple, neighbors from the Westchester enclave where Grace and Benson lived, approached, waiting for Grace's attention. Carter silently monitored the interaction and her response. While Grace appeared sad and pensive—even numb with grief, which was perfectly understandable—it was hard for him to tell how she was really doing under the strain of the last week.

He tried to imagine what it must have been like getting the call that notified Grace of her husband's collapse while at work and then rushing to the hospital an hour later, only to be told he was already gone. Carter wondered how she'd felt learning that Benson had died almost instantly, felled by an aneurysm, even before the call to her had been placed. Afterward, she would have had the terrible task of calling her mother-in-law, Marjorie, to tell her that her only child, her beloved, handsome, and brilliant son, was dead. And there was Grace herself. How was she doing?

Carter looked at the time and checked out the remaining guests. He saw Grace's father, Ward Mathison, chatting and laughing with several former classmates of both Benson and Grace from NYU, where they'd gotten their undergraduate degrees, and where they'd met. Ward caught his gaze and nodded briefly, continuing with his conversation. Carter paced along the side of the room, thinking that he should leave as well. He guessed that after a week of ceremony, testimony, tears, and the prevailing shock that hovered over everyone, Grace probably just wanted to be alone.

Grace's simple two-piece black ensemble made her look elegant and slender, and offset her tan complexion. Her only make-up, lipstick, had worn off during the last few hours. Her hair, which was as long as when he'd first met her five years earlier, was brushed back from her face and rolled into a neat twisted knot at the back of her head. She wore no other jewelry besides her engagement and wedding rings, and both sparkled on her left hand, an ever-present reminder. She had been appropriately named, Carter thought, as she *grace*fully handled everyone else's surprise, grief, and memories. What would she do with her own?

Carter raised his gaze to Grace's face to find her studying him as well. He looked for signs of distress but saw only wide-eyed bewilderment, a kind of stunned appeal. Their mutual regard narrowed the distance between them across the salon, but only for a few seconds as someone else claimed her. He watched as Grace sat with the guest, patiently attentive while they expressed their condolences about her husband.

Carter stood alone. He knew he should be leaving. He wasn't sure what more he could do here now that the memorial service was over. But something kept him slowly circulating around the room, reluctant to say good-bye. He looked around for Benson's mother, Marjorie. Not seeing her, he was sure that she was sitting alone somewhere, closeted with her pain. He'd always liked Marjorie. Perhaps she was a little too devoted and maternal, a bit too much the stage mother to an ambitious son, but Carter admired what she'd managed as a single parent. She'd raised a son and kept him out of the seductive clutches of street life and away from other bad influences.

Suddenly, Carter saw Marjorie emerge through a door that he thought led to a small library in the vast complex of the club. She was blowing her nose in a wad of tissues balled in her hand. A stout woman of average height and in her sixties, Marjorie was considered a pretty and curvaceous woman in her youth. She had given her life to nurturing her only child, and with him gone, Carter knew Marjorie had aged virtually overnight. She straightened her

6

back, but her shoulders were still curved from the weight of her loss. The perfect hairdo of her stylish wig was the only thing about Marjorie that was not in disarray.

"Can I get you anything?" Carter asked, placing a solicitous hand on Marjorie's back and bending slightly toward her.

"All that food going to waste. It's a shame, but I really couldn't eat a thing," Marjorie said, looking distressed at the very idea.

"Why don't you sit down? I'll get you something to drink. How about hot tea?"

Marjorie nodded and gave her consent with an absent gesture of her hand.

Carter walked silently across the carpeted floor. The room seemed so much bigger now that most of the guests had left. On his way, he once again searched out Grace. Finding her, he could see the first signs that the long afternoon, indeed the past ten days, was taking its toll. He could detect strain between her eyes and a tightening of her mouth, which prohibited a natural smile. She was absently twisting her wedding ring round and round her finger, sliding it up to the knuckle before pushing it back into place. Halfway across the room, Carter hesitated a moment before continuing. At the console table, which was laden with light refreshments, Carter poured hot water and made a cup of tea for Marjorie Haley. He carefully carried it back to her. After a moment's hesitation, he took a seat by her side.

"Thank you, Carter," she murmured. Her voice was hoarse and deep from crying. "I appreciate that you stayed to help with everything."

Carter took her hand. "Benson was my best friend. He knew I'd do anything for him. I'm sorry that it came down to this."

"Yes," Marjorie said, her voice warbling and her hand trembling around the cup of tea.

"You're going to be fine," he soothed.

Marjorie raised her head proudly, her eyes red and watery and filled with despair. "The good Lord willing. He saw fit to take my child, but I'm blessed to have Madison and Becca. I don't know what I'd do without my grandbabies."

"And Grace," Carter added, watching the older woman. "You know she'll be there for you always."

"We'll see," Marjorie said cryptically.

"I wish there was something more I could say to you besides I'm sorry. Benson was a good man, and he did you proud."

"He could have become a judge one day," Marjorie prophesied. "Maybe a state senator."

"Maybe." He glanced around. There were only a handful of people left, but Grace was nowhere in sight. He stood up. "Will you be all right for a while? I'm going to check to make sure that everything's taken care of."

Marjorie silently nodded as she sipped her tea.

Carter headed to the same room that Marjorie had appeared from, but it was empty, as were the two small alcoves next to the fireplace. He proceeded through a passageway leading to a series of rooms. One was being used as a staging area for the preparation of the refreshments for Benson's memorial service. A second room housed a photocopier, fax machine, and several cartons of paper. The door of the third room opened, and a man stepped out, closing it behind him. He was carrying a sheaf of documents as he walked toward Carter.

"Yes?" the man inquired, raising his brows and blocking Carter's way.

"I'm looking for Mrs. Haley," Carter responded.

"She's in my office, but I don't think she wants to see anyone just now. It's been an emotional day."

"Yes, it has. I'm a close friend of the family. I want to make sure she's all right."

"She seemed a little weary so I gave her my office for some privacy. Can I help you with anything?"

Carter was amused that the man, in his own way, was being protective of Grace by running interference. "I'm just going to let her know I'm leaving."

The man finally acquiesced and stepped aside. Carter waited until he had gone before reaching for the door. From within the room came the low but distinct sound of Grace crying. For a moment Carter considered leaving, weighed down with the feelings of loss, even his own. But as the sounds became more plaintive and heart-breaking, he went against what was perhaps the best thing to do under the circumstances. He opened the door and quietly slipped inside.

Grace was sitting, ironically, on a love seat positioned next to the door. She was hunched forward with her elbows on her knees, her shoulders shaking as she sobbed into a tissue. It was pressed against her mouth, held in place by both hands. Her eyes were closed, but tears leaked beneath the lids to trail down her cheeks and through her fingers. For a moment Carter could do nothing but watch help-lessly, mesmerized and miserable as he bore witness to what she was going through.

His jaw and throat tightened, and he felt a sudden anger, which took him by surprise. He stood in front of Grace and squatted down on his haunches. He was so close to her that he could see the veins in her temple, filled with the coursing blood of stress and emo-tion. He could smell the faint but fragrant scent of her perfume. The tissue she held was sodden. Carter looked around for a box of Kleenex and placed it next to her on the sofa. He pulled several fresh ones from the top and carefully touched Grace's hand to give them to her.

She jumped, her crying abruptly cut off as she opened her eyes, startled to find him there. Carter put his hands on her arms, gently rubbing them to calm her. She stared at him, her eyes wide, slightly red, and watery.

"I'm sorry I scared you," Carter said softly. "I wanted to make sure you were okay."

Grace suddenly got up from the sofa, stumbling away to stand next to a massive oak desk. Her chin trembled, and her eyes filled with fresh tears. "I'm not okay," she said tightly.

Carter stood up. "I'm sorry," he said, feeling foolish. She began crying again. "I know this is hard for you, Grace. Benson was a great guy. . . ." She turned away from him. "I wish there was something I could do. . . ."

With a great wrenching sob, Grace turned and looked at Carter. The expression on her face was more than he could stand. He barely had time to think about what he was doing before he opened his arms. Grace stepped into them and allowed him to hold her. Her crying was quiet now, but just as intense and poignant. Carter applied everything he could think of to comfort her. He slowly rocked back and forth. He softly murmured sympathetic but unintelligible words. He rubbed a comforting circle on her back. He closed his eyes, fully experiencing the weight of her in his arms. He pressed her face to his chest, absorbing her anguish as he fought his own.

"You loved him very much, didn't you?" he found himself asking, holding his breath as he awaited an answer.

There was no response from Grace beyond her turning her head to rest a cheek against his jaw. The warm fanning of her breath was against his neck. That was, oddly, enough for Carter.

Neither of them heard the office door quietly open and then close a moment later.

One

"Grace, it's Brian. Come in."

"Yes, Brian. I'm here."

"I thought I'd let you know what's going on. We have a few problems."

Grace Haley moved slowly and unnoticed on the periphery of the crowded party as she answered the call on her walkie-talkie. She was on duty at the evening gala, overseeing the arrangements and details, while three hundred formally dressed guests were occupied with boisterous conversation and laughter. Their collective joie de vivre was fueled by several open bar stations, as well as unlimited glasses of champagne being served by a circulating waitstaff. The din was so loud that the music of the quartets playing at each end of the hall could barely be heard. Grace pressed her earphone tightly to hear above the noise.

"Go ahead," she said, talking as discreetly as she could, hoping not to draw attention to herself.

"The ladies' room outside the hall is out. I'll have to close it off until maintenance can deal with a malfunctioning stall."

"Get a sign up as soon as you can. We'll reassign the men's room to the ladies for the rest of the night and direct the men to the lower-level restrooms."

"Okay."

"And let the attendants on duty know ASAP about the change so they can inform guests looking for the facilities."

"I've already notified the supervisor. . . ."

Grace positioned herself in the shadow of the Ionic pillars just inside the entranceway to the hall, where a meet-and-greet reception was being held for employees and guests of a large financial institution. She'd passed by several times, checking out the arriving guests. She was familiar with the sponsoring company and knew one of the employees from an affiliate office.

From where she stood, she could also take in most of the main hall and the attendees. Her gaze roamed absently over the gathering. In a brief parting of several people across the open space, she suddenly caught a fleeting glimpse of a tall black male guest and did a double take. A sudden stomach spasm signaled recognition. Then she lost sight of him.

". . . Arranged beforehand."

"Sorry, Brian. Say that again," Grace instructed, searching for that face that had stirred to life part of her past, giving rise to disturbing and conflicting feelings within her.

"I said one of the corporate bigwigs wanted to know if the guests could walk through the exhibits on the main floor. I told them it wasn't possible because there wasn't adequate security on duty to cover those areas."

"Good response, but tell the attendants to keep an eye out, anyway. So far, everything seems to be going well," Grace commented while she began her slow patrol again. She observed the guests intently, even as she wondered if she'd imagined what she thought she'd seen.

"So far. We've had the usual stuff happen. Spilt drinks and squashed canapés, glasses and plates left all over the place. Somebody got sick near the corridor to Gallery 3, but it's been cleaned up."

"Thanks," Grace said, giving up her search. She'd made a mistake. "I'll be outside the rotunda as the guests are directed to dinner. I'll notify the caterers to begin breaking down the bar as soon as the hall is empty. Is that everything?"

"Caught a couple who'd sneaked into one of the exhibition halls."

"Nothing embarrassing, I hope."

Grace watched as a tuxedoed staffer from the communications office maneuvered his way to her, silently indicating a need to talk with her.

"I'm told it was limited to kissing and hugging. . . ."

"Brian, hold on a minute. What is it?" she asked the staffer.

"Sorry to interrupt. There's someone who says he'd like to speak with you. He's over there."

He pointed, but all Grace could see was a densely packed group of people engaged in their own conversations.

"What about?"

"He didn't say."

"Did he give you his name?"

"No, but I think I can take you to him."

Grace shook her head. If it was important, if it was who she thought, he'd find her again. She held up her hand to the staffer.

"I can't leave now. If you see the gentleman again, give him my apologies. Maybe Steve Milton can help him. Steve should be with the caterers."

"I'll go check," the staffer said as he walked away. At that moment she could hear a gong being sounded to signal to the guests that they were to proceed to another hall for the formal sit-down dinner.

Grace spoke again into her walkie-talkie. "Brian, I have to go."

"One more thing. Security has calculated that there are probably fifty to seventy-five more attendees than the guest list allowed for. I had two of my staff using counters as people checked in."

"Review the numbers, and give the development office a head

count in the morning. Let them decide what to do about any added expense."

When Grace finished relaying instructions, she was already in motion, hurrying off to make sure the guests were being properly ushered into dinner. She tried not to let her attention wander.

She stood to the side as the main hall emptied and the guests filed past her into the rotunda. She allowed herself a few moments to study the beautifully dressed women while indulging in a private game of picking out the dresses she liked the best. She smiled to herself as she also realized that she no longer had occasion to wear anything so elegant. While she was nicely dressed in a simple, black, cocktail-length dress appropriate for the event, she certainly couldn't compete with the glamorous women guests decked out in expensive designer gowns.

It took almost twenty minutes for everyone to find their table and then covertly switch places with one another as invariably happened. The caterers then served the first course, offering each guest a choice of red or white wine with dinner. The noise dropped to a low hum, and Grace breathed a sigh of relief. She'd managed to keep things moving through half the evening without any serious mishap or griping by the sponsors.

Part of Grace went into a new alert mode as she took in the seated guests. She resisted the urge to try and identify any one person. Ten minutes into the first course, she signaled for the attention of a technician, waiting discreetly behind a screen with the audio-visual equipment to make sure the microphones were ready for use.

At one of three main tables where the corporate higher-ups and their wives were prominently seated, one man suddenly stood up. Grace automatically turned her attention to him. The lights were very low, and the room was softly illuminated by cleverly designed centerpiece candles on each table. She could not see his features clearly but didn't need to. She experienced instant recognition and a feeling that was akin to fight or flight. Grace was quickly able to overcome the surprise factor and had time to compose herself before she heard him call out her name.

Someone else did the same from several feet away. Grace turned around as the catering supervisor approached to request instructions on what to do with the leftover food and the extra bottles of liquor. When she'd finished conversing with him, she pivoted slowly and found herself face-to-face with the man who'd called from across the dinner hall.

She lost her sense of time and place. She remained controlled, but her smile was stiff, her hands cold. She rested her gaze upon him, cool and distant.

His dark eyes were watchful and discerning. His wide mouth showed signs of a smile. His brows were black and finely arched over discerning eyes, which watched her through thin, wireless glasses that were almost undetectable until he was right in front of her. His skin was a rich earth brown, and his face was clean-shaven, with masculine contours and angles. Grace kept her gaze on his face but avoided direct eye contact. Finally, in self-defense, she resurrected those impressions she'd formed of him at their first meeting, some eight years ago. She held those memories up like an invisible shield, as if he was somehow a danger to her.

He tucked his chin as he thoughtfully considered her. "Why do I get the feeling you were trying to avoid me?"

His voice was confident. Although strong and deep, Grace knew that it could also be very quiet, a steadying force. Ignoring his astute observation, however, she hid her embarrassment behind a smile.

"Carter. My goodness. What are you doing here?"

"First thing's first," he said. "How about a proper hello?"

Grace started sharply, thinking he was going to embrace her right there in the hall. Instead, he merely bent forward to kiss her on a cheek.

"I know you're working, but I don't think that was too out of line."

She stood stiffly at his greeting, feeling the warm imprint of his lips on her skin, lips that momentarily quickened her breathing. "It doesn't matter. By tomorrow someone will ask me, 'who was that man?'"

"And your answer?" he baited smoothly.

"I'll say you're a family friend whom I wasn't expecting to see," she said indifferently. She could tell that he was monitoring her reaction to him. "But to get back to my question—"

Carter stretched his arms out to the sides so that she might see how he was dressed. "I was invited. I'm one of the guests."

Grace gave him a quick up and down glance. She'd seen him in a tuxedo before. He did it justice, appearing not only urbane and sophisticated, but with an air of authority that could be intimidating. It had taken her a while to learn he could be otherwise.

"A guest? You mean you flew in from Chicago just for the evening?"

He slipped his hands into the pockets of his formal slacks. "More than just an evening. Actually, I'm in New York for about ten days to take care of business."

"Really. Where are you staying?" She couldn't help asking.

"Through my company, I have guest privileges at a midtown club." He took a moment to study her features and said quietly, "I thought of calling to let you know I would be in." ·

"Checking up on me?" Grace shook her head. "You don't have to do that. I'm doing fine, and I know you're busy. You do have a life that has nothing to do with Benson and his family. And he's been gone three years."

He nodded, considering her words. "I know that. But, like you just said, I am a family friend. I'd like to stay in touch. I'd like to—"

Grace put her hand out to stop him, taking a deep breath. "Look . . . you're here for a party. I can't keep you standing here, and I'm supposed to be working. Please, go back inside and finish dinner. I've got things to take care of. . . ."

"You're right. I don't want you to get in trouble on my account."

16

Carter put his hand around her elbow for a brief moment, squeezing it before releasing her. "I'll catch up with you later."

Throughout the rest of the evening, Grace found herself constantly distracted and a little off balance owing not only to Carter Morrison's sudden appearance, but also to the one unsettling memory she'd retained from their last encounter. It had been at the memorial service for her late husband, Benson.

Grace now moved briskly, not giving herself any more time to let her mind or attention slip into reflection, or to process the fact that Carter was not only in New York, but would be here for nearly two weeks. She oversaw the timely cleanup and dismantling of the bar. She accepted the praise of one of the corporate honchos, who was pleased with the level of service from her staff. Of course, Grace had to put his comments in perspective, given the distinct possibility that he may have had too much to drink, or was expecting her institution to concede another favor.

But for the rest of the night, there was no denying that a part of her was absorbed by the presentations, speeches, laughter, and applause that flowed out from the guests dining in the rotunda. She was surprised when Carter was introduced to accept an award. She stood listening to his humorous acceptance speech, which drew laughter and applause. Also evident was the effortless way Carter showed himself as someone who could be trusted. Nonetheless, later, as the guests trickled out of the rotunda after dinner, she made a point of being someplace else.

After nearly everyone had left, one of the female guards approached Grace as she talked over the evening with her coworker, Brian. The guard was holding a square glass vase with an exotic arrangement of hothouse flowers. They had been part of the decoration for the night.

"I saved this for you, Ms. Haley," said the chubby woman as she smiled at Grace.

"Carmen, you know we're supposed to leave everything for the night crew to clean up."

Carmen made a dismissive face. "Why should they get everything? You know they are not going to throw out these beautiful flowers and the vase. They're going to take 'em home. The way I figure, it's like taking the centerpiece home when you go to a wedding reception, right?"

Grace laughed but still didn't accept the arrangement being held out to her. "Why don't you keep them? I'll pretend you didn't say anything to me about it."

"I already got one," Carmen said conspiratorially.

"Carmen, I really don't think I should. How will it look if the events coordinator for the society is caught sneaking off with the floral arrangements? Even if it were okay, I can't take those home with me on the train."

"Tell you what. Don't worry about it, okay? If you come into your office in the morning, and there happens to be this big thing of flowers on your desk, you can act surprised and say you have a secret admirer or something like that."

"Whatever." Grace gave in with a grin as Carmen walked away, carefully balancing the vase.

There was plenty to take care of, and Grace was glad that her duties kept her away from the exit and the departing guests. She reasoned that she wasn't really avoiding Carter, but that she was fulfilling her responsibilities for the evening. When she finally switched from black, high-heeled pumps to her winter boots and put on a stylish black wool overcoat, Grace realized she had a mere thirty-five minutes to catch her commuter train. She said good night to the last of the cleanup staff and exited the building through a side security door.

Despite the late hour, there was plenty of traffic on the Midtown Manhattan street, and Grace had no qualms about walking the six blocks to Grand Central Station alone. But she'd gone no more than a few yards when the driver's door of a town car double-parked near the corner suddenly opened and out stepped Carter.

Grace slowed her steps, astonished to see him again.

"You're not waiting for me, are you?" she asked.

"Are you done for the night?"

He stood with the car door open and the engine running. He wore no coat over his tuxedo, and his breath vaporized in the late January air. The streets still had piles of dirty snow from a heavy snowfall the previous weekend.

"Yes. I'm on my way to Grand Central to catch my train. I've really got to run." Grace waved casually to Carter as she walked away.

He beckoned to her. "Get in. I'll drive you home."

She shook her head. "That's nice of you, Carter, but crazy. You don't want to go all the way up to Westchester at this hour."

"It's my invitation, my decision. All you have to do is say yes. Unless you really want to ride the train alone this late. Or maybe it's me?"

Grace was forced to stop completely. She regarded him with wary embarrassment. To her, Carter sounded neither angry nor hurt, but was simply speculating.

"That's not true," she said quietly. But even to her ears, her disclaimer came across as insincere. "I just assumed you'd want to hang out a while with some of your associates."

"That's why we all attended the dinner. I'm off the clock now. This is my time."

"Right. But you don't have to spend it with me every time you come to the city," Grace said, trying to walk away.

"Benson was my best friend, Grace. I was there at your wedding. I'm godfather to one of your kids. So far it's fair to say I haven't really been here for you when you've needed anything, especially after Benson died. And he did ask me to keep an eye on his family if anything ever happened to him."

Grace faced him squarely. She also remembered Benson making that request. It had come right after Carter, the best man, had given an eloquent toast at their wedding reception.

"I can't hold you to that, Carter. It was eight years ago. . . ."

Two men passed behind her, deep in conversation. A lone woman on a cell phone passed in front. Grace was standing in the middle of the sidewalk, and it was cold.

"Come on. Get in," Carter repeated and waited.

Grace took a deep breath and slowly walked toward the car. By the time she'd reached the passenger side, Carter had come around the front of the vehicle to open and hold the door for her. She settled herself in the front seat and waited for him to get behind the wheel. In the few seconds it took for him to climb in and put on his seat belt, she had accepted the situation. Besides . . . the car was deliciously warm, with a luxurious leather interior, and she was grateful that she'd been spared a grim late night Metro-North train ride to the suburbs.

Neither said anything for several blocks, as Carter navigated traffic and headed to the east side of the island and the FDR Drive. It was the quickest route to the Major Deegan Expressway and north into Westchester County.

"Are you warm enough?" he asked, making a turn at an intersection.

"Yes, thank you," Grace said, pulling off her gloves and stuffing them into her tote bag. She noted that Carter knew his away around the city like a native. She stole a glance at his profile, noticing the familiar firm set of his jaw and his unconscious habit of flexing the muscles there. Her gaze went to his hands, curved around the steering wheel. His nails were clean and his fingers were long, tapered, and capable. She stared out the windshield at the traffic and the city lights as they sped along. "I'm sorry I was rude to you tonight. I didn't mean to be, Carter."

"Not consciously, maybe. But I don't think you were particularly happy to see me."

"I didn't expect to see you. It's been a long time."

"Only seven months."

"You came in for a quick meeting before flying over to Germany."

20

"It was also Becca's birthday. We're going to go through this every time we see each other."

It was a statement, not a question. Grace felt bad that she'd given him the impression that she didn't want to see him, but she also felt that she'd been put on the defensive.

"I was working. I was distracted. There was so much going on at the gala, and . . ."

"Relax, Grace. Apology accepted, okay?"

She glared at his profile. "That wasn't an apology."

"Look, I'm going to rewind the tape back to the beginning of the evening, and we're going to start over."

Grace was surprised at how relieved she felt that Carter had adroitly smoothed over the awkwardness. It also annoyed her that he didn't seem nearly as unsettled as she felt.

"If you want," she agreed.

"You first," Carter said, giving her a brief glance.

"Carter! It's so great to see you," Grace exclaimed with exaggerated excitement. "Why didn't you tell me you were going to be in New York? I would have baked a cake."

He grimaced and shook his head. "Be careful. Don't overdo it."

Grace stared ahead. "I'm being real now. I was shocked to suddenly see you. And it *is* nice to see you. Honest."

He chuckled, his wide smile showing white, even teeth, and his eyes almost squinting in amusement. "Okay. I'll accept that. Sorry I didn't let you know I was coming, but I didn't find out myself until early this morning."

"Why so last minute?"

"Actually, not so last minute. I knew a few days ago that the firm was offering me a new position that would mean moving to New York."

"Oh."

"There was a lot to consider. Did I want to move to the city?"

She waited, not hearing any definitive answer. "Did coming to the dinner tonight have anything to do with the offer?"

"As a matter of fact, yes. I flew in early enough to meet my new colleagues, to see my new office, to look over a few apartments I can choose from to lease until I decide on more permanent housing."

"Oh."

He started laughing. "Oh? I can't decide if that means you're surprised, happy, disappointed, or what."

"It just means oh," Grace said noncommittally.

"Fine. Anyway, once I knew I was attending the gala, I called your office. They said you were busy getting ready for an event this evening, so at least I knew you'd be on hand. I thought I'd surprise you."

"Well, you certainly did that," Grace murmured a little dryly. She glanced at him. "Are you really going to move to New York?"

"Looks like it," he said, glancing her way again. Silence spread between them for almost a full minute before he spoke again. "Is that going to be a problem?"

Grace shrugged. "Why should it?"

For the rest of the ride to her house, they managed to keep the conversation on the safe topic of his job, which was as financial executive for an international corporate firm. Grace got questioned about her position as events coordinator for a private library, a major step up from working in guest services. They talked about mutual acquaintances and family. About Madison and Becca, her two young children. About Benson. They reached the quiet and orderly suburban community in Westchester, which lay immediately north of the city, in about forty minutes.

"You'll have to take me to the station. I left my car there this morning."

Grace gave Carter directions. Her late-model Honda Accord was among only five cars remaining in the commuter lot. She got in and started the engine, and Carter followed closely behind her as she headed home.

They finally reached Grace's house in a quiet residential neighborhood of spacious detached homes. The raised ranch, which she and Benson had considered their starter house, intending to move once he felt more secure in his position as one of several deputies in the mayor's office, was on a quarter-acre lot set back from the street. It had a modest circular drive and was landscaped with several trees that provided a natural but subtle screen from passing vehicular and pedestrian traffic. There was still quite a bit of snow around the property.

Grace turned into her driveway, and Carter pulled in behind her, turning off his engine. She thought that he would get out of his car to say good night, and when he didn't, she climbed inside instead. Immediately, the suburban stillness closed in around them. The warmth from the car heater began to quickly dissipate.

Grace wasn't sure why, but she waited for Carter to say something first.

"Before I forget, I have something for you," Carter said. He reached behind her seat and grabbed a small, gold-toned shopping bag with red and gold ribbons tied to the handles. He sat it in her lap.

Grace stared at the bag without touching it. She felt a peculiar sensation, a cross between surprise at the unexpected gift . . . and suspicion.

"What is it?"

"It's the goody bag the company prepared for all the guests. I took one for you."

She looked at him and half-smiled in exasperation. "First Carmen and now you?"

"Who's Carmen?"

"Oh . . . never mind. Why are you giving this to me?" Grace asked, poking through the red tissue paper to look inside.

"Because there won't be a thing in the bag that I want or can use. The goody bags are for the women guests. It's yours."

"Thank you. But isn't there someone else you can give it to?" she asked.

Carter shifted in his seat so that he could fully face her. His gaze was thoughtful, but also faintly amused.

"Is that your way of asking whether I'm seeing anyone?"

Grace turned her head away in a haughty manner. "I wasn't trying to be nosy."

"There is someone I'm interested in. The relationship is still new, but I have high hopes," Carter explained.

"Well. That's nice," Grace murmured, checking to make sure she had all her things. Taking her house keys from her purse, she added, "You never liked any of the women Benson tried to set you up with."

"Benson had no idea what kind of woman I want."

"He could be opinionated, but I know he meant well."

"I know he meant well, too," Carter agreed.

Grace waited. She realized she was waiting for Carter to elaborate on who he might be dating. He changed the subject instead.

"Tell me about the kids. How are they?"

She suspected this was a diversionary tactic so she'd stop tiptoeing around the issue of his personal life. She sighed in resignation. "Good. Becca is—"

"Going to be a heartbreaker," Carter chuckled.

"My father says the same thing. Of course, she's got him wrapped around her finger. Madison is going to be tall, like Benson."

It was a natural comparison, but Grace felt awkward saying so. Carter never missed a beat and didn't appear to find the reference uncomfortable.

"I bet he's a handful."

"Sometimes. He's got more energy than he knows what to do with. Definitely all boy."

"Do you think I could see them while I'm here? They probably won't remember who I am."

"I think they might. You must have promised Madison you'd take him to a basketball game, because he talks about it now and then."

"I'd like to keep that promise."

"I wouldn't worry about it," Grace demurred. She played idly with the gold ribbons on the gift bag. "I owe you an apology."

"Why?"

"I never thanked you for sending Becca that sweet Valentine's Day candy last February. Or that little stuffed lamb for her birthday. She's very attached to it. It's filthy"—she broke out into a rich laugh—"but I'm afraid to wash it. She might throw a fit."

"Then I wouldn't if I were you."

She glanced at him openly. "And I never thanked you for the flowers and candy you sent me, either. It was very thoughtful, Carter."

He shrugged, embarrassed. "No need to thank me. I hope you enjoyed everything."

"I loved the flowers. Never got any of the candy. The kids beat me to it."

Carter laughed again. For some reason, it made Grace feel good that she could make him laugh. Carter had always struck her in the past as too serious.

"I guess I'll have to do something different this year."

"Don't," Grace quickly said. "It's not your responsibility."

He sat up straight in his seat. "I'm sorry. I forgot that you might be seeing someone."

"I'm not. At the moment," she said, quickly qualifying her answer. "The kids and my job take up a lot of my life. That's not a complaint, by the way."

He silently nodded. "How's Marjorie?"

"Marjorie is doing fine. She adores the children, of course. I don't know what she would have done if her only child had died before making her a grandmother."

"Do I hear a bit of—"

"No, you don't. Marjorie can sometimes have a one-track mind, but don't you think it's understandable that she misses Benson?"

"What you're saying is, she hasn't let him go yet."

Grace sighed. "Maybe we can't expect her to. How do you put a time limit on grief?"

25

"How about you? Do you hold him in your memories?"

She stared straight ahead out the windshield. "I have two children with Benson. Of course, I think about him. They remind me every day of my life."

"That's not what I mean," he said quietly.

Grace searched blindly for the door handle. "You know, it's really late, and I better go in. And you still have to drive back to the city. I appreciate the ride, Carter. It was nice of you to go out of your way."

He lightly touched her shoulder, and it stayed her as she glanced back at him.

"I'm serious. I'd like to see the kids. Do you think that's possible? I have to return to Chicago in about a week to wrap up some business and arrange for the move here. Can I see all of you before I go?"

There was an element of appeal in his voice that touched Grace because it came across as sincere. But rather than responding, she found herself weighing the ramifications. She was about to suggest that perhaps getting together should wait for another time, hoping that by then his interest would have waned, when he spoke again.

"How about this coming Saturday?"

She thought about it. In all honesty, there was no reason why he couldn't visit for a few hours, even though she was reluctant to encourage his sense of responsibility to her children.

"I've got a couple of household errands and chores to do in the morning. Madison and Becca have a swim class. Afterward, I'm taking them to a local ice-skating rink. Then I treat them to lunch at the local mall."

"Why don't I join you for lunch?"

"If you want," Grace said in an offhand manner before finally getting out of the car.

She heard the driver's door close and realized that Carter intended to walk her right up to the front door.

They stood under the entrance light and faced each other.

Carter's gaze seemed to roam her face, taking in all of her features. She tried to ignore the fact that he was staring.

"I know you have to go inside and relieve the babysitter. . . ."

Grace shook her head. "The kids are with Marjorie tonight. She's very good about volunteering to keep them when I have to work late. I'll pick them up in the morning and drop them off at school before heading to work."

He nodded his head to indicate he was listening, but Grace was starting to feel a little uncomfortable under his persistent scrutiny. Finally, Carter broke his trance.

"Sounds like you have a system that works. What do you do when you want or need time to yourself?"

She laughed. "Haven't you heard? Mommies don't get time off. We're not allowed to get sick, either."

He shook his head sadly. "All work and no play. Gotta do something 'bout that."

"I'm open to suggestions."

"I'll get back to you," Carter said lightly. "I should let you go in. It's great to see you again, Grace."

"Thanks again for the ride."

Carter slowly raised and opened his arms. There was only a fleeting instant of awkward hesitation before Grace took one tentative step forward into them. Their embrace was loose, brief, not at all romantic, but familiar. She patted his shoulder, like she often did with her children when they needed comforting. Carter glided his hand back and forth across her back before they stepped apart.

Again memories of the past came back to Grace, and she felt a brief but heavy sense of guilt. She inhaled the cold air to shake it off.

"I'll see you Saturday," he said, returning to his car.

"Good night, Carter. Drive safe."

"Oh, by the way," he said, about to climb back into the driver's seat. "I really like your hair cut short that way. It's very becoming."

Grace didn't respond to the compliment. Benson had liked her hair long, but it was more work that way. Cutting her hair had been one of the first things she'd done once things had settled down after Benson's death. The new grown-up style was her declaration of independence and break from the past. She saw no point in looking back. She tried to remember that as Carter turned over his car engine.

She turned to unlock her door as he reversed the town car into the street and drove away.

Two

"Madison, put that book away, and go get your coat. We're going to be late. Becca, honey, you don't need any more raisins in your cereal. Eat one more spoonful, and then we have to go," Grace said firmly to her children, who seemed inclined to dawdle.

"Oh, Grace, do stop fussing at them. You'll make them nervous," Marjorie Haley complained in her own maternal nagging tone.

"I asked you to please have them ready by the time I arrived. I have a train to catch," Grace said, trying not to sound annoyed.

She was standing at the kitchen counter in the home of her former mother-in-law, checking her son's knapsack to make sure all of his school things were inside. She then approached her daughter, removing the nearly empty cereal bowl and instructing her to find her boots and put them on. Marjorie, a pleasant looking late fifty-something woman of average height but slightly overweight, was meticulously packing a lunch for each of the kids which she then put into each of the children's schoolbags.

"I told you I could take them to school myself, but you kept telling me you want to do it. I think you get the children all mixed up."

Grace decided not to point out to Marjorie that she was hardly ready to drive Madison and Becca to school since she was still in her bathrobe and nursing a cup of coffee. The only thing already in place was Marjorie's fashionable wig, one of several she owned in different styles. Instead of arguing, Grace placed Madison's schoolbag by the front door of the house and bent over to help Becca as the child tried stuffing her tiny foot into her boot.

"I can do it," Becca told her mother, sitting on the floor to make it easier to pull the boot on.

Grace glanced over to Marjorie. "I know it would have been easier, even made sense. But I wanted to see my kids before they went to school this morning."

"Do you have to work late again tonight?"

"No, but I don't like going such a long time without seeing them."

"I suppose that means you don't think I know how to take care of my own grandchildren."

"That's not what I mean, and that's not what I said," Grace corrected calmly. She was holding Becca's pink parka to help her into it.

"I want to remind you that after my divorce, I raised a son alone. He turned out good enough to attend Harvard. *You* found him good enough to marry."

"Mommy, Nana Marj said that if me and Becca come to stay with her, she's going to take us to see Monsters, Inc., an ice show."

"When is this?" Grace asked, grateful to Madison for the distraction.

"It's performing for the next two weeks, but I thought maybe this Saturday," Marjorie said. "The kids can stay with me for the weekend."

"Can we?" Madison asked.

"Did you forget we have plans for Saturday?" Grace asked.

Madison groaned dramatically, his face scrunched up as he recognized the conflict.

"I wanna go ice-skating," Becca piped up, not to be left out.

"Can we go with Nana on Sunday?" Madison negotiated.

"We'll talk about it tonight. Right now, we have to go. Do you have everything?"

"What's going on on Saturday?" Marjorie asked as she walked Grace and her grandchildren to the door.

"Madison, take Becca and get in the car. I'll be there in a minute."

"I thought you said we have to hurry?" Madison protested.

Grace sighed and sent Madison a silent, telling look. Taking the warning to heart, he went to his grandmother, arms outstretched for a perfunctory hug.

"Bye, Nana."

"Have a good day in school, sweetheart. Come on, Dumplin'. Give Nana a kiss," Marjorie cooed, bending over to scoop Becca into her arms.

Becca returned the affection but quickly pulled away to run after her brother. "Wait for me!" she whined, dragging her red, blue, and yellow schoolbag by a strap, her bright knit hat askew over the four thick cornrows of her slightly curly hair.

"I'll call you later," Grace said to her mother-in-law, heading for the door.

"Grace, you can spare five minutes to tell me why I can't see my grandkids this weekend," Marjorie complained.

"You make it sound like I deliberately keep them from you," Grace said carefully. "You had them for a full weekend two weeks ago. I told you we already have a lot to do. Madison is going to a sleepover on Friday night. Then he, Becca, and I are going skating. They've been looking forward to that."

"Then bring them to me in the evening. They can stay until Monday."

Grace shook her head patiently. "Not this weekend. It's too

much running around for them and me. I do enough of that during the week. Besides, Carter Morrison is in town. He asked to see the kids, and I invited him out for the day," she finished casually.

"Carter Morrison?" Marjorie repeated. "What's he doing in New York?"

Graced stared at her, taken aback by Marjorie's scathing question. "He's here on business. He happened to attend the corporate event I worked last night. As a matter of fact, he's gotten some sort of promotion and will probably leave Chicago."

"Oh, really? I suppose he's moving here?"

"Why do you say it that way? I thought you liked Carter. I mean, he's . . . was Benson's best friend."

"*Was* is right. Carter may be smart and good-looking, but he always thought he was better than my son. He's very ambitious, and you know what I'm talking about."

Grace suddenly forgot all about the time. She took a quick look out the window next to the door and saw both children in the backseat of the car, waiting. Madison had once again buried himself in a book, and Becca had fallen asleep in her car seat.

"I haven't a clue what you're talking about," she said, turning back to Marjorie.

"I saw you, you know," Marjorie drawled in a low, nearly menacing tone.

"What?"

"Don't think I don't know what's going on. I saw you and Carter together after the memorial service for my son. Couldn't believe my eyes. Benson not in the ground forty-eight hours, and I catch you fooling around with another man."

Grace felt her heart thudding wildly at the accusation. She swallowed hard as Marjorie's words drained all of her body heat. She narrowed her gaze on the older woman.

"How dare you say that to me. I wasn't fooling around with Carter, then or at any other time."

"I know what I saw," Marjorie said with equal indignation.

"Benson was a good, honest man. He deserves a wife who holds his memory dear. But you couldn't wait until he was gone to turn to someone else."

Grace realized that she was squeezing her gloves so tightly in her hands that her fingers were cramping. Her mouth was dry, but when she spoke, her voice had a steely edge to it.

"You're my children's only grandmother, and I know you love them very much, so I'm not going to trade insults with you. It's really none of your business, and I don't owe you any explanation, but what you saw three years ago was Carter trying to comfort me. I was in Reverend Daniels's office. He found me crying. I was overwhelmed with the changes that I knew would take place after Benson died. I was scared, and hurt. I . . . I realized that my daughter will have no memory of her father, and that Madison might soon forget.

"I loved Benson. He was too talented, too smart, and much too young to die, but he's gone. I'm trying to do the best I can for my kids and myself."

Marjorie stood listening to Grace's recital with interest, but skepticism was still apparent in her gaze. But by the time Grace had finished, Marjorie's demeanor had changed. Her shoulders slumped, and she averted her eyes to hide the evidence of tears.

"Benson was my only child," Marjorie moaned. "My . . . baby. Lord, not a day goes by that I don't think about him. I miss him so much. He was my life."

Grace took another moment to let her tumultuous feelings settle down. She was not unsympathetic to Marjorie's loss. She sucked in a deep, calming breath and reached out to rub her mother-in-law's arm. "I know you do." Grace looked down at the head, with its synthetic hair, bowed in grief, and suddenly felt sorry for Benson's mother. "Maybe I can bring the children over after Sunday school. I'll call you later."

Grace couldn't stand to see any more of Marjorie's pain, or to explore the bald assumptions that had been made about herself. There was no time to react fully to the astonishing news that she and Carter has been seen together that afternoon three years ago. The cold morning air gave her a jolt back to the present. Grace resolutely buried that singular memory. She drove away with her children, knowing now that the past was not so easy to let go of after all.

Grace took a quick glance at Madison, who was already laced up and on the ice with fifteen or so children his age. There were two ice attendants but no rambunctious teenagers to interfere or take over the PeeWee Period on the ice. Assured that he was okay, she bent to tie the laces on Becca's ice skates. Suddenly, she felt a hand brush her shoulder. She swiveled her head and, in a state of disbelief, saw Carter looming over her. His sudden appearance was disconcerting.

"Carter," Grace said. She went back to securing her daughter's skates. She fumbled the laces and had to start over.

"Mommy, hurry up," Becca complained.

"I'm almost done, honey."

"I know I'm early, but I wanted to watch the kids skate. I hope you don't mind."

"Why should I? How did you find us?" Grace asked, getting to her feet and helping Becca stand on the double-edged training blades.

"I let my fingers do the looking. This was the only public rink in the area. Hi, Becca. I'm Carter. Remember me?"

He held out his big hand to the little girl, who after getting a reassuring nod from her mother, shyly put her hand in his to let Carter gently shake it.

"Hi," she murmured, pulling free and looking up at her mother. "I want to go skate."

"All right, but stay close to the side of the rink. I'll be watching you, okay?"

Grace led her daughter to the entrance gate. She held Becca by both hands as the little girl stepped off the protective rubber matting and immediately lost her balance as her feet slipped out from under her. Grace pulled her upright and held her until she got her footing.

"Mommy, let go. I can do it by myself."

Grace reluctantly did as she was asked, watching as her baby shuffled along the ice. Becca wasn't going fast enough to be in any danger, and she was low enough to the ground that if she fell, there'd be minimum damage. Still, Grace hid her anxiety over her daughter's safety.

"She's pretty fearless," Carter chuckled admirably, standing behind her.

Grace didn't realize he was so close, as she was intent on making sure that Becca was managing. "Frighteningly so," Grace sighed. "Madison! Keep an eye on Becca!"

"Okay," he yelled back.

But Madison was involved in a game with several other boys to see who could spin around without falling. Not knowing the correct move, their actions consisted of trying to force their bodies to turn in one big effort, a movement that was unsteady and clumsy.

"I'm not going to look," Grace murmured as she walked to a bench and sat facing the rink.

Carter laughed quietly but stood alone, watching the children. Assured that her children were doing fine without her, Grace returned her attention to Carter, checking him out. She realized that this was probably the very first time she'd seen Carter dressed down. He had on sturdy Timberland boots, corduroy slacks, and a black turtleneck sweater. The rolled collar hugged his neck right up to his jaw and chin, and the stark color seemed particularly bold and attractive on him. Carter was hatless and stood with his olive drab barn coat gathered and tucked under one arm. He looked and seemed different. Somehow stronger and more solid than a few nights ago, when he'd materialized formally attired. It was strange to see the difference. But both times Grace recognized in Carter a man who was self-possessed and indomitable.

Watching him, however, she was also reminded of that strained conversation with Marjorie. And it wasn't as if her mother-in-law was totally wrong, Grace conceded. She and Carter *had* hugged after the memorial service, although Marjorie's spin on the situation was pretty nasty. And yet, Grace admitted to herself, there had been a brief moment when she'd wondered, *what am I doing? What is Carter thinking?*

It was equally disturbing to recall that when Benson had asked her to marry him, he'd said that he couldn't wait for his best friend to meet his future wife. He'd told her that Carter was straight-up and dependable, worth going to the mat for. It was a very guy thing to say, and she'd found it funny at the time. Now she was finally coming around to seeing exactly what Benson had meant. What he'd said about Carter was true.

Carter turned to find her sitting on the bench. He slowly approached and sat next to her. He glanced at her, with humor brightening his eyes. The rink lights created glare on the lens of his glasses so that all she could see was his smile.

"I bet your heart leaps into your throat every time you have to let them go off without you."

"I want them to do things on their own and have fun. But I don't want them to get hurt."

"But they will. It's part of going off without you. Why don't you join them? Do you skate?"

"Not if I can help it. To be honest, I'm a little afraid that I'm the one who'll get hurt; then I can't take care of them. I mean, there is my father or Marjorie, but . . ."

"I think I'll join them," Carter suddenly announced. "Do you mind?"

Before she could tell him that wasn't necessary, Carter had dumped his coat in her lap and marched off to rent skates. He came back, sat down again, and laced up the skates. Afterward, he stood, took off his glasses, and silently handed them to her. As he made his way to the entrance gate, Grace was struck by how much taller he was in skates. Gigantic. They made him appear invincible. She also noticed that he stepped onto the ice with amazing confidence, although it was quickly apparent that he moved with the stiff, careful gait of an adult trying to overcome inexperience and lack of control.

Grace got up from the bench to stand closer to the rink so she could observe through the Plexiglas barrier. She was curious and followed Carter's progress. He seemed to be deliberately headed for her kids. She spotted Madison showing off as he awkwardly skated backwards in front of his sister, teasing her, while she scuttled along trying to catch him. Carter caught up to them, stopping to speak. Grace could see Carter reintroducing himself and then holding out his hand to Madison. The boy listened and then looked to her for guidance. Grace raised her hand and waved, signaling her okay.

Madison shook Carter's hand. In the meantime, Becca, unable to grab ahold of her brother, had nothing to help steady her as her arms flayed, and she fell. Carter, not much more steady himself, nonetheless bent to lift her back to her skates and then released her. Grace raised her brows and grinned. How smart of him not to patronize the kids.

It was hard for her to tell after a while if Carter was really keeping an eye on her children, or was out there having a good time himself. His ease and grace improved considerably with time. Only a few times did he engage Madison and Becca in brief conversation, mostly just leaving them to enjoy skating. Madison fell only once, and Becca several times, once close enough to Carter to wrap her small arms around his leg and pull herself upright.

It was inevitable that Carter himself would end up on his butt. Madison thought it was very funny and laughed merrily at the grown man sitting on the ice, trying to figure out how to get up. Even Grace allowed herself to chuckle. Then she watched in amazement as

Madison and Becca each took hold of one of Carter's hands and actually tried to pull him to his feet. When that didn't work, Madison turned his back and told Carter to use him for balance. And Carter didn't hesitate to take the boy up on his offer. Bracing his large hands on Madison's shoulders, he positioned one foot on the ice and quickly levered himself up, not actually putting any weight on the boy at all.

Grace was not only glad but relieved when Carter indicated that he'd had enough and headed off the ice. Madison and Becca followed him. Madison was sniffling from the cold air of the rink. Becca's nose was running, and the knees of her jeans were wet from her many falls. Grace gave her attention fully to her children, letting Carter take care of himself.

"Mommy, I only fell down a little bit," Becca boasted, wiping her nose on her sleeve before she could be stopped.

Madison chortled. "You fell down a lot. I only fell once."

"You both were great," Grace complimented them.

"I helped Carter get up. Didn't I?" Madison said proudly.

"You sure did. You're pretty strong," Carter agreed.

"Mommy? Did my father know how to ice-skate?" Madison asked.

Grace glanced briefly at Carter, who was engrossed in pulling off his skates. "No, sweetie, I don't think he did."

"Know what, Madison? Your dad was a pretty good soccer player, and he knew his way around a basketball court."

For just a moment Grace's gaze met Carter's. She didn't have to smile her thanks but knew that he'd gotten her silent message.

Madison thoughtfully considered that before asking, "Are you still going to take me to a basketball game? You promised."

"Absolutely," Carter said and nodded smoothly. "I'll check out the games for the rest of the season, and we'll set it up, okay?"

"I want to go, too," Becca complained.

"Mommy, tell her she can't go," Madison fussed.

"We'll talk about this later, Madison. Right now you can do me a favor and return the rental skates."

"Well, I don't know about you guys, but I'm ready for something to eat," Carter said as he stood to return his skates and get his boots.

"I'm hungry," Becca suddenly decided.

"We're going to the mall for lunch. I want to go to Mac-Donald's," Madison called out as he raced to the rental desk.

"No! I want Friendly's," Becca piped up in her tiny high voice.

A final decision was postponed until everyone had made a bathroom run and they'd left the rink. Carter followed behind in his town car, which looked so out of place among the SUVs and suburban sedans. The local mall was the zoo that Grace knew it would be on a Saturday afternoon, but it suddenly didn't seem so bad as she watched with interest the interaction between her children and Carter. What was even more pleasing was that he was effortless and totally comfortable when talking with them, and did not talk down to them. She was pleased with his ability to make both of them laugh; sometimes four-year-old Becca laughed only because Madison did. For the most part, Carter seemed to ignore Grace's presence. His decision, conscious or otherwise, went a long way toward putting her at ease in his company.

Grace wasn't sure how Carter managed it, but he successfully, and without a fuss, persuaded the children to have lunch at a café and not a fast food restaurant. Madison and Becca were still able to have hamburgers and fries, and Grace was thrilled to be able to order Oriental Chicken Salad.

A waitress brought the children each a coloring book and small boxes of crayons. They contentedly occupied themselves with coloring after eating their fill, while Grace and Carter talked.

"I saw you fall on the ice," Grace said.

"Are you going to hold that over me?" Carter asked smoothly, eating a grape tomato from his pasta dish and putting aside the menu he'd been reading, which advertised Valentine's Day special meals.

"I thought you hurt yourself. I was a little worried."

His gaze was warm as he regarded her. "I'll probably feel it later tonight or tomorrow, but I'm okay."

"I think they like you," Grace observed honestly. "Madison tends to be a little more reserved. You won him over again pretty fast. Becca is more open and trusting."

Carter nodded silently, wiping his mouth with a napkin. Then he rested his elbows on the table and thoughtfully stared into his empty bowl.

"Becca reminds me a lot of Benson. Madison is more like you." He looked steadily at her. "On the other hand, both of them look more like you than their father."

"I know. Marjorie said once that she wished that at least one of her grandchildren looked like Benson or herself."

Carter shrugged. "Luck of the draw. It's all in the genes. They're beautiful kids, Grace. Nice kids. Benson would have been really pleased about how you're raising them."

Grace couldn't think of how to respond other than to murmur a thank-you and busy herself finishing her Diet Coke. When she next glanced up, she found Carter staring openly at her.

"Do you still miss him?" Carter asked quietly.

Still miss him, Grace repeated to herself. She thought quickly, again remembering the painful conversation she'd had several days before with Marjorie. The question was a minefield, and she trod with caution.

"I'm sorry that he'll never know his children, or they him. Benson had a larger-than-life personality, didn't he?" she asked rhetorically. "His presence could fill a room, and he was such a natural-born leader. I think he would have been a great success if he'd ever run for office."

Carter pursed his mouth. "Yeah, he would have. But do you miss him?"

She shifted restlessly. "Benson's death was so . . . so unexpected. In a way, I still haven't adjusted. It's like my life was stopped short, and it's taken a while to get it back into gear." Carter was still waiting for her answer, and she looked squarely at him. "I guess I miss the promise of what we might have been together."

Nothing in his facial expression changed, and Grace wondered what Carter was thinking. Why did he ask that particular question? Why couldn't she be straightforward in her answer?

"Are you coming home with us?" Madison asked, gazing up at Carter.

"Are you inviting me?"

"Yeaaaaah," both children chimed in unison.

"Did you get your mother's permission? Maybe she has things to do."

"Can Carter come to visit for a while?" Madison asked his mother.

"For a playdate?" Grace asked her son.

Madison got the joke and laughed. "Not a playdate. He's too old. I know how to play chess," Madison boasted to Carter.

"Really?" Carter said, impressed. "So do I."

"Me, too," Becca said, not to be left out.

"No, you don't. You're still a baby," Madison teased.

"No, I'm not," Becca whined.

Grace intervened. "I know you have something else you probably want to do for the rest of the day, so don't pay attention to Madison. . . ."

"I'd love to stop by. I think I just got challenged to a game of chess."

"I wanna play, too," Becca said.

"Mom, tell her she can't," Madison pleaded.

Becca's whine turned to slow tears.

"Okay, time to leave. They're getting tired," Grace said. She slid out of her seat, lifting Becca. "I'll be back in a minute," she said to Carter as she and her daughter headed for the ladies' room.

When Grace returned to the table, Carter had already taken care of the bill. Together they headed in the direction of the parking lot, meandering their way through the mall, which was crowded with shoppers, aimless teens, a plethora of baby strollers, and children.

Grace suddenly felt a stilted silence between herself and Carter. And she was very much aware of his physical presence. In a strange, intimate way, he made her more aware of herself. Grace wondered suddenly if she looked attractive in her black stretch pants and white cashmere sweater set. She absently fingered her hair. Was it fluffy and cute like when she'd combed it that morning, or had the cold, breezy air left it a mess?

They slowly followed behind the two children, who seemed to be enjoying the noisy bustle of the mall. Grace was very mindful of the one probing question Carter kept asking her about Benson. She worried that somehow her answer was inadequate. Why hadn't she been more forthright? And she couldn't stop herself from replaying in her mind the things Marjorie had said to her. Had she wanted Carter to hold her?

Grace took several more steps before she realized that Carter was no longer beside her. She looked quickly around and spotted him approaching a jeweler's window to browse the brightly lit display of rings, necklaces, and bracelets.

"Madison. Becca. Come over here," Grace called to her children.

Becca skipped over and squeezed in front of Carter, and then she stood on tiptoe to peer into the showcase.

"I can't see," she complained.

Carter obliged by lifting her into his arms. Madison grew bored and walked away to a nearby water fountain. Grace kept an eye on him but joined Becca and Carter at the store window.

"What are you looking for?" she asked.

"It's that time of year again," Carter said.

Puzzled, Grace followed his gaze to the cutout red hearts, confetti, and curled ribbons, which hit shoppers over the head with the reminder that Valentine's Day was just around the corner.

"I want that," Becca said, pointing with a small finger.

"That's too expensive," Carter replied, shaking his head.

"What's she pointing to?" Grace asked, searching the display. She caught Carter's gaze over the top of Becca's head. He silently shrugged and raised his brows as if to say, what difference does it make?

Grace grinned and went back to examining the jewelry. She took in all the things a man could give a woman to show his love. Benson had never succumbed to such ploys.

"What do you want for Valentine's Day?" Carter asked Grace as he set Becca back on her feet. The little girl immediately joined Madison at the water fountain.

"Nothing," Grace said, waiting until the kids had caught up to her and Carter.

"I don't believe you."

"I'm serious," Grace said, holding out her hand to her daughter.

"Are you telling me that your husband never did it up right on February 14?"

"He made up for it at Christmas, on our anniversary, and on my birthday. That was fine by me," she said, and it was true.

Still, Grace had a sudden and overwhelming sensation of isolation, almost abandonment. She distinctly recalled her last Valentine's Day celebration with Benson. It has been three months before he'd suffered a fatal aneurysm while standing in a corridor of City Hall with colleagues. He'd gotten her flowers, and they'd gone out to dinner. But he'd spent the whole evening discussing his problems with the mayor's staff. He'd taken a cell phone call and made several of his own. It had not been a special night to her at all. But then, she'd always known about his intense focus on his career.

"Why are so you interested in how Benson and I spent Valentine's Day?" Grace asked Carter.

"Just curious. Last year I wanted to send something to Marjorie.

I realized that with Benson gone, there was no one to remember her. So, when I sent flowers to my mother in Virginia, I sent some to Marjorie as well. I know it's been tough for her."

"Is that why you sent me flowers and candy?"

Grace was a bit surprised by the intensity with which Carter returned her gaze before he finally responded.

"That was one of the reasons."

Her stomach churned. She wasn't going to ask what other reasons he had. "Well, it was very—"

"Romantic?" he asked with a smile.

"Nice," she corrected.

He shook his head. "You say that like you thought I was either a confirmed bachelor or gay."

She couldn't smile at his attempt at humor. It would never enter her mind that Carter might be gay, especially since Benson had told her about some of Carter's girlfriends and love affairs when they were in law school together.

And there was certainly something genuine about the comfort she'd received from his embrace that one time.

While her own thoughts and questions were putting her through an emotional wringer, Grace absently consented when Carter asked if it was okay to get Madison and Becca ice cream. She declined his offer to get some for her as well.

After accepting his waffle cone, Madison raced to hold two recently vacated bistro tables and chairs so they could all sit down.

"What's your idea of a romantic Valentine's Day?" Carter asked Grace as he slowly consumed his ice cream. "What would really do it for you?"

Grace sighed. "Are we back to that again?" But she pensively gnawed her lip. "I don't know if I should tell you. It's going to sound indulgent. Foolish. Whiny."

"I'll let you know if it is or not."

Grace gave him a crooked grin. She got over her shyness and decided to treat Carter's question like a game of what-if.

"Well, first of all, I get to sleep late. Somebody else has the kids. There will be flowers all over the house. Inside my croissant, I'd find a pair of diamond ear studs. . . ." Carter laughed at that. "In the refrigerator, a bottle of Perrier Joet champagne. The local spa would call to tell me I have an appointment for a massage, *and* they're sending a car to pick me up. After that, we're flown by helicopter to a secret retreat for three days and two nights of . . ." Grace stopped, remembering that her children were within earshot of her recitation. "You get the idea," she concluded.

"Who's the other person in the 'we' part?" Carter asked.

Grace reined herself in. Fantasy over. She was back at the mall with her kids, Carter, and a cast of thousands. She pursed her mouth. "I don't know. I was just making it up."

"Can I come with you?" Madison suddenly asked.

Carter grinned broadly. Grace glared at him. "I'm not going anywhere, baby. Mommy was just pretending." She felt Becca pulling on her arm.

"I wanna go home."

"We're leaving now," Grace said, standing up and taking her daughter's hand.

Once they all arrived back at Grace's house, Carter became the sole and exclusive playmate of Madison and Becca. And while Grace was amazed and relieved that her children had taken so effortlessly to him, she couldn't wait for Carter to leave.

It wasn't so much that he'd gotten too comfortable too quickly in her children's lives, but that Carter was insidiously burrowing into hers. It wasn't that she didn't enjoy his company, his bantering, and his thoughtfulness. It was the other possibilities that could be part of the package. Every time her mind ventured into the unknown, Grace was pulled back to reality by two things. The first was the notion that she'd somehow been unfaithful to her late husband's memory. The second was a fear of falling.

Without interruption, and with nothing else to keep her company but her own thoughts, Grace did chores. First, she did the laundry, and then she repaired a hole in one of Madison's pants. All the while something was definitely happening inside her. It was a gradual recognition of her loneliness. It was a desire to live again, and to love.

"I guess I should have offered to help."

Carter's voice startled her, and she looked over her shoulder to find him standing in the doorway of her kitchen, hands in his pockets.

"You are helping. You're keeping the kids from fighting and getting in my way. Where are they?"

"In the family room, watching a DVD. Square Bob something."

Grace couldn't help laughing. "It's *SpongeBob SquarePants*. Who won the chess match?"

"We didn't actually play a game. I thought it wiser to just show Madison a few moves, see what he could do. Who taught him? I don't remember Benson playing."

"He didn't. My father taught Madison."

Carter was watching her fold small T-shirts belonging to her son. "I guess it's true what my mom once said to me. A woman's work really is never done. What do you do to relax?"

"Relax? What's that?"

He nodded. "I get you. Look, I think I'm going to get on the road back to the city."

She put a half-folded T-shirt on a pile and followed Carter into the front room, where he'd left his coat.

"Thanks for being so patient with the kids."

"Thanks for letting me come to play with them," he grinned.

Carter put on his barn coat but left it unbuttoned. "When can I see you again?" he asked.

The question struck a nerve in Grace. She knew he wasn't talking about being with her kids. "The next few weeks are going to be busy."

He grinned knowingly, well aware that she had deliberately misunderstood. "Tell you what. I have to go look at some apartments the next time I fly in from Chicago. Can you come with me?"

"Call me when you get back," she said coyly.

"Great. I'd like your opinion."

"You might be sorry you asked."

With his hand on the doorknob, he looked at her for a long moment. "I seriously doubt it."

"Do you have to go?" Madison asked, wandering into the front room in his stocking feet.

"I'm afraid so. I have plans tonight, and I have to go get ready."

Grace folded her arms across her chest and fixed her attention on the middle of Carter's chest.

"Can you come back to see us again?" Madison asked.

"I hope so," Carter said comfortably, watching Becca as she soon joined them, sucking two fingers and leaning against her mother's side. Coming from the family room were the screechy, frantic sounds and dialogue of cartoon characters on the TV.

"Have a good trip back home to Chicago," Grace said.

"New York is going to be my home," he replied. Then he playfully pinched Becca's nose. "Be sweet." He turned to Madison and asked solemnly, "Is it okay if I kiss your mother good-bye?"

"Carter—" Grace started to object, but her disapproval was lost in Madison's response.

The boy shrugged. "Sure. I don't mind."

"Madison . . ." she complained anew.

She barely had time to prepare herself when Carter stepped in front of her. She'd imagined something highly inappropriate. Her wild imaginings had already worked it out. But Carter's kiss, light and affectionate, caressed her lips briefly and was done.

"I'll call you before I leave the city," he said.

He was gone before she could react.

"I'm hungry," Becca announced.

"I'm going to do dinner right now, hon. Madison, please put

your chess pieces away. And if you're not going to watch that movie, turn it off."

Madison knelt on the floor and swept together all the chessmen, putting them in a box. "Carter's fun. I like him," he said simply.

Grace grimaced ruefully to herself as she moistened her lips with her tongue.

What's not to like?

Three

"Hi, it's Grace. Can I help you?"

"You got a minute?"

Grace sighed. "I have a little more time than that for you, Marjorie, but I'm going into a meeting soon. Is everything okay?"

"As well as can be expected. I was wondering what you're going to do in May for Benson's anniversary?"

Grace, who was multitasking as she talked to her mother-in-law, furrowed her brow. "Benson's anniversary?"

"Of his passing."

"I don't have any plans to celebrate, Marjorie," she said smoothly.

"Good. 'Cause it's no occasion to celebrate. I'm talking about recognizing the day, all of us visiting his grave."

Grace quickly bit back her immediate reaction to Marjorie's suggestion. "By all of us, I take it you want to include Madison and Becca."

"Yes, I do. I think they need to show their respect."

"I'm sorry, but I don't agree with you."

"Benson was their father," Marjorie defended firmly.

"The key word here is *was*. Don't you understand that the children don't remember Benson? They see his picture, even pictures of him with them as babies, but they don't really make a connection. He's just a man in a photograph."

"That's your fault. You could do more so Madison and Becca don't forget who he is. It's your responsibility as my son's wife."

Grace closed her eyes and rested her forehead in her hand, speaking patiently. "Marjorie, look. I'm raising my children, and I know very well what they need to know. I can't begin to tell you how many times I've sat them down to tell them all about Benson. I tell them stories about how he and I met, about Benson asking me to marry him, and about what he did when each of them was born. They're just stories to the kids right now.

"One day about a year ago, Becca comes home after preschool and asks me, what's a daddy? She was having trouble with the concept, let alone attaching it to Benson. Now she knows that he's died and gone away, but that means nothing to her because she never knew him to begin with. I don't think I can force a memory that's not there."

"That's all the more reason why I think you need to mark that day. It's time she learned about him."

Grace looked at the time. "Look, I'm sorry to cut you off, but we can finish this later. I have to go. I promise I'll think about it, but I'm not fond of the idea."

There was only silence for a moment before Marjorie finally responded.

"Have they met Carter?"

"Yes, they have. I told you he was coming out on Saturday. Don't forget, Carter is Madison's godfather. So why would I deny him a chance to see the children? They like him. You'll be pleased to know that Carter told Madison a lot about what a good athlete Benson was, and how they became good friends."

"That was nice of him," Marjorie said grudgingly. "I still feel—"

"I know how you feel. I get it. If it's not too late this evening, I'll call you after the children are asleep."

"Don't forget that I go to bed myself at ten," Marjorie said and hung up.

Grace replaced the phone, but instead of feeling angry at her mother-in-law's imperious attitude, she felt consumed by guilt.

She had no desire to visit Benson's grave, and even less interest in dragging her children out to stand over a granite marker in the ground with his name carved on it. She was not interested in playing the grieving widow, or in pretending that his death was an unbearable loss. Benson's death had been hard at first for reasons that neither Marjorie nor anyone else could ever understand. But there was no point in revisiting the past.

Shame at her thoughts forced Grace out of her chair. She snatched up her folder of notes and headed out the office toward the meeting in a nearby conference room. She'd gotten as far as the office door when her phone rang again. She wavered between taking the call and leaving it to her answering machine. She looked at the time again. There was still five minutes to spare. She had been expecting a call.

But it was her father on the line.

"Hey, baby. Am I interrupting something?"

"Hi, Daddy. As a matter of fact, I'm about to go into a meeting. Is this important?"

"Yeah, but not urgent. It can wait. Am I going to see you and the children anytime soon?"

"Do you want to come over for dinner this weekend? Madison has some new chess moves, and he wants to try them out on you."

Ward Mathison laughed in his booming voice. "Tell him to bring it on. Who's he been playing with?"

"Carter Morrison. You remember him, right? He spent the day with us last weekend."

"Carter Morrison," Ward murmured. "Is that right?"

"Madison and Becca really took to him."

"How 'bout yourself? What do you think of the man?"

"Did you want to talk to me about anything in particular?" Grace asked, ignoring her father's question.

"Nothing that can't wait 'til I see you. But some time soon, okay?"

"Now you've got me curious."

He chuckled. "Now you'll have to wait. Bye, baby. Call me when you can."

This time Grace actually made it through the office door into the corridor when the phone rang again. This time she ignored it and went to her meeting. An hour later she was back in her office, listening to her voice messages, including one from Carter. He was just getting to his reason for calling when a staffer stopped by her office, knocked gently on the door, and announced that there was someone waiting to see her at the entrance. Carter's voice message made it clear that he was on his way to her office and was going to take her to lunch.

Grace sat for a moment, processing the unexpected visit, analyzing the past and present, and speculating on the future. The very first thought that came to her was the lingering impression of Carter's good night kiss. In truth, it could hardly be called a kiss. But she still remembered it. She wondered at the wisdom of encouraging a relationship with Carter, even for the sake of Madison, for whom, she admitted, she couldn't have picked a better role model. But Carter was part of the past as well, and she wanted to be done with that. At least, she kept telling herself that.

He was in conversation with the security guard when she arrived at the entrance. As she approached, Grace noticed that he was dressed less casually than when he visited the weekend before but was definitely dressed down from business attire. He was wearing a winter overcoat, and a long chenille scarf was wound rakishly around his neck. At his side was a packed folding garment bag made of black leather, with numerous pockets and straps. He looked so worldly. He seemed so together. He was so . . .

"Hi," Grace said, drawing his attention.

"Hi, yourself. I was hoping you'd be free. Sorry I couldn't give you more warning about getting together. I'm leaving a day early for Chicago."

"It's a busy day, but I can do lunch."

"My treat," Carter said, lifting his bag and walking with her out to the street.

"You better believe it," she responded tartly, making him laugh. "Where would you like to go?"

"Downtown," he said, walking to the curb, where the town car was again double-parked.

"Downtown? Why? There are plenty of good places a few blocks from here."

"I want to show you something first. It won't take long, and then we can find a place." He opened the passenger door and held it for her.

Grace didn't move. She was puzzled and more than a little suspicious. "What's going on?"

"Remember I told you about viewing some apartments? I want your advice. Are you with me?"

She slowly nodded. "Okay."

"Good."

During the ride, Carter told her about the apartments that had been arranged for him to see in Battery Park City, an enclave several blocks away from the site of the former World Trade Center towers. Grace listened as he tried to describe the area, but she confessed that she didn't know anything about that part of Lower Manhattan. She was surprised that he would consider living there but flattered that he cared about what she thought. Grace also felt a rising apprehension that Carter's move to New York was becoming real. He'd be able to spend time with Madison. That meant spending time with her.

For all the new construction and the contemporary sleekness of the high-rise buildings, the manufactured parks and promenades, and upscale shops and restaurants in Battery Park City, Grace found the setting sterile and artificial. Carter parked behind one such rectangular high-rise and led her through a maze of security procedures. Before they'd even boarded the elevator, Grace hated every inch of what she'd seen so far. This was a place for men and women whose lives were ruled by work and the clock. It was a residence, but not a home. It was fine for singles and couples, but terrible for a family.

As Carter led the way into one of the apartments on his list, on a floor high enough to induce a nosebleed, Grace couldn't help but wonder if this was really the way he wanted to live. The rooms were rather small, except for the master bedroom, which had a walk-in closet, a large dressing room area, a Jacuzzi in the bathroom, and heating racks for towels. One wall of the bedroom was almost entirely glass and overlooked the Hudson River and the undistinguished shoreline of New Jersey on the other side. She watched Carter's broad shoulders and his erect posture as he stared silently out the window.

"There isn't much room for . . . do you expect to get married some day? Do you see yourself having kids?" she asked carefully, not sure if she was crossing the line of "too personal."

He turned to face her and seemed mildly surprised by the question. "Definitely. What do you think?" Carter asked.

"It's nice," Grace said politely.

"You hate it," he said without rancor. "Be honest with me; that's why I brought you to see it."

"Carter, it really doesn't matter what I think. I don't have to live here, or raise a family here."

"But you have a woman's point of view, and that's important. I trust you. You won't hurt my feelings."

Grace felt trapped and sighed helplessly. She looked around again, hoping to find one redeeming quality, one positive thing to say about the space, for his sake.

"It will work fine for your lifestyle," Grace began, trying to sound enthusiastic. "You have a fast-track life right now. You could make this place comfortable, simple, and easy to maintain. And it's not permanent, right? You can always get something different in a few years, if anything changes."

"I expect it to," Carter said, watching her move about the empty rooms.

They went to see two more apartment units, but to Grace's thinking, there wasn't much difference between them. It was hard to generate excitement about places that seemed little more than compartmentalized boxes. It was hard to imagine Carter living in any of them, with or without a significant other.

They finished seeing the last place and headed back to the elevator. The presence of other passengers forestalled any conversation until they were both back in the car. She was relieved when he didn't question her further right away but turned the conversation to his work and what his new responsibilities would be. He drove in search of someplace to eat. Grace could tell that he was excited about starting again in New York, but she was sure she detected an edge, almost an uncertainty, to his excitement. It was understandable, given all the changes Carter was going through in such a short period of time.

He took her to a small, well-known restaurant near South Street Seaport. Grace was very familiar with its name and reputation but had never eaten there herself. She hadn't done much fancy dining of the adult variety beyond the children's birthdays, Christmas, and Halloween. She'd looked forward to lunch with Carter, but as they were seated, Grace felt a warm lethargy overtake her, which she didn't understand. Carter also seemed pensive, with a disquiet underlying his conversation all through the meal. It was over cappuccino that she finally addressed his quiet mood.

"Is everything okay? You seem a little distracted. I hope it wasn't because of what I said about those apartments."

The rest of her comment stuck in her throat as Carter reached across the table and took hold of her hand. She stared at his hand and then into his eyes, their expression protected behind the lens of his glasses. But she could tell by his eye movement that he was closely monitoring the changes on her face.

"Maybe I was testing you."

"Testing me? What for?"

"I wasn't sure if you still hated me."

Grace stared at him. "Where on earth did you get that idea? I don't hate you."

He adjusted his glasses but finally took them off and laid them, folded, next to his plate. He regarded her silently. To Grace, it somehow felt as if they were much closer together. She felt enveloped by Carter's gaze, by the memory of two small moments between them that had changed everything.

"When Benson first introduced us, six months before you two got married, that's how I felt. Those were the vibes you seemed to be sending me."

Slowly, the shock faded, and she became reflective. "You know, it's funny you would say that," she murmured. "I always thought you hated me. And what has any of that to do with where you're going to live when you move to New York?"

"I needed to know what you really thought about me. How well do you know me? How much do you care?"

He paused, but Grace remained still and silent, her insides roiling. She felt an overpowering sense of intimacy, drawn into his dark gaze.

"If you were indifferent, it wouldn't matter if I wanted to live at the Plaza or a Ramada Inn, in Battery Park or Harlem. But I felt like you were really considering what was right for me."

"I can't believe you'd be happy in any of those places we saw."

"That's what I wanted to find out, Grace."

She was still confused. "But, why?"

"Was I just Benson's best friend, or can I be your friend, too? Can we start with that?"

"I don't hate you," she repeated. "But when we first met, I

thought . . . well, I thought you were arrogant and unfriendly. I felt like you looked down on me, like you didn't think I was good enough for Benson. You never seemed to smile when I was around, and you never made much attempt to talk to me. What was I supposed to think?"

Carter's expression looked strained. He seemed both surprised and sad by her observations, and shook his head.

"I didn't realize I was coming across that way. I'm really sorry you felt that way all those years, but you did touch on something that was partially true."

"What?" she questioned cautiously.

"It's not that I thought Benson was too good for you. It was the reverse. I thought you were probably too good for him."

"Really?"

"Don't get me wrong; Benson was a great guy. He was street-smart and ambitious; he was basically an honest man. But he was a player." Seeing the shock that came into her eyes, Carter held up his hand to keep her silent. "I don't think he fooled around. As far as I or anyone else knew, he was totally faithful to you.

"I'm talking about what he wanted to do with his life, where he wanted to rise to. Getting appointed to the mayor's office was a real coup, but Benson had plans to go much higher. You can't have that kind of drive without knowing you have to play ball, cut deals, compromise, maybe even gloss over the truth when necessary. Well, that was fine for Benson, but I always had the feeling that that's not the kind of life you bargained for when the two of you got married. He went from being just another district attorney to being in 'the game'."

"How did you know how I felt about his career?" Grace asked, not denying any of Carter's statements.

"You seemed not in awe of Benson, but overwhelmed. Like he was moving too fast, and you were afraid you'd hold him back. I think you wanted to be a partner in a marriage, not in his career goals. I think you wanted to know he would give as much quality time to his family as he did to outfoxing his opponents and enemies. Benson had them, you know."

"I . . . I don't know what to say," Grace murmured. "I never realized anyone was paying attention to my relationship with Benson. Everyone liked him, and he was so popular, but I wasn't jealous of that."

"I came to understand that after a while," Carter nodded. "But I thought you hated me because you believed I thought you were holding him back. On the other hand, Benson really loved you. He said you were a class act, not like those other bi . . . women he'd known before. You gave him a son, and that made a huge difference in his outlook. But I wondered what would have happened down the road."

It was a lot for Grace to think about, putting together all the puzzle pieces that made up the relationships between her, Benson, and Carter. She'd never seen before that their relationships were such a complicated triangle. The revelations about her and Carter's misconceptions about each other also had an effect on her. Grace suddenly felt as if a door had opened to reveal secrets that might give closure to the past.

"I wasn't sure that becoming a father would make a difference to Benson. When Madison was about two, I started to think Benson was getting a little restless. Like he wanted and needed something else. Like . . . I wasn't doing it for him anymore. I even asked him if he wanted a divorce. That sort of shook him up, and he said no. Shortly after that, I got pregnant with Rebecca. But deep in my heart, I *knew* that having another baby was only a Band-Aid on a bigger wound. I knew I couldn't keep up with him."

"I'm sorry," Carter said quietly. "I had no idea. Which makes what happened three years ago so unreal, doesn't it?"

"What do you mean?"

"When I found you alone and crying after the service for

Benson, you looked like your heart had been broken, and I felt it was proof positive of how much you loved him. Then you lost him."

She grimaced ruefully. "I never had Benson. You don't hold someone like him. I never really belonged to him. Maybe I wanted something from him he couldn't give. Maybe, after a few years and a couple of kids, he felt the same way. But I don't believe in looking back, Carter. I'm not still in mourning."

"I wanted to be sure."

"How come?"

"That day when I tried to comfort you, I knew that the timing couldn't have been worse. I finally got a chance to show a little of how I felt, and your husband had just passed away. Was I just Benson's best friend or could I be your friend? Maybe take it from there. Do you understand what I'm saying?"

Grace felt disoriented by Carter's admission. Suddenly, every word, every action in their time together lately fell into place and began to make sense. Benson's mother had seen more three years ago than she could have realized.

"I . . . don't know what to say."

He leaned across the table. "How about, for starters, that I'm not making a fool of myself. That it's not too late, or a big mistake."

There was something poignant and vulnerable about his honesty.

"I'm a little nervous and confused, but I think you're on to something," Grace quietly confessed.

"It took three years for me to get up the courage to say something. I know you didn't feel the same way."

"Do you think Benson knew how you felt?" she asked, suddenly horrified at the thought.

"I would have broken off the friendship if I thought I couldn't keep it to myself. I didn't want to hurt Benson or you."

She shook her head in amazement. "But to stay silent for all those years."

"Until now," Carter quietly reminded her.

"Is everything okay here?" The waiter's overly cheerful voice broke into their mutual reflection and brought Grace and Carter back to the present. "Can I get you anything else?"

"No, this is good," Carter reassured the young man. He glanced at Grace. "This is very good."

By the time they left the restaurant, Grace felt as if everything had changed and the world looked different. She was giddy and disoriented, her head spinning with Carter's revelations. She felt awkward and shy and exposed. Carter had tapped into something between them that she had only begun to question herself. But she wasn't there, yet.

They left the restaurant, and he took her hand.

"Don't say anything right now."

"I can't," she agreed, bemused.

"I guess I could have planned this better. Maybe I should have said something sooner. Maybe waited until I'd already moved here. I hate that I have to leave you like this."

Grace smiled kindly at him. "Don't take this the wrong way, Carter, but I'm glad you have to go back to Chicago for a while."

He looked a little grim, but stoic. "Got it," he nodded.

She waited in numb silence while he hailed a cab for her and paid the driver to return her to her office. They faced each other suddenly like total strangers. But she finally realized how much courage it had taken for Carter to come forth with his feelings about her. And how much more it had taken for him to remain silent for eight years. Despite that spontaneous but electrifying encounter between them, Carter had never taken advantage of her. She stood before him now, appreciating and admiring the risk he'd taken. He had shown strength of character and had opened his heart. Could she do any less?

Grace took a tentative step toward Carter and raised her arms for a hug. It was gentle and comforting, and took them back to that time and place when the moment called for understanding.

"Have a safe trip," Grace said softly. "Hurry back."

*   *   *

"Thank you so much for understanding. I'm sorry I couldn't give you more warning, but something came up, and I have to stay in the city a little longer this afternoon."

Grace, on the phone with her babysitter, felt a little uneasy about having to change her children's routine. It was rare that she was forced to rearrange her schedule and theirs, and it was always work-related, something that she had to accommodate when necessary. Yet going into emergency backup mode for Carter Morrison struck her as not only out of character, but pretty spur-of-the-moment. Her life was not geared to spontaneity, or to taking chances. Grace realized she was making concessions for him that she hadn't made for any other man since Benson.

Why?

"I've already spoken with the children's grandmother, and she'll pick them up at your place at the time I normally would," Grace informed the babysitter. "Here's her name and phone number. . . ."

Why not? she thought.

Because with Carter, she could talk about more than Pokémon and Bratz dolls, she thought, realizing how limited her vocabulary had become. Because he liked her kids, and they liked him. Because Madison had been asking when Carter was coming to play chess with him again. Was it because the myth that had been dispelled between them had allowed for another feeling to sneak in?

Now it could be said.

"Yes, everything will be back to normal tomorrow," Grace assured the babysitter. "I'll pick up the children after work as usual. Thanks so much. I'll call my mother-in-law and let her know you'll be expecting her. Bye."

Grace sat forward in her chair, turning to her computer to finish an e-mail. She was tired of trying to analyze her decision. What difference did it make? There was nothing to read between the lines as she made arrangements so she and Carter could see each other.

He was becoming a good friend. There was nothing wrong with having a good friend.

Right?

Grace had known exactly when he'd returned to New York. He'd called on his way up the New Jersey Turnpike to say he'd taken a year lease on one of the three apartments they'd seen together. He already had a phone number, had arranged for movers to arrive with his things, and had driven himself back in his Lexus.

He'd wasted no time in asking to see her.

Grace was breathless with anxiety. Was he moving too fast? Was this whirlwind of feelings more than friendship or curiosity? Or just a momentary apparition?

Carter's phone call an hour earlier, asking if she could possibly stay late and meet with him, had not only caught her off guard but had stirred an odd anticipation. When she left work that afternoon at almost five-thirty, it was raining lightly. She walked briskly toward the subway only to realize that Carter was standing at the top of the entrance, under the protection of a large umbrella.

"What are you doing here?" she asked, sounding more annoyed than she'd intended.

"Waiting for you."

"Afraid I'd get lost in the subway? Or that I'd stand you up?"

"Aren't you glad I came to drive you in the comfort of my car, saving you the hassle?" he said, waving a hand to the Lexus parked near the corner.

"Yes," Grace conceded as a gust of wind tried to tear her pocket umbrella from her hand.

The drive downtown was stop and go as the traffic was hampered by the weather and the usual insanity of rush hour in the city. He'd made reservations at B. Smith's.

She realized that she was nervous to be with him—to the point of trembling. She crossed her legs after they were seated to keep her knees from jumping. Seeing Carter again after their parting conversation ten days earlier made Grace wonder what they could say to one another now. How they would behave. But the one surprising difference that she'd noticed at once was that she was glad to see Carter again.

He ordered glasses of champagne. They toasted his return to New York, finding an apartment, beginning a new life. But Grace realized it was a new start for her as well. Then Carter proposed a second toast.

"Let's hope the joys of the future will be strengthened by those of the past."

She found his remark thoughtful and somehow profound. Grace had always thought of Benson with genuine feeling and warmth and regret, and without guilt she smiled at the man sitting opposite her. Grace began to relax in his company.

After they'd placed their order, Carter took a purple envelope from his pocket and slid it across the table to her.

He said nothing, offered no explanation, and Grace stared at the envelope suspiciously. She did not ask what it might be; but her sudden rapid heartbeat and her flushed skin signaled that she'd reached her own conclusion.

"Does this have anything to do with Valentine's Day? Because if it does, you're a day early."

He shook his head as he watched her. "To my way of thinking, I'm a few years late. Better late than never."

Grace finally reached for the envelope. It was flat, but thick. She slid her fingers inside and removed the contents. As she leafed through them, her surprise increased . . . as did a new anxiety. There was a card with a sweet, romantic, but tasteful, greeting. It made her smile as she read it through twice. Then she realized that the other contents consisted of two cruise tickets—one issued in her name, and one in Carter's—although they had different staterooms. She was unable to utter a single word.

"This is my way of saying that not only do I want you to be my Valentine, Grace, I want you to be mine period. I want to go back to square one, start over, and court you. I want us to get to know each other. We have a lot of catching up to do. I want to do all the him and her things I've never done before, and I want to do them with you."

She couldn't breathe. She felt dizzy, like the room was slowly turning on its side. "I guess I can't say this is so sudden."

"Maybe for you, but not me. I told you the last time we saw each other that telling you my feelings was a long time coming."

She silently put everything back into the envelope; her gaze upon him was troubled but pleaded for understanding. "You're asking me to go away with you. I don't think I'm ready."

"Am I wrong to believe you have feelings for me?"

There it was. Truth or dare.

"No," she said with some relief.

"Are you worried about the kids, and about how Marjorie will react to our being together?"

"Yes."

"Are you worried about being alone with me?" he asked more gently.

She merely nodded.

Their dinner was served, and Carter wisely guided the conversation to a general discussion of all the places he wanted to travel to in his lifetime. Grace eventually confessed she had her own short list. On it was a trip to Disney World, which didn't need an explanation. Ever since Benson's death, she'd imagined the rest of her life alone, as if she'd been banished forever to widowhood. There were the children, of course, but Grace had prepared herself for living without a partner, a lover, and soul mate. She was ready to accept her fate. Carter's interest and his intentions had not eliminated that, but had added a new wrinkle in the fabric of her life that was not so easy to deal with.

Grace knew that Carter was disappointed in her response. He

watched her closely throughout dinner, trying not to look like he was staring. She knew he was looking for a sign of hope or encouragement, rather than an outright no.

Silence eventually took over as her mind went into free fall, and a flurry of vignettes and episodes from the past, moments that had been charged with emotion, innocent yet titillating, exciting but dangerous. All the wishful thinking she'd ruthlessly suppressed rose to the surface. She'd married Benson because she loved him; he had been a good man with enormous promise, but he was gone.

So, why did she continue to feel guilty and ashamed?

Carter took care of the bill. They stepped out into the cold February night. The rain had turned to a light snow. He began walking to his parked car, then realized that Grace hung back.

"Carter, I . . . I'd rather go home by myself on the train."

The muscles tightened in Carter's jaw, and he nodded. "All right."

She touched her temple. "My head is spinning. I can't think straight. I'm sorry."

He took her elbow. "I'll drive you to the station."

They were both silent, both deep in thought, neither having any idea what the next step was. Outside the gate to her train track, they stood facing one another. He held out the envelope. After a moment she silently took it.

"I don't think this came at you out of left field. I kept my distance out of respect for Benson. But then I asked myself, what am I waiting for?"

"But . . . to go on a cruise together," she stammered.

He grinned gently at her. "You gave me the idea. I counted on that when I asked you what you would want."

"You were pretty sure of yourself," she said grimly.

"Only about wanting to be with you. But I'm not out of the woods, it seems. You could still turn me down. If that happens, I'll deal with it. The cruise leaves in ten days. I want you to come with me, Grace."

She was afraid to ask what if she didn't?

An announcement echoed through the terminal about the departure of train 317 to Westchester, leaving on Track 29.

"No matter what else happens, there's something I have to do before you go," Carter began.

Grace stood waiting. She knew exactly what it was. Carter put his arms around her, drawing her to his chest. She knew instantly that this was more than caring, more than affection. His mouth descended, and she closed her eyes and tilted her head so he would fit properly atop her open lips. The first touch went to her head, his mouth gently moving and caressing hers. She became pliant and willing and easy and breathless.

The euphoria was like a drug that she'd been without for so long; the sensation was dramatic and overwhelming.

Grace let Carter take his fill. Even she held nothing back, enjoying the delicious expertise of his embrace, the sensual dance of his tongue around hers. It was a sweet awakening.

And, very possibly, a bittersweet good-bye.

Four

"Gracie, I'm not going to tell you what to do. Besides, that's not why you called me all in a tither about Carter asking you to go away with him. You expect me to get upset and defend your honor? You want my permission? You're a grown woman."

"Okay, I don't want you to tell me what to do, but I need help!"

"You don't need help, either, girl. You just need to make up your mind about what you want. You either feel something for the man, or you don't. Simple." Ward Mathison began to laugh heartily, as if the punch line to a joke had just come back to him. "Lord, what's going on in the world! Your Mama and me sure had it easy. Nothing like the pretzel twisting y'all put yourselves through these days."

Grace, sitting in bed with her knees drawn up to her chest, began to relax under the nonjudgmental sound of her father's voice, and his wisdom. It was the reason why she'd finally called him.

"Do you like him?" she asked.

"Do *you* like him? is more to the point."

"Yes."

"Okay, now we're getting somewhere. I've only had a chance to talk with Carter maybe half a dozen times in the eight years since you met him. He strikes me as a very smart man. A good man."

"A lot like Benson," she murmured thoughtfully.

"Right. But different. If Benson hadn't died so unexpectedly, you two might have made a go of your marriage for a long time. Maybe forever. But it didn't work out that way. So now Carter shows up and has the guts to admit he's always cared about you. It's your move. The ball is in your court, if you'll pardon the sports analogy.

"Grace, this is a no-brainer, baby. If you're developing real feelings for him, I'll watch the kids for five days while you go have a good time and figure it out. If you decide to stay home, then I'm coming over on Sunday for dinner like I always do after church."

Grace wasn't sure her father fully understood that the force driving her was not about what she might feel for Carter, but what to do with what she used to feel for Benson. The question of loyalty might raise its ugly head, but maintaining her children's memory of their father was more important. That really only left, as her father said, what she wanted to do. Grace started by asking herself two simple questions: What's the worst thing that could happen? And, what was the best possible outcome?

Grace had put herself through such a night of what-ifs that now, as she got out of the cab she had taken from Grand Central, she felt a preternatural calm combined with the excitement of a child. She hoped she'd be able to find Carter at the check-in point at the pier, but she also wondered if it had been a mistake not to call and let him know she was accepting his Valentine's gift. What if he'd gotten so discouraged he'd changed his mind?

She didn't see him anywhere in the lines of people waiting to show passports and get their ship IDs, so Grace refused to let the porters tag and take her luggage. For all of her ambivalence about traveling with Carter, she had no desire to go without him.

She found a public phone and used a calling card to reach her father, checking with him for the second time since he arrived at her house to stay with the kids while she was away. Grace knew that Madison would do fine without her, but Becca was still likely to call her in the night if she woke up from a bad dream or needed to go potty. Grace hoped that her father's presence would be enough for the week that she'd be away.

And then she remembered the call to Marjorie. . . .

"Hey. You made it."

Grace looked up from putting her calling card away and saw Carter approaching. Her reaction was swift and telling. Caught off guard, she fumbled and dropped her purse. He bent to retrieve it, holding it out to her.

"I'm really glad to see you," he said, returning her purse.

"Me, too," she admitted.

"Are you sure you're okay with this?"

"I'm fine. I'm really sorry I gave you a hard time."

Carter grinned slowly at her, and it was another minute before Grace understood the innuendo.

"Right now it doesn't matter. I had to have faith that you'd come. That you'd trust me."

A porter appeared again and took their suitcases, Carter's garment bag, and Grace's tote. Then they were directed to one of the lines. In a few moments they were issued onboard IDs, which served as room keys and ship credit cards. Grace was relieved that she had her own stateroom.

Finally, they were directed to board the ship. As they moved along behind other passengers, Grace felt Carter's hand lightly on her arm as he ushered her along. She looked up into his face and met his gaze.

"I'm very nervous," she said honestly.

Carter took hold of her hand as they walked. "Me, too."

Once onboard Grace became completely turned around, unable to figure out the front of the ship from the back, or to remember the nautical terms for both. There was so much to learn right away, including how to get to their staterooms, where to report for the safety and evacuation drill on deck, and how to put on the life vests. To Grace's way of thinking, she was already under enough pressure being isolated with Carter for six days and five nights without feeling truly like a fish out of water.

When the drill was over, they returned to their staterooms, and each disappeared inside to unpack. Grace was still hanging up clothes when there was a knock on her door. She stepped over the open suitcase on the floor to answer it.

"Man," Carter chuckled, stepping into the small space. "I didn't know the staterooms were so small. If you sneeze, you're in trouble."

"The bed doesn't look long enough for you to sleep in," she observed. "Are you going to be okay?"

"I'll manage. Leave that for now," he said, pointing to a pile of clothing on the bed. "Let's go look around."

Grace grabbed her room key and purse and joined Carter in the narrow corridor. He took hold of her hand and started walking.

"Do you know where we're going?" Grace asked him.

"I haven't a clue. But sooner or later, we'll end up right back where we started."

Grace was content to follow Carter's lead. He quickly figured out how the ship was laid out; where the theater, gym, casino, and lounges were all located; and the shortest way back to their rooms. Out on one of the decks, they realized they were already under way. The ship had backed out of the slip and was coasting down the Hudson toward the mouth of New York Harbor. It was much too cold for them to stay outdoors and watch as they passed by the Statue of Liberty and beneath the Verrazano Bridge. Carter suggested that they go up to the top deck lounge, The Crow's Nest, and watch from there. He ordered drinks for them, and they sat in soft leather chairs, watching through a panoramic window as the New York skyline fell away behind them. Carter made a bon voyage toast, and they clinked their glasses gently together.

"Here's to smooth sailing, sandy shores, and not getting seasick."

Graced laughed. "Here's to winning in the casino, midnight daiquiris, and a facial in the spa."

Carter took a sip of his drink and grew serious. He rested his head against the back of the chair and closed his eyes. "Thank you for coming, Grace."

Grace watched him for a moment and then took up a similar position in her chair. "I'm glad to be here. Thank you for asking me," she said softly.

They relaxed in companionable silence as night settled around them and the ship headed out to sea.

Grace was convinced that Carter had changed his mind about her. It had taken her a full day to become used to being with, and seeing, him so often in the confines of the ship. They were assigned a table for two. Each evening they got dressed and met for dinner. With Carter escorting her, Grace felt like she was on a date. He was accommodating and polite, and their conversations covered everything under the sun . . . except personal matters or themselves. During the first afternoon at sea, Grace indulged in several spa treatments, while Carter spent time in the gym and napped in a lounger. It was companionable, and although he seemed to be enjoying himself, Grace wondered whether he'd become bored with the slow-paced activities onboard, or with her.

At night they sat in one or another of the many ship lounges, each with its own musical theme. They found the one that played contemporary rock and danced to familiar songs from high school and college. Grace quickly realized that she'd not been out dancing since her wedding reception, but she didn't tell Carter. She especially liked the slow numbers, when he'd hold her against his chest, their thighs rubbing as they moved, and their hips pressed together. With her eyes closed, Grace let herself be lulled by the seductive swaying of their bodies, feeling a gentle heat building in her veins as she wished for more.

At any time she could invoke a complete replay of the way Carter had kissed her at the train station the night he revealed the way he felt about her. And yet, now that they were alone, he'd done nothing to act on his feelings, nothing to encourage her to act on her own. The first night onboard the ship, she'd lain in bed awake, half expecting to hear a knock on her door, which never came. Grace was grateful; it was as if she'd been given a reprieve. But at the end of the first day at sea, she was better prepared and anticipated some sort of overture from Carter only to be surprised when again, night after night, nothing happened.

By the afternoon of the second day, the ship was farther south, and the air was a little warmer. It was not warm enough to venture into the outdoor pools, but it was warm enough to walk on deck or stretch out in the loungers on the sunny side of the ship. Grace and Carter placed their deck chairs side by side in reclining positions. He reached for her hand and held it. But it wasn't enough. She knew it wasn't enough.

"Why haven't you ever married?" Grace suddenly asked.

"Who said I was never married?" he responded lazily, turning his head to squint at her through his dark glasses.

Her head swiveled sharply toward him, and she stared back. "Were you?"

"For about four years."

"Benson never said anything about it to me."

"There was no reason to. It happened before I met Benson and ended in the second year of law school."

"Oh. Maybe I shouldn't have brought it up."

"I'm glad you asked."

"Really? Why?"

"Because it means you're thinking about me. You're wondering who I was before I knew Benson, and before I met you."

Grace was thoughtful for a moment, conscious of their fingers linked together and the firmness and warmth of his skin.

"I can't believe I was so wrong about how you felt about me."

"It was better that way, believe me. You were married. I was on the outside looking in. It didn't matter how I felt."

"I thought a lot about you. It always made me feel guilty. Like I was cheating on Benson."

"You never would have. I never would have asked."

"You're right."

"That would have been a sure way of losing you."

She closed her eyes. "Right again."

The ship docked in St. George's, Bermuda, on the third day out of New York. Neither Grace nor Carter had ever been to the island before, and Grace was completely charmed by the quaintness of its old towns and by the English customs that were maintained by the locals.

She did not object when Carter suggested renting a scooter for getting around. Although nervous about this open mode of transportation, Grace trusted Carter to keep them both safe. After a few hair-raising turns on the twisty roads, she got into the adventure. They stopped a number of times at historic points and found a lovely outdoor café overlooking a pink sand beach. At Tobacco Cay, Carter rented snorkeling gear, and again overcoming her initial fears, Grace let him teach her how to use the gear to watch sea life just beneath the water's surface.

They lay stretched out in the sun on towels brought from the ship. Everything was beautiful. Warm. Colorful. Friendly. She was very glad that she'd overcome her qualms and followed her instincts to accompany Carter on this trip. But Grace had more than a few moments of feeling overwhelmed by how much she missed her children. She was anxious about them being okay without her there.

A cloud blocked the sun and covered half her body in shadow.

She opened her eyes and saw Carter leaning over her. She waited for him to say something, but his actions were much more eloquent and to the point. He lowered his torso and his head and his mouth, and kissed her. Caught unprepared, Grace felt an instant languid swirling of sensation. A release of pent-up energy and longing softened her limbs, and she responded naturally. She'd been holding herself in check for the last few days, hoping for a blissful return of the magic. How had Carter known she was ready?

Grace's thoughts of Madison and Becca were replaced by images of making love in the sand.

Instead of being worn out from too much sun, sea air, and the intoxicating taste of hot kisses, Grace felt awakened, as if she'd been set free. She examined her face in the mirror to see if anything else had changed. Her mouth was fuller, poised for smiling. And her eyes were bright. As she dressed for dinner that evening, while the ship sailed on to the next port on the island, Grace wondered if Carter would notice. Could he tell, as she had been able to on the beach earlier in the day, that there had been another shift in her awareness?

Even Carter's knock to summon her to dinner was new. It was quiet. And on the other side of the door, he seemed expectant, waiting, alert for some signal from her. They stood silently, staring at each other across the threshold. By some agreement, he stepped into her stateroom, and she stepped back. The door closed behind him, and they both knew.

They came together, still silent, communicating only with what had already been building between them. They'd had three days to synchronize their rhythm, and it was finally coming together. They embraced and began kissing, not in a tentative or exploratory manner as before, but with knowledge of what they each wanted from the other. No half-measures, no precipitous moves, no memories of the past. Grace knew in that instant that she'd finally gotten beyond the past and stood firmly in the present, ready to take on the future.

Her hands shook as she helped Carter remove his shirt and unfasten the belt at his waist. While kissing her, his hands expertly lowered the zipper on her dress and slid it from her shoulders. Working as a team, they rid themselves of the rest of their clothing.

His hands and fingers were everywhere, stroking and caressing and teasing. With bold intent, he thrust his hips against her, cupped her breasts, and massaged the nipples. Grace explored with her hands the hard planes of his chest, the erect stiffness of his penis, and let herself feel as a woman who desires a man should. She took a step back and lowered herself to the bed, and holding on to her, Carter carefully followed.

The steady and gentle listing of the ship aided them when Grace raised her open thighs and encouraged Carter to join with her. To the rocking of the vessel, their bodies locked together as he thrust and she heaved, and they moved with perfect choreography, timing, and release. They clung to each other, having already waited for three years before even allowing themselves the freedom to speak of their feelings.

"We're going to miss dinner," Grace observed, panting.

"We could order in," Carter suggested, his lips nuzzling across her cheek to her lips.

"Maybe later. Unless you're hungry." Grace arched her back, making it easier for Carter to take the tips of her breasts in his mouth.

"This will do for now."

She laughed, but her laughter was abruptly cut short and turned to a long moan when he began making love to her again.

Afterward, they felt little need to eat and less desire to leave the cabin. They finally did, however, for one of the famed midnight buffets. Although common sense told Grace that no one should be eating Chocolate Decadence Cake at that hour, her body demanded it. They discovered an empty whirlpool, and risking that at almost one in the morning no one else would join them, Grace and Carter got in, the steaming bubbles hiding their nakedness.

They missed breakfast the next morning but woke in time for lunch. Carter never did make it to the gym again for the rest of the trip, and Grace missed a reflexology appointment at the spa. But whatever they missed of what the cruise had to offer, they made up for in the privacy of their cabins. There they had the joy of discovering that what they were experiencing together had been well worth waiting for.

Five

"Boy, that must have been some vacation."

"What are you talking about?" Grace asked one of her colleagues, who'd just handed her a copy of the budget for the next year.

"You came back looking fabulous, but you've been really distracted. Like you'd rather be back on vacation."

"That sounds about right," Grace responded dryly as her colleague laughed. "Unfortunately, it will have to last me through the summer and fall. I want to spend as much time as I can with my kids once school is out."

"That's too bad. I know you love your kids, but that's not a vacation."

Grace was about to say that that was just the way it was but thought better of it. She and Carter had already had their first argument because she wasn't willing to consider alternatives like day camp, or visiting his brother and his family in Arizona, or letting the kids spend more time with her father. Or with Marjorie. It didn't help that spring was one of the busiest times at the society, with almost nightly outdoor sponsored events, which meant working late.

Grace wasn't spending as much time as she would have liked with Madison and Becca, and even less time with Carter.

As she worked to get her budget in order, she also tried to conjure up those glorious six days at sea with Carter. It was one of the ways that she had of recapturing the glory of their time together. It all seemed like a wonderful fantasy now that they were back home. It had been next to impossible to continue with any intimacy when they'd returned to the city from the cruise. She was uncomfortable with his staying over at the house, and they'd been unable to find time when Grace could stay with Carter. The relationship, at least the physical part of it, seemed at a stalemate before it had even gotten started.

"What happened to the line item on the budget for hiring part-time help?" Grace frowned at the Excel spread sheet on her computer screen.

"It was taken out while you were away. There's just no money for more staff."

"What about the money I requested to buy a new printer?"

"Gone."

Grace sighed, agitated and aggravated. "I need another vacation," she mumbled.

But that would not solve her problems, and she knew it. She was seriously off track. She found it difficult to balance work and family. She had to pick the kids up from school and drop them off in the mornings, not to mention playdates, team sports, laundry, cleaning, church, grandparent visits, and trips to the mall. There was barely time to sleep. And nowhere on her list of things to do was there room for Carter.

Grace knew he was trying his best not to make a big deal about what little time they spent together, but she had yet to find a balance she could live with.

And it was inevitable that Marjorie would find out that she was seeing Carter—when she could see him, that is. It was understandable that the idea of her dating again touched a raw nerve for her mother-in-law. It was unfair of Marjorie to feel betrayed and abandoned. But so far Grace had found it impossible to have a clear, friendly conversation with her former mother-in-law about both of them moving on with their lives. She tried to put herself in Marjorie's place. It wasn't fair that her only child had died.

In a gesture of helplessness, Grace put the budget down on her desk. "I can't deal with this right now. Maybe tomorrow I can think my way through it. By the way, I really appreciate you doing the event this evening in my place."

"Sure, it's no problem. But I can't help you out next week. I have a class that night."

"Fine. I'll arrange something else."

"Why don't you ask Ricardo?"

"Good thought," Grace said as her phone began to ring. She eagerly snatched it up. "Hi, Dad."

"Just checking to see what's going on this weekend. Am I the baby-sitter or what? Have you changed your mind and asked Marjorie?"

"To be honest, I don't know what's happening. I haven't talked to Marjorie yet, and I also haven't heard from Carter."

"Oh, oh. Trouble in paradise?"

Grace was in no mood for teasing. "I don't know. We've had a hard time finding time to spend together. And he's had to travel back to Chicago a few times; plus he's trying to pull his place together. He's still waiting for the furniture delivery. There's not much more than a bed there."

"Well, if I remember anything about being in love, that's all you need. Not just love, but the bed."

"Very funny."

"Look, I know it's been difficult, but you'll figure it out. Now, I'll take the kids if you need me to. . . ."

"Thanks. I'm going to talk to Marjorie, if you're okay with that. She's been very difficult since finding out about me and Carter. And I think she's been trying to influence Madison. He's been asking a lot of questions he shouldn't even be thinking about."

"Like?"

Grace sighed. "There's the whole question of Carter staying with me. Marjorie has been asking Madison if Carter ever stays over. But how do I have a personal life and do the right thing?"

"Carefully. Very carefully," her father teased gently.

Grace had just gotten Becca into her pajamas when she thought she heard a car in her driveway. She didn't pay it much attention since drivers were known to use any driveway on the street when they wanted to turn around. Then she heard the front doorbell.

"Mommy, someone's at the door," Madison called out from his room.

"Who's that?" Becca added.

Grace gave her daughter a stuffed animal and her favorite blanket to hold. "I'm going to find out. You stay in bed. I'll be back to kiss you good night, okay?"

She navigated around the children's things still in the living room and headed for the front door. She looked through the security hole and was stunned to see Carter there so late at night. She opened the door.

"Carter. What are you doing here?"

"I came to see you."

"But it's late."

"I knew I'd catch you at home," he said meaningfully.

"I'm sorry. Come in."

Carter stepped into the house and at once reached for her. Grace made a feeble attempt to wiggle away from his grasp.

"Carter! The kids are still awake. . . ."

That was as far as she got because she was in his arms and was being kissed in such a way as to remind her of what she missed, among other things, when she and Carter were apart. She gave in to the seduction and returned his kiss with equal ardor.

Grace heard childish giggling and tore herself out of Carter's arms, speechless and embarrassed.

"Hi, Carter," Madison waved.

Becca, who'd also gotten out of bed, was too busy sucking two of her fingers to do more than stare sleepily at the visitor.

"Hey, Madison. I'm sorry for coming by so late. I wanted to see your mother."

"When are you coming back so we can play chess?"

"I can play chess," Becca asserted, but no one paid her any attention.

"Okay, back to bed, both of you. Right now!" Grace said in her sternest parental voice.

Carter touched her arm. "Wait. Before you make them leave, I'd like to ask Madison and Becca something. It will only take a minute, okay?"

"You can ask me anything," Madison said, delighted at being able to help in some way.

"First, let's all sit down."

Carter took a seat on the sofa, perching on the edge, and leaned forward to rest his forearms on his thighs. Grace sat down not far from him and beckoned to her daughter. Becca crawled onto her mother's lap and leaned back against her. Madison came to sit on the sofa arm nearest to Carter.

"When are you coming back to play with us?" Madison asked Carter again.

Carter sent a knowing glance to Grace. "Soon, I hope. I've been busy at work and traveling a lot, and I just moved into a new place."

"Can I come and visit?" Madison asked.

"Me, too," Becca whined. "I want to visit 'partment."

"Yes, I want you all to come and see me. That's what I want to talk to you about," Carter said, looking around at the gathering. He reached out for Grace's hand and held it fast as she would have pulled away. "How would you guys feel if I visited more often?"

"Mommy, can he? I want Carter to come see us."

Grace was watching Carter, hope burning bright in her gaze that there was a way to resolve the issue, and others.

"I think that would be wonderful, if you and Becca don't mind," Grace said.

"Becca, wake up! Don't you want Carter to come visit us?" Madison shouted.

Becca was almost asleep in her mother's arms. Grace held her small daughter closer. "Madison, we can hear you."

"Is that okay?" Carter asked Grace.

"Yes. I think we all would like it very much if you did."

"Good. Now second question. This is for Madison since he's the man of the house. Will it be okay if I take your mother out?"

"Where to?"

"Lots of places. Dinner. Maybe a movie. Long drives. Maybe away overnight," Carter ventured.

"You mean like sleepaway camp?"

"Yeah. Something like that." Carter smiled. "I enjoy your mother's company. And sometimes, it's really important that she gets to spend some time with other grown-ups. Like . . . going out on a date."

"I guess," Madison shrugged. He came over and leaned against Carter's knee. "Maybe you can come and live with us. I don't mind if you share my room."

"Is he going to be here?" Marjorie asked Grace, walking into the house as if she was on a death march.

"Carter wanted to come, but I told him I wanted just you and the kids for dinner. I'll invite him another time."

"Please don't do it just for me."

"I won't. I'll do it for all of us."

"It's not going to make any difference to me. I don't approve of you and Carter getting together, and I don't like you doing it around my grandchildren."

"I'm sorry you're unhappy about my relationship with Carter, but it's not going to end because you want it to."

"Then I don't know what you hope to prove by this dinner."

"Just that the children like Carter, and they're very comfortable around him. They consider Carter a friend. Actually, they think he's *their* special friend. I want to be careful introducing a different relationship to them. I want them to know and understand the difference between Carter and Benson."

"Lord, have mercy," Marjorie moaned, dropping into a chair and quietly crying.

Grace sat next to her and patiently patted her shoulder. "It's going to take time, but you've got to see that the children are always going to have other people in their lives, Marjorie. Other men. No one is ever going to replace Benson, but he can't and won't be the only important figure in their lives. I'll always want them to know who he was and what he was like, but please try to accept that there's no way Benson can be a part of their lives."

"You're going to take them away from me."

"I would never do that. But you could drive them away, if you're not careful." Grace stood up and went to the stairs to call up. "Madison, Becca. Come down. Nana Marjorie is here. We're going to have dinner soon."

Madison was the first one down the stairs, and he dutifully greeted his grandmother with a hug.

"Nana, how come you're crying?"

Marjorie attempted to dry her eyes. "Oh, I guess I'm a little sad, baby. I still miss your father very much."

Madison was sweet and kind with his grandmother, wanting to make her feel better. He laid his cheek on her shoulder. "Don't worry, Nana. You can love me and Becca and Mommy just as much. I bet my Daddy won't mind."

* * *

Grace preceded Carter into the apartment and put down her tote. There were still precious few pieces of furniture, but the absence of fully outfitted rooms no longer mattered. The first time she and Carter had been able to spend a full day and night there alone had changed her mind about the apartment. Without it, she and Carter might have been reduced to rendezvousing in the guest rooms of friends' homes or, if desperate, at a midtown hotel. Only a few times had they been able to enjoy the cozy comfort of her own bedroom. On those rare occasions, the children had been overnight guests of either grandparent.

Carter took her coat and hung it in the hall closet. He immediately led her to the bedroom, where the queen-sized platform bed had been joined by a comfortable chair, a small bureau, and a few lamps. His single-mindedness made her laugh. As long as they could be together, it was home sweet home.

"I never thought you'd hear me say this, but I'm so glad to be here," Grace said as Carter offered a comforting hug.

"I'm so glad you're here, too," he agreed.

"Thank you for waiting for me. I didn't expect to have to stay that extra thirty minutes."

He kissed her forehead. "No problem. I'm getting used to it."

"I guess we should think about a more permanent arrangement," Grace mused boldly, not just to herself.

"Sooner or later," Carter said, stepping back. He began undressing her, and Grace stood like an obedient child, letting him.

"Do you want to keep this apartment?"

"It has its uses."

"I could get a bigger house."

"The kids will be leaving home soon. You don't need bigger."

She chuckled. "Carter, Madison's only six. He's got a long way to go before he leaves for good." She turned to look at him, with a loving, warm regard. "We've never talked about you and me having children."

"It's on the list."

"Carter?" She was down to her underwear and pressed against him, with her arms around his neck.

He kissed her nose, her mouth briefly. "What?"

"I never told you before, but I used to be afraid that I would love you so much more than I did Benson."

"That was never a requirement. Come on. Take off your things and get into bed."

"Are we having dinner here?" she grinned, remembering the last few nights of the cruise, when they'd more or less barricaded themselves in their staterooms and lived on room service.

"Maybe later," he said, looking down at her as she curled up beneath the covers, waiting and watching him remove his own things. "I have something else in mind for now."

She pressed close to the long, hard warmth of his body. "Carter? What if you'd never gotten that promotion? And had never considered moving to New York?"

"We would have found each other eventually, Grace. I always knew, it was you and no other."

Love Lessons

Deirdre Savoy

Prologue

Another day, another forty-six cents.

Cara Williams muttered that familiar sentiment as she walked the distance from the front of the building to where her car was parked in the school parking lot. There had been days when the amount she credited herself earning and when teaching twenty-three kindergartners didn't seem to cost her closer to two dollars worth of aggravation, but that was a long time ago. At thirty-seven, she'd been teaching for fifteen years—long enough that the prospect of a sabbatical made her mouth water. However, the newly dubbed Department of Education had seen fit to decline her application for a sabbatical for the second time in two years.

It wasn't that she didn't love her job, because she did. She loved the kids. But she was tired. She could really use a year away from the classroom to renew herself, to study, maybe to travel somewhere. Her brother Alfred nearly laughed himself silly when she told him she wanted to take time off.

"You teachers get every other day off as it is. You want to take a whole year off and still get paid."

Telling him that a sabbatical would not be at full pay did nothing to stifle her brother's incredulity or his humor. Cara had merely shrugged to herself. Anyone who didn't understand the necessity of a sabbatical simply didn't work with kids.

With her one free, gloveless hand, she gathered her collar closer around her neck. The evening was frigid as only a night in the northeast Bronx could be—windy, with an icy blast coming off the waters of the Pelham Bay. As usual, she was the last one in the school building, working on the lessons and projects she planned for her class. Unlike most of her colleagues, Cara reserved her time at home for herself. Any work she needed to complete was handled on school premises or not at all. The only exception to her rule was filling out report cards, which usually demanded more time to complete than she possessed at the end of a typical school day.

During the day, teachers' cars filled the lot; however, at this time of night, every car besides hers most likely belonged to one of the residents of the surrounding neighborhood. She trudged over to her car, a red Ford Taurus, and set her schoolbag on the hood. She first opened the driver's side door and tossed her purse onto the passenger seat, on top of the gloves she'd forgotten to wear inside the building. She started the engine before retrieving her school-bag to store it in her trunk. Surprisingly, the trunk to the car beside hers was wide open. Debris littered the ground behind the car, as if the trunk had been cleared haphazardly.

Cara sighed. Although this wasn't a high-crime area, a certain amount of vandalism of cars in the lot had been known to occur. That's why the school had hired a guard to look after the lot during the day. For a moment Cara debated what to do. She didn't feel comfortable leaving the car the way she found it. Leaving the trunk open was an invitation for further abuse. For all she knew, the car belonged to one of the students' families, who though not poor, could ill afford to come out the next morning to find a stripped car. She gazed around the lot and saw no one who might be returning to the open car.

Oh well. Using the palm of one hand, she pushed the trunk closed. Even if she was wrong, and the owner of the car had left the trunk open for some unknown reason, they would certainly have the key to open it up again. At worst, she'd caused them a little inconvenience.

She stowed her bag in the trunk and got into her car. As she drove the length of the lot to the entrance, she scanned the area, still looking for a possible owner of the car. Finding no one, she grew more certain that her first assumption had been the correct one. Hopefully, she'd saved that car from any further vandalization. Chalk that one up as her good deed for the day.

One

"The fingerprints came back on the Randazzo case."

Joe Malone looked up as one of the clerks dropped a file folder on his desk and kept moving. Isidor "Iggy" Randazzo had been found in the trunk of a stolen car earlier that morning, with a couple of chunks missing from the back of his skull where two bullets had gone in. So far, they knew little about him, except that the coroner had set a preliminary time of death as sometime the previous afternoon, and that according to his sheet and his sister, he was a petty criminal with possible Mafia connections. The last bit of information had prompted Joe to put in a call to a guy he knew on the organized crime squad to see if Randazzo was on their radar.

"Thanks," Joe said to the woman's retreating back.

"You talking to me?" the voice on the phone asked.

"Sorry. The fingerprints just came in."

"Who do they belong to? Any name I should know?"

Joe flipped open the file and scanned the sheet inside. He didn't find a name Gus would recognize, but one that he did. Cara Williams. His first thought was that there had to be more than one Cara Williams in all of New York City. Then he checked the address given for her—her parents' house in the Bronx, four blocks from the house he'd lived in as a kid. What the hell did she have to do with some mobster wannabe from Brooklyn? Why was there a perfect set of her fingerprints on the car in which Randazzo was found? The last he'd heard from his sister Allison, Cara Williams was a schoolteacher, not a hitwoman for the mob.

He scanned the file. She'd been arrested four years ago as part of some animal rights protest. The charges had been dropped, but as was pretty typical, her fingerprints had not been removed from the database. His gaze settled on the photo that came with the file. Even in the dated picture she didn't look much different than she had twenty years ago when he'd known her in high school. The same corkscrew curls floated around her oval face. The same expression that said "whatever" molded her features, even though that saying hadn't been popular back in the day. He'd changed; he knew that. Lines had etched themselves around his eyes and mouth, and a bit of salt now peppered his hair. Apparently, time had been kinder to her.

"What's the name?" He detected a hint of impatience in Gus's voice.

"Cara Williams."

"Doesn't ring a bell. I'll see what I can find on her, too."

"Thanks." They set a time and place to meet, which was the purpose of the call, and hung up. That done, Joe's thoughts returned to Cara. The girl he'd known had been a bit of a pacifist, an opponent of the death penalty. He couldn't imagine what circumstance might have caused her to alter her views so radically enough for her to be involved in an execution-style murder. He was looking forward to seeing her and finding out exactly how she figured into this mess.

Actually, he'd been looking forward to seeing her ever since he'd gotten the notice from St. Xavier High School that their twentieth reunion was right around the corner. Although he'd kept up with few of his friends from those days, he'd been tempted to show up just to see if she would. He hadn't formulated any plan for what he'd do if and when he saw her. For all he knew, she was still married to that dentist. In a way, he hoped she still was, since that would mean she was happy. Cara wasn't the type of woman to put up with much foolishness from a man. He'd learned that the hard way.

He dialed his sister's number at the PR firm she owned. Allison the "Walking Palm Pilot" would probably have some idea where Cara worked. If he moved his butt, he could make it up to the Bronx to see Cara and get back to Brooklyn in time to meet Gus. Of course, he could wait until later, until after she got home, to talk to her. But he'd rather hear her story and, if possible, remove her from the scope of the investigation before she got too embroiled in it.

Allison answered her phone on the third ring, made a few acerbic comments about his lack of brotherly devotion, then provided the information he wanted. She didn't know the address of Cara's school, but she knew the school name and number and the cross streets. She didn't ask him for a reason why he wanted the information. Joe didn't volunteer one, either. Knowing her, she'd probably invent some scenario in which he was, after all these years, trying to get back with Cara, and nothing as prosaic as the truth would get such romantic notions out of his sister's mind.

Let her think whatever she wanted. His only interest was keeping Cara out of trouble, if indeed she didn't belong in it. The only way to find out was to see her. He got up. *Time to get going.*

Every Tuesday afternoon during sixth period, Cara and the other three kindergarten teachers at P.S. 158 got together in her classroom to discuss lesson plans for the following week. Although the teachers were free to implement lessons for their own classrooms as they saw fit, general topics for reading, writing, math, social studies, and science were decided on according to the curricula.

The four of them sat around the kidney-shaped table at the front of her room, Cara on the only "grown-up" chair she had in the room, the others on kids' chairs. "I think that about covers it," Cara said, looking over her notes, which she would xerox for the others. "We just need one more word for the week. We only have four."

"How about . . . hello," said Monica, the teacher who had the room next to hers.

Cara had her head down, poised to write. There was something odd in Monica's voice, which made Cara look up. "We've already used that. . . ." She trailed off upon discovering that the other three women were looking not at her, but behind her toward the classroom door.

A man stood in the open doorway. Not so much time had passed that she didn't recognize him. Her eyes wandered over him as she tried to swallow. Her throat had suddenly gone dry. Aside from a little gray at his temples and a few lines around his eyes, he looked exactly the same—the same gray-brown eyes, the same boyish face, the same wiry body beneath the suit he wore. The only thing missing was the sardonic smile that used to be his trademark. Instead, he wore a somber expression, which made her wonder who'd died.

But the first words he spoke belied the seriousness of his expression. "Hey, Face."

They were the first words he'd ever spoken to her, a lifetime ago when they'd both been freshmen at St. Xavier High School. She'd been late to Spanish class after her English teacher had kept her a few minutes after class to discuss a paper. By the time she'd arrived for her Spanish class, all the seats at the front, where she usually sat, were taken. She was forced to take the one desk that remained, in the row next to him.

The school term had just started, but already she knew his reputation. He thought himself some kind of wit, handy with a sarcastic comment or joke just when it wasn't wanted. Since she didn't want to be the brunt of any of his supposed humor, she'd avoided him. She hadn't had a choice on that day. She'd slipped into the seat beside him, hoping he wouldn't notice her.

Luck wasn't with her, though. She felt his gaze on her, even though she refused to look at him. She focused on Señora Martin, who was teaching the class the various body parts in Spanish.

"Face," Señora Martin said, using a pointer to indicate the image of a woman's face drawn on the board with chalk. "*En Español, cara.*"

While thirty-one of the students had dutifully repeated the word, he had leaned closer to her and whispered, "Hey, Face."

Heat stole into her cheeks as a few of the kids around them snickered. She'd looked back at him with as much disdain as she could muster. "*Cara* also means expensive," she'd informed him. "And since you couldn't possibly afford me, maybe you should keep your mouth shut."

It was a silly thing to say, and in some ways, mean. Everyone knew he had to take a job after school to help his family financially. But he'd flustered her with his unwanted comment.

He'd shrugged, apparently unfazed by her attempt to insult him. "I didn't know you were for sale."

She'd gritted her teeth as he straightened in his chair. She hadn't had a handy retort for that, and besides, Señora Martin was looking her way. He might be on a first-name basis with the dean of students, but she wasn't, and she wanted to keep it that way. Instead, she'd opened her notebook and had drawn a hangman figure. The face on the stick figure looked surprisingly like Joseph Alan Malone.

Cara blinked and focused on the present. Everyone was waiting for a response from her. She gave the only one that popped into her head. "What are you doing here?"

"Can I speak to you for a moment, privately?"

"Of course." She glanced at her three colleagues, who seemed reluctant to leave. She couldn't blame them. They all knew that she hadn't been involved with a man since her husband died two years before. They probably had Joe pegged as some sort of romantic interest, and therefore he was of interest to them. In that case, they were bound to be disappointed. Whatever purpose Joe had in showing up there, it wasn't to pick up the thread from the past. Cara stood as an encouragement for them to leave.

Once the three women had filed out of the room, Joe stepped farther inside and let the door close. The sober expression returned to his face, reminding her that this wasn't a social call. She sank down to her seat, still facing him. She would have offered him one of the kids' chairs, except he would never have fit his six-foot-plus frame on one of them, or if he had tried, he would never have gotten back up. "What can I do for you, Joe?"

He stepped closer to her. As he moved, he pulled a minicassette recorder from his pocket. He didn't ask her if he could tape their conversation, which was fine, since she wouldn't have objected, anyway. She had nothing to hide.

"Do you know an Isidore 'Iggy' Randazzo?"

That name didn't sound familiar, and she was sure she would have remembered it if she'd heard it before. "Should I?"

"He was found dead this morning in a car that bore your fingerprints."

"My fingerprints?" That surprised her, though it didn't surprise her to know that Joe was there on official business. She'd heard from Allison that he'd become a cop out in Brooklyn or Queens somewhere. "This is your case?"

"Yes."

A simple, straightforward answer. That did surprise her. The Joe she'd known hadn't been capable of responding without some sort of smart-aleck comment. Obviously, more had changed about him than solely his appearance. "I don't know what to tell you. I don't know any Iggy Randazzo. What kind of car was it?"

"A black Lexus. Does that ring a bell?"

She wondered if he'd asked that question idly or if her reaction had shown on her face. "Last night, around six o'clock, when I was leaving school, I noticed that the trunk of the car next to mine in the school parking lot was open. There was glass on the ground and some other stuff. I thought someone had broken into the car. I closed the trunk, thinking I was doing its owner a favor."

"Where in the lot?"

"The second spot from the top. I usually get here early enough to take the first."

A bell rang that was meant to announce the change of period. But since the PA system was off, it served as more of a two-minute warning that class was about to end. She stood. "I have to go to my students to dismiss them."

"Go ahead. I have some more questions for you. I'll need you to show me where the car was parked once the lot is cleared."

"All right. Where should I meet you afterward?"

"Here." He opened the classroom door.

Cara walked through it and turned left toward the stairs. Her class was in the second-floor art room. As she ascended the stairs, she wondered what exactly she'd gotten herself into trying to be a Good Samaritan. As the saying went, no good deed ever goes unpunished. She hoped her minor involvement in this murder didn't cost her too much.

Joe waited until Cara left to close the classroom door and pull out his cell phone. He needed to alert his superior to what he'd learned and to get a crime scene unit to inspect the school parking lot. He didn't expect to find anything pertinent, given the number of people passing through the area during the course of a day. That accomplished, he went to the principal's office to announce his presence and to ensure that those parked in the lot would move their cars immediately. The principal, a portly Hispanic man, went to the general office to make the announcement that all teachers should be out of the building by 3:15.

With the help of a local squad car, Joe blocked off the near entrance of the parking lot, which was across from the spot where Cara said the cars had been parked. Within a few minutes, the area was alive with teachers, kids glad to be out of school, and an assortment of school buses and caretakers to take the children home. Joe felt a little buzz of excitement. At least they now had some handle on how Randazzo had spent part of his day—or at least the car in which he'd been entombed. So far, Joe had come up with nothing from Randazzo's tight-lipped mother and sister. For all Joe knew, they were as crooked as Iggy Randazzo had been, though his mother exuded a purely maternal vibe that suggested otherwise.

The parking lot was a clue, though Joe had no idea to where it would lead. What would a Brooklyn-born boy be doing up on the edge of the Bronx, so far from home? The car had been found with the VIN numbers filed down and without license plates. Hopefully, the lab would be able to lift the numbers, and the crime scene guys would be able to provide him with some answers as to what had gone on in the lot. He suspected that the parking lot was where Randazzo had first made acquaintance with the interior of the trunk. Otherwise, why leave it open? Which led him back to what Randazzo was doing in the Bronx. Maybe his friend Gus would have the answer for him.

Joe looked up and noticed Cara approaching. Just as when he'd seen her picture, he thought the years had been kind to her. Aside from the grown-up clothes and demeanor, she looked as she had in high school. Her wild hair was contained under a fuzzy black hat, and her feet were encased in a pair of high-heeled boots. He hadn't noticed the boots before. Maybe she only wore them in and out of the building. She stopped a few feet away from him, on the other side of the crime scene tape, which had been put up to ward off the curious, her hips canted to one side, a fist on her upturned hip. He knew what she was thinking. How could she wait for him inside when all the teachers had been thrown out of school?

He ducked under the tape and went to her. "Where's your car?" he asked. The lot was now clear of all vehicles save for those belonging to the police.

"I parked in the high school lot." She gestured over her shoulder to the larger parking area. "I hope I don't have to answer your questions standing here."

Just then, as if to punctuate her reasons for not wanting to remain outdoors, a gust of wind blew past, whipping her hair into her face. With a delicate gloved hand, she brushed it back, a familiar gesture.

"Why don't you show me where around here we can get some coffee? I'll follow you in my car."

Since he was parked at the curb, he drove her back to her car, then waited for her to pull out so he could follow her. He remembered that there was a coffee shop almost around the corner, but she didn't stop there. She drove to a Dunkin' Donuts on Conner Street, which was at least five minutes out of the way. Obviously, she didn't want to be seen with him. Considering the glances on the faces of her colleagues, and her lack of explanation as to who he was, he figured she liked to keep her business to herself. That hadn't changed, either.

Once they both had a cup of coffee and a doughnut, which he paid for, they sat at one of the low, narrow tables along the window. Even though he suspected his comment would be unwelcome, he said, "You're looking well. In fact, you don't look a day older than the last time I saw you."

He knew the last of what he said was a mistake, even before a slight frown turned her lips down. "You have some questions for me?"

He pulled out his tape recorder, set it to record, and placed it on the table. "You said you left the building around six o'clock?"

"Yes, maybe a little after. I got home at six-thirty, and I only live ten minutes from school."

"Did you see anyone else when you came out?"

"No one, and I looked. I thought whoever owned the car might be nearby."

"Had you ever seen the car before?"

"Not to my knowledge. I figured it belonged to one of the neighboring families. The school sits in the middle of a large housing complex. I don't know the owners of most of the cars that park in the lot after school."

She took off her gloves and picked up her coffee, seeming to savor the warmth that flowed through the Styrofoam cup into her fingers.

"What happened to your gloves that day?"

A hint of a smile turned up her lips. "I forgot them in my car."

He found himself smiling, too. He used to call her "the absent-minded student," since her nose was always in a book, and wherever she went, she left a trail of her belongings behind. "I would have thought you'd grow out of that."

She lifted one shoulder in a delicate shrug. "For the most part, I have."

He put away his notebook, having nothing more to ask her, at least nothing that had anything to do with his case. He sipped from his cup and surreptitiously checked his watch. He should have left then to meet Gus, but he couldn't find the will to get his butt out of the chair. He set his cup on the table. "How's your mom?"

"She's fine. Florida agrees with her. She's made new friends, a new life."

He knew she meant after her father died. He'd heard about the funeral a couple of years back but hadn't been able to make the wake. At the time, he'd thought it was for the best, as he had no idea if she would want to see him or not. "I'm sorry about your dad," he said, anyway.

She shrugged again. "The man was a walking advertisement for a heart attack. Everyone in the world knew it was coming but him."

Still, his passing must have pained her, Joe thought. His own parents' passings had been more sudden. He sipped his coffee, searching for something to say. Eventually, he settled on, "Did you get the invitation to the Valentine's dance?"

She laughed. "I would think St. Xavier's would have given up on that by now."

"I guess they have for the young folks, since they made it old home day."

"I guess. Are you going?"

He shrugged. If he'd entertained the thought at all, it had been for the possibility of seeing her. "How about you?"

She offered him a wicked smile. "And pass up the opportunity to see old man Hayden try to do the Shake?"

He rubbed the back of his neck with his palm. "That would be something to see."

"I'll skip it, if you don't mind." She took one final sip from her cup. "Is there anything else?"

He switched off the tape recorder, thinking he'd have to erase the last of what they'd said. Yet at the same time, he wasn't ready to let her go. In the few minutes he'd spent with her, he'd realized how much more he wanted to know about her, not about her past, but about the woman she was today. "Have dinner with me?" he asked impulsively, forgetting his own plans.

She tilted her head to the side, considering him. "Why would I want to do that?"

He didn't have a ready answer for that, considering there was no good reason for her to do so. "I suppose, for old time's sake wouldn't be a good enough answer."

She shook her head. "I like to be in early on school nights. I have a lot of work to do."

He scanned her face, finding no evidence of a lie, but not quite believing her, either. "Some other time?"

She offered him a half-smile that told him nothing. Before he could think of something else to say, she stood. "If you need anything else, you know where to find me."

He rose to his feet. "If you think of anything else, give me a call." He pulled out one of his cards and handed it to her.

She surveyed it a moment, then glanced up at him. "Thanks." She adjusted her bag on her shoulder, then walked away.

It occurred to him belatedly that he should have walked her to her car rather than watching her through the donut shop's large windows. He had no reason to continue occupying their table and would, in fact, be late to meet Gus as it was. Being in her presence had sabotaged his common sense, as it always did. Shaking his head at himself, he cleared the table and left.

Cara walked into her house on Ely Avenue a little after four o'clock. Misty, the little kitten she'd recently adopted, came out of her hidey-hole, a quizzical expression on her tiny face. Even her pet didn't expect her home this early. She set down her bag and picked up the kitten to nestle it in the crook of her arm. "What have you been up to today?"

The cat purred and adjusted itself to receive Cara's petting where she wanted it.

Cara sighed. In the two years since she'd moved back into her parents' home, she'd often considered renting out one of the bedrooms upstairs just to have some human, adult companionship on occasion. The kitten was no great conversationalist; her friends from school all had men or children who claimed their time away from school. Most of the neighborhood families she'd known in her youth had long since moved on. She hadn't bothered to make friends with any of the new ones, considering most of them were young families with children. Her situation left her feeling isolated and lonely.

That probably explained her reluctance to walk away from Joe and her simultaneous determination to do so. Any relationship between them was the province of the past. She didn't know what prompted his dinner invitation, and it was in her best interest not to think about it too much. Otherwise, she might change her mind. She pulled his card from where she'd left it in the pocket of her skirt. The card boasted his name and several numbers where he could be reached. She got a pushpin and tacked the card up on the bulletin board that hung above the wall phone. She didn't know why she kept it, considering she really knew nothing about his case and had no reason to call. *For old time's sake*, she told herself, then went up to her bedroom to change.

Two

Joe pulled into the parking lot of Il Trattoria, an Italian restaurant in the Canarsie section of Brooklyn. The sun had long since set. He spotted Gus sitting at one of the tables lining the front window before he made it to the door. With his dark hair combed back from his forehead and his black leather jacket over a camel-colored sport shirt, Gus looked every bit like one of the Mafiosi he investigated, though his heritage was Greek, not Italian.

Joe slid into the seat opposite him. "How's it hanging?"

Gus raised his glass in salute. "I bet I'm doing better than you're doing."

Joe couldn't argue with that. "Have you got something for me?"

"Other than the calamari I ordered?"

"Yeah. Other than that."

Gus pushed a file toward him. "Randazzo is small potatoes as mob guys go. As far as I can tell, he hasn't progressed much from being Anthony DiMarco's errand boy. And there's nothing to suggest that Tony would want him taken out."

Joe picked up the file and skimmed it. Randazzo had been picked up for "finding" the contents of a lost trailer carrying electronic equipment and for a few other minor offenses. Nothing had stuck, which wasn't surprising considering he'd been bailed out and presumably represented by a high-powered mob lawyer—the same lawyer his boss used. It looked like Joe would be paying said boss a visit.

"You got anything else on him, anything personal?"

"He lived with some broad in Brooklyn Heights, but that's about it. He wasn't really on my radar."

"Thanks." Joe stood, grasping the file.

Gus grinned. "Aren't you going to wait for the calamari?"

"Only if I'm handcuffed to the table." Joe jiggled the file. "I'll get this back to you."

"Take your time. We're not looking into him for anything else at the moment."

Outside, Joe returned to his car and got in. He set the file on the seat beside him. Even though having an obvious mob connection for Randazzo's murder would have simplified his investigation in some ways, he was glad no such connection existed. Simply being a witness to any kind of Mafia activity could put Cara in danger. But Randazzo had pissed someone off enough to kill him. Now, all he had to do was find out who.

Joe had bought his house years ago, when he'd first been assigned to the 76th precinct in downtown Brooklyn. The neighborhood was quiet, and there had been a time when the good reputation of the surrounding schools had mattered to him. Angie, his once upon a time fiancée, had approved of both the location and the spaciousness of the three-bedroom home. Every now and again he felt a twinge of regret at calling off their engagement, but tonight was not one of those nights. Tonight he had another woman on his mind.

He went to the refrigerator and extracted the bottle of beer he'd wanted since seeing Gus enjoy his. He shut the refrigerator, and the pink sheet of paper fastened to the front of it with a magnet fluttered. He'd been thinking about her ever since the flyer had arrived in the mail heralding the twentieth reunion Valentine's Day dance for their graduating class.

For a moment his mind drifted back to that first night, to that long ago dance that he wasn't supposed to attend. His friend Willis had talked him into it, though he'd never explained why he'd considered it important for Joe to go.

The only formal event at the school, aside from the senior prom, the Valentine's dance that year had revolved around the theme of the movie *Footloose*, which had come out two years before. That meant that the gym looked like any other high school gymnasium decked out with a bunch of pink and white balloons and a half-assed disco ball. The girls were a bunch of Lori Singer clones; the guys wore an assortment of bad tuxes that would make Vinnie Barbarino throw up.

Joe had stood with his shoulder leaning against the wall, his hands in his pockets, looking for Willis amidst the crush of bodies on the dance floor. Not that he had really expected to find Willis there. Not unless some generous sister had taken pity on him and dragged him onto the floor. Willis had neither the temperament, the looks, nor technique to approach most girls. If Joe had been smart, he would have concentrated on searching the tables for a lone and lonely figure.

He saw Cara then. She was sitting at a table of laughing girls, her head tilted back, her face bright with humor, unself-conscious. He wondered if that would change if she knew he was watching her. He was neither vain nor cocky enough to think she'd care one way or another, but he knew his own mostly undeserved reputation. Besides, she seemed to be enjoying herself too much to wonder what any nearby stranger might see in her expression. He wasn't sure what he saw there himself, yet he felt the pull of attraction to her.

"She's something, isn't she?" said Willis, who'd slipped up beside him unnoticed, as if his words offered a complete explanation of something.

Joe slid a glance at his friend. "Who?"

"You're looking at her."

And she still didn't notice either of them. All in all, that wasn't a bad deal, since it occurred to him that she had something to do with the reason Willis had begged him to go to the dance.

He slid his glance to Willis. "No."

"I didn't ask you anything."

"But you're going to, and the answer is no."

Willis hung his head. "That's cold, man. I just wanted you to introduce me to her. You know her; I don't."

He cast Willis a sour look. The fact that she was in one class of his and he'd spoken two words to her didn't mean he knew her. Judging by her reaction to that one ill-timed remark in Spanish class, she didn't like him, either. He had a mind to tell Willis that, but maybe it was better if he hurried up and got shot down so they could both go home.

Joe pushed off the wall. "Fine. But don't say I didn't warn you."

Willis grinned. "I know."

Joe led the way through the crowd to her table, with Willis following behind. But as he neared her table, he noticed her mood had changed. Instead of laughing, her face bore an annoyed, defiant expression, making him wonder what had happened to cause the shift in her mood.

When Joe reached her, she stood and turned to him before he had the chance to open his mouth.

"Do you want to dance?" she asked him, but she didn't speak with the anticipation of being with someone she wanted to be with. It was apparent that what she wanted was to escape, and any warm, mobile body would do. Too bad Willis hadn't been first, he thought.

She grasped his hand, and without waiting for an answer from him, started pulling him toward the dance floor.

More amused than anything else, he let her lead him to the edge of the floor. Despite the fast beat of the music, he pulled her into his arms.

Not moving, she glanced up at him, a quizzical expression in her eyes. "This isn't a slow song."

No, it wasn't, he thought, but that didn't change anything. "If you want to dance with me, you have to do it my way."

She shrugged and looked away from him. But she did allow him to lead her in a slow, circular sway to the music. Without thinking, he pulled her a little closer, making it easier to appreciate the softness of her body and the sweet smell of her perfume. With a little effort, he reminded himself that he didn't even want her. He'd only approached her because of Willis. At least that's how this had started.

She pulled away from him slightly, shaking her head. "I'm sorry about the way I dragged you out here."

"Why did you?"

She sighed. "Carol was starting in on me again about her cousin Harold. She invited him again tonight, and I didn't feel like dealing with that."

He smiled, hearing the exasperation in her voice. "You're not interested?"

"Not even if he dipped himself in molten gold and allowed me to sell him."

"That bad?"

"No worse than your average egotistical jock with delusions of grandeur. What is it about you guys that makes you physically incapable of appreciating the word 'no'?"

He knew how guys could be but didn't want to be lumped in with that knucklehead. "I don't remember saying no when you asked me to dance."

She rolled her eyes. "So you're the one grand exception."

"Are we done yet?"

He held his breath, his eyes intense, waiting for her answer. He knew what he, surprisingly, wanted to hear from her, but he didn't want to make himself into another Harold.

She cocked her head to one side, her gaze drifting over his face, scrutinizing him in a feminine way. Then her tongue darted out to moisten the corner of her mouth. "When I'm done with you, I'll let you know."

As the tempo of the music shifted to a slow ballad, he'd pulled her closer still, and let the wistfulness of the song and the sway of her body work their magic on him. After that night, they'd been inseparable, or so he'd thought, until she'd gone away to college, and distance caused a rift between them. Or rather his own inability to remain faithful at a distance had done that.

He'd never really gotten a chance to explain to her what had happened, how he'd felt. All these years, he'd wanted to see her, to tell her his side of the story, but he'd never gotten the chance. Or rather, he'd never taken it. He'd known when she moved back to town, but he hadn't sought her out. Maybe he hadn't been as ready to hear what she thought of him as he wanted to pretend.

But now he'd seen her, anyway, and she didn't seem interested in hearing any explanations he hadn't bothered to offer. They were both adults, and whatever water had passed under the bridge between them was old news and best forgotten. There was no point in pretending now. He should throw the flyer away, he reasoned, but he didn't. He went instead to the smallest of the bedrooms located on the second floor, the room he'd converted into a den of sorts, with a large-screen TV and a desk for his computer. He checked his e-mail, most of which came from his sister. How did any one person collect so many ribald jokes in a day? Then he went back to the kitchen to start his dinner.

"Okay, girl, get ready to spill it."

Cara had wondered how long it would take her colleagues to question her about Joe the next morning. She had her answer now:

not long. Cara had been in her classroom a scant five minutes before Monica showed up at her door. She doubted the others would be far behind.

She folded her arms, a posture she recognized was defensive. "There's nothing to tell."

Monica folded her arms, mimicking Cara's stance. "Don't tell me you left here with that gorgeous man, and nothing is going on between the two of you. I know I'm not mistaken in thinking there was some sort of sexual vibe going on."

"If there is, it's a long dead one. We were a big thing in high school. That was over a long time ago."

Monica tilted her head to one side, and her eyebrows lifted. "Maybe not as long as you think. Or maybe not as over."

Cara let out a heavy breath. She couldn't speak for Joe, but she knew she'd felt a misguided thrill seeing him again. It had taken considerable willpower to get up from that table in the doughnut shop. If nothing else, curiosity about how he'd spent the last twenty-five years could have held her there, even though she knew that wasn't all there was to it. The same pull exerted itself on her now as it had before, the same attraction, even if she was wise enough now to ignore it.

But she couldn't tell Monica that, partly because Monica would run with any ball she was thrown. More importantly, to Cara, those feelings—both the ones from the past and the present ones—were private, something secret and sacred that she wouldn't share.

She fastened a hard look on her friend. "Maybe you just have a hyperactive imagination. Besides, I thought you'd be more interested in what he was doing here in the first place, since everyone was forced to go home."

Monica waved a dismissing hand. "That someone's car had been broken into? What's news about that? I'm surprised anyone showed up to investigate that."

She couldn't argue with Monica's logic, given that the story being circulated about the investigation was as Monica described.

For now, anyway. In a couple of days, the rumor mill would whip the episode into a double homicide committed in the principal's office. As if there wasn't enough real crime in the area for folks to get excited about.

Monica glanced up at the clock that hung above Cara's door. "Anyway, I gotta run if I'm going to make it to the bathroom before I have to pick up my kids."

Cara watched her friend go, knowing that Monica had let her off easy because at lunchtime she and Katherine, the other woman they lunched with, would have a chance to triple-team her over sandwiches and coffee.

Reaching for her own neglected cup of morning coffee, Cara sat back, momentarily pensive. She couldn't fault Monica for figuring out that there had once been some romantic connection between her and Joe. She and Joe hadn't parted badly; neither of them had ever hated the other because of what happened. Cara didn't blame Joe, at least not the way she suspected he thought she did. Especially since there were things he didn't know, things she'd deliberately kept from him. Never in her life had she been a completely innocent victim.

She'd walked away from him mostly because she feared opening old wounds. The pain of her husband's death was still too fresh for her to want to compound it by picking at long-healed wounds. Maybe one day she would have the wherewithal for that, but today was not that day.

She much preferred to remember that first night, when he'd taken her in his arms on the dance floor. As the band eased into a surprisingly good rendition of "Almost Paradise," she'd drawn closer to him, resting her head on his shoulder. She'd never been too impressed with him before, but something about his closeness had called to her. At the time, she'd told herself that she was simply grateful to escape Harold, but even then she'd known better. There had always been something quietly compelling about him. She'd felt it the day before at the doughnut shop as strongly as ever.

But considering that she had no more to offer his case or the man himself, she doubted she'd see him again. She sighed, annoyed at herself for her own disappointment.

When Joe walked into the squad room the next morning, his partner, Brian Caffey, was already at his desk. Caffey, whom Joe had nicknamed the "Eager Beaver," wasn't the worst guy a cop could partner with. A little too, well, eager to "prove his mettle" to the powers that be, but perhaps that went along with being a police captain's son.

Caffey was reading over the Randazzo file but looked up when Joe came in. "Interesting stuff. How'd this lowlife manage to get himself whacked?"

Joe pulled out his chair and sat. "That's the sixty-four-thousand-dollar question."

"The what?"

Joe looked heavenward. *Kids!* "It's the million-dollar question, with no lifelines."

Brian grinned, displaying his Black Irish good looks. "I knew that." Then he sobered. "Seriously, what's this guy's story?"

"Your guess is as good as mine. He was knocked off execution style, but as far as I can tell, he hadn't pissed off any of his connected friends. The most I've got is the car they found him in, which was seen in a school parking lot close to the time of death."

"Near Arthur Avenue?"

Caffey said that with a note of hope in his voice, considering Arthur Avenue and its environs were the Little Italy of the Bronx. "No, in a predominantly Black and Hispanic neighborhood."

"What was a goombah doing over there?"

That's what Joe wanted to know. Although there were pockets of prostitution, drug trafficking, and other nonsense all over the northeast Bronx that would attract a mobster's attention, this neighborhood wasn't known for any of that. Besides, something about this killing bothered Joe, though he couldn't say what. They'd make the rounds of Randazzo's regular associates, wait for the dumps of his cell and home phones, and see what the lab turned up. Randazzo's autopsy was scheduled for that afternoon. Maybe the man's corpse could tell them something he could not.

That evening Cara walked to her car at the usual time, a little after six. The sun had long since set on a day that had promised snow but hadn't produced any. The frigid, humid air felt raw in her lungs, making her steps heavy. She was tired. The only thoughts in her head were of a nice warm bath and a hot dinner in front of the tube before bed.

As usual, her car sat at the top of the school parking lot. As she approached, she pressed the button on her key chain to unlock the doors and headed for her trunk. She was in the process of putting her bags down when a man's voice caught her attention.

"You need any help, Miss?"

Cara glanced over her shoulder, alarm racing through her. That man hadn't been there a second ago, when she'd come out to the car. She had no idea where he'd come from, but dressed all in black, he had an ominous appearance. Maybe the experience last night had made her paranoid, but she didn't think so. "I-I'm fine," she stammered.

She turned to slam her trunk closed, but she could feel the man's rapid approach. As soon as she could, she turned to face him. Already, he was close, too close. And they were alone. She was sure of it, even though she hadn't looked. Sound in this area carried. If anyone was nearby, they'd have to be silent as a tomb not to be heard.

"It's no trouble at all," the man said. He smiled at her, his teeth flashing white against his swarthy complexion. "It's not safe for a woman to be out alone at night."

She backed away from him, all the while fumbling with the can

114

of pepper spray she kept on her key chain, trying to get it into position to use it. With her other hand, she felt behind her along the side of her car, hoping to find the door handle.

The man's smile stretched into a feral expression, which sent a chill through her. "I'm not going to hurt you."

He had that straight. She had no intention of letting this stranger do anything to her, particularly since he appeared to be unarmed. She might not get out of this unscathed, but if an ambulance needed to be called, they'd need to get into it together.

"Stay away from me," she warned, just as a car pulled into the lot, its headlights drawing both their attention. For Cara, it was a momentary fascination. As soon as her assailant turned to look behind him, she pivoted, yanked her car door open, and flung herself inside. In a second she had the car door shut and locked. In another second, she had the car in gear and was backing out of the lot. Once out on the street, she fishtailed to head in the right direction before peeling away, leaving the man standing in the same spot she left him.

She knew she was driving like a lunatic but couldn't seem to make herself slow down until a red light made her stop altogether. She sat back in her seat, breathing heavily, trying to will her heart to slow down. She brought her hand to her mouth as tears stung her eyes. She didn't know what she'd averted back there, or why, but she was certain that man had intended to harm her.

She had no idea if this incident had anything to do with her discovery of the car in which some mobster had been found, but she was scared. There was only one person she trusted to tell about this. She dug her cell phone out of her purse and dialed his number. When he answered, she told him, "Joe, I'm on my way home. I need you."

Three

Joe pulled up in front of Cara's house a little over half an hour after she'd called. Since he was coming from the opposite end of the city, the trip should have taken almost twice as long, but he'd driven like a madman to get there. He wouldn't describe Cara as a fearless woman, but it took a lot to get to the girl he'd known. Hearing her distressed voice pleading to him over the phone had gotten to him, too. Once they parted the previous night, he didn't figure on seeing her unless something untoward turned up linking her to the case.

He parked and strode up the walk to her house. She opened the door before he knocked. Her hair was a bit tousled, and her feet were bare. He could see smudges around her eyes where her make-up had run, but there was a hint of an embarrassed smile on her face. He understood that smile. She regretted calling him. But that didn't mean that she shouldn't have.

She licked her lips and met his gaze. "You got here quicker than I thought you would."

Which meant she'd been contemplating calling him back to tell him not to come, he thought. "I didn't want to keep you waiting." He took a step toward her. "May I come in?"

She nodded and stepped back to let him enter. He did so, crossing the small foyer, walking past the steps on the right, and stopping by the entrance to the living room. Her mother hadn't been much of a decorator, but from what he could see, Cara had turned the home into a warm, inviting place. If he wasn't mistaken, some of her own artwork hung on the walls.

He glanced back at her. "I like what you've done."

"Thanks." She walked past him to enter the living room. She motioned toward the sofa. "Why don't you have a seat? I'll make some coffee."

As he stepped forward, he took her hand and led her over to the sofa to sit beside him. "Why don't you just tell me what happened?"

She sighed, tucking her feet underneath her. "It seems silly now."

"It usually does. That doesn't mean it isn't important." He sat back, draping his arm along the top edge of the sofa behind them. "Tell me."

She sighed again, this time with a touch more resignation than exasperation. "When I came out from school tonight, a man approached my car. There was something about him that made me nervous."

"What did he look like?"

"Italian or maybe Hispanic. Dark. Dressed all in black. I don't know where he came from. I didn't see him near a car."

"Did he say something to you? What did he do?" He listened as she described the encounter, becoming increasingly certain that whoever this man was, she'd been lucky to get away from him the way she did. "Did he follow you?"

She shook her head. "No. He was just standing there when I left. Which is why I started thinking that maybe I'd overreacted when I called you. Do you think he had anything to do with the murder?"

He couldn't honestly answer that question. For all he knew, it was some unrelated guy looking to mug her or worse. Joe had looked into the crime rate in the neighborhood and knew that such an occurrence wouldn't have been completely out of the ordinary. But it was her description of the man that caught his attention. A Hispanic man in the neighborhood wasn't unusual; an Italian was.

He lifted one shoulder in a shrug. "I don't know." He squeezed her hand, which he still held. "How are you doing?"

"Better now. At the time I was scared out of my wits." She licked her lips. "What happens now?"

He doubted much benefit could come from reporting the incident to the local police department, considering that the man hadn't really done anything. "Can you tell me anything else about the man you saw?"

"Sure." She turned to retrieve a sheet of paper from the occasional table beside her. "I drew a sketch of him."

He took the sheet of paper from her and scanned the image. She'd captured her assailant down to the scowl on his face and the scar that bisected his left eyebrow.

"Can you use that?" she asked.

He didn't want to give her his true answer, which was probably not. If she'd had a photo, and if he knew someone in homeland security or at one of the other agencies pioneering face recognition software, that would be another story. He could feed the sketch into a database of mugshots, and it would hopefully spit out a name. In the morning he'd fax her sketch to his friend Gus and to her local precinct to see if either of them could identify the man she'd seen.

He folded the sketch and put it in his pocket. "We'll see what turns up."

If she were any other witness, he would have handed her his card, with the promise to keep in touch if anything developed. But neither was she the average victim nor did he want to leave her. That had nothing to do with his responsibilities as a cop or even with making sure she'd survived her ordeal unscathed. It had everything to do with their past together and his fear that he'd never get the chance to explain himself to her.

Still, it wasn't a topic he felt he could jump into with her, either.

He thought he could broach another topic, though, one just as painful, but not as treacherous.

"How did you get into teaching? I thought you wanted to be an artist."

"I did. I am. I started out as an art teacher in an elementary school."

"What happened?"

"My school did away with its art program to focus more on academics. If I wanted to keep working, I had to teach a regular class. This was right after Marcus had been diagnosed, so I didn't have much choice."

"I was sorry to hear about your husband's death."

A wan smile crossed her face. "I know. I got your flowers."

That was the only contact they'd had since that fateful November day nearly twenty years ago. "Do you miss him?"

Her smile deepened. "He was a good man, Joe. You would have liked him. In some ways, he reminded me of you."

That surprised him. "In what way?"

"He couldn't dance a lick, either, unless it was to a slow song. Imagine any one woman knowing two Black men with no sense of rhythm."

It was on the tip of his tongue to remind her that he had plenty of rhythm when it counted, but he didn't say anything. It wasn't the time, and it wouldn't get him anywhere, besides. He also knew he couldn't stall any longer. He needed to say what he wanted or leave.

He inhaled, screwing up his courage. "I never meant to hurt you all those years ago. You know that, don't you?"

A patient look came over her face, as she'd known he would broach the topic but found it unnecessary. He read something else in her face as well but couldn't decipher it. "We were kids, Joe. We should have known better than to think we could maintain a long-distance relationship when grown folks can't even do that. I told you then that I didn't blame you. It was only a shock the way I found out."

It had been a shock for both of them. She'd come home a day early from college and found them together. Ironically, he'd only met Janet that day to tell her that Cara was coming home the next day. In the months after Cara had left for college, he'd seen her only three times. She'd come home for Thanksgiving and Christmas, and the first day of the break between semesters, when her parents had whisked her away on a trip to Florida. They were thinking of buying a house down there, so the trip was a mix of sightseeing and house hunting.

Even though he had been on break himself, her parents hadn't bothered to invite him along, as they had done on other occasions. He knew they liked him, but they also disapproved of how serious they believed he and Cara had become, fearing their continuing relationship would interfere with her dedication to her education. Even now, he believed the timing of that trip had been a means of driving a wedge between them. Whether that was true or not, the effect had been the same. In Cara's absence, he found himself growing closer to one of her friends, a girl in the same situation as he, but in reverse. Both of them had been left behind, but Janet made no pretense of waiting around for her beau.

But now Cara would be home a few days—enough time for him to have a conversation with her, which he'd wanted to conduct face-to-face. He'd been careful not to let anything happen between him and Janet that he might be ashamed of or be unable to look Cara in the eye and tell her. He hadn't even kissed her. But as they sat on one of the park benches that surrounded the sandlot in Haffen Park, he'd slid his arm around Janet's shoulders and told her about Cara's pending arrival.

Her response had been to plant the kind of kiss on him designed to knock a guy's socks off. He knew Janet had been impatient to discuss their budding relationship. She, like Cara, was an up-front person. That similarity of disposition was one of the main reasons he liked her. Their being together wasn't a secret, but neither of them admitted to being anything more than friends.

When she'd pulled away from him, she'd tossed her hair and said, "That's what's waiting for you after you tell her."

For an instant he'd stared back at her, bemused, until he heard Cara's unexpected, angry voice. "There's no need to tell me anything. I can see for myself."

Cara whirled around and stalked off toward the entrance to the park. His first impulse was to go after her, to explain the scene she'd just witnessed. He rose to his feet to follow her, then remembered Janet sitting there. This situation had to be as humiliating for her as it was for him. For a moment he was trapped between his obligations to both women.

"Go," Janet had whispered.

He'd taken off after Cara. Even though he caught up with her, she wouldn't listen to him. Honestly, he couldn't blame her. That day saw the end of both his relationship with Cara and with Janet, though it took longer for the death knell on the latter relationship to sound.

But looking at Cara now, he thought he understood that other emotion he at first couldn't place. He'd seen it that day: a hurt she tried to mask with bravado. "I know what you said," he said finally.

"No matter what happened, or what I said, or what you said, it all happened a long time ago." She stood. "It's getting late, and I have to be at school early in the morning."

It wasn't that late, and she didn't go in that early. He supposed that was her way of saying she'd had enough of the blast from the past. He stood also and started toward the door. When he reached the foyer, he turned to face her. "I don't suppose I need to remind you to lock the doors and windows tonight?"

She shook her head. "Got that covered."

He opened the door and stepped outside. "I'll see you in the morning." She didn't ask him where he'd be staying, and he didn't volunteer the information. Besides, she had his cell phone number if she needed him. He reminded her, anyway. "You know how to reach me?"

She leaned against the doorframe. "Yes, Joe."

Although he sensed her impatience to have him out of her house, the unintentionally soft look on her face drew him in. If he was going to beat himself up about the way he'd treated her, he might as well have something decent to be sorry for. He leaned toward her, cradled one side of her face in his palm, and kissed her.

She surprised him by kissing him back. Their tongues met, and he drank in the sweet, familiar taste of her. A host of memories flooded him, all of them good. When he forced himself to pull away, she looked up at him with an amused expression.

"I see some things haven't changed," she whispered.

Before he had the presence of mind to say anything or question what she meant, she closed the door on him. "Good night, Joe," he heard her call from the other side of the door.

Shaking his head, he walked down the path to the sidewalk. If anyone had told him his day would end with kissing Cara Williams, he would have told them they were nuts. But his lips still held the taste of hers, a heady sensation.

He left his car where it was and walked down and across the street to his parents' house, which was now occupied by his sister and her family. Although he had a key, he rang the doorbell and waited.

A few moments later his sister answered the door. Her gaze changed from one of curiosity to out-and-out surprise. She planted one hand on a slender hip. "Well, if it isn't the prodigal brother returning home. I'd thought you'd forgotten my address."

Humor as well as chastisement laced her words. "I was in the neighborhood, so I thought I'd drop by."

Allison leaned out of the doorway enough to scan the block. Undoubtedly, she noticed his car parked in front of Cara's house. She leaned back and glared at him with a knowing smile. "Been visiting anyone I know?"

"Let me in, and I'll tell you."

She stepped back, gesturing for him to enter. He walked past her and headed to the kitchen, his sister's preferred room for sitting and talking. He took the chair beside the one she'd obviously been occupying. A half-full glass of iced tea and a *Times* daily crossword, three-quarters complete, sat at her place.

"Are you hungry?" she asked.

"I could eat."

"You're in luck then. I made beef stroganoff tonight, which didn't go over too well with your niece and nephew. If it had been fried chicken and french fry night, you'd have been in trouble."

Neither of them said anything until Allison presented him with a plate fresh from the microwave. He sampled a forkful. "Your kids have no taste."

"Nah, they're just kids. They're proponents of the three main food groups: fried, chocolate-covered, and dipped in sugar. They think 'vegetable' is a dirty word."

But if he knew his sister, she provided them with wholesome food and told them that they better not complain too much about it, either.

"So tell me. What are you really doing here? Brooklyn too small for you all of a sudden?"

Joe put down his fork. "No, you're right. I was at Cara's. Some guy tried to threaten her earlier tonight."

"What? And she called you?"

"To make a long story short, her fingerprints turned up in an investigation, so when some menacing guy approached her, she called me. No big deal."

"No big deal, huh? Maybe not for her, but for you?"

"What is that supposed to mean?"

"Don't think I didn't notice that you seemed to forget your way here the moment she moved back into her parents' house. You've been avoiding her, so forgive me if your seeing her came as a bit of a shock."

Since he doubted that protesting otherwise would get him anywhere, he didn't bother. Instead, he told his sister what she wanted
to hear. "She looks good."

"I know that." She leaned over and brushed her thumb against
the corner of his mouth. "If you don't want people to know what
you're up to, you should be more careful about who you allow to
leave their mark on you."

He swiped his mouth with his napkin. "It was nothing."

"Right," came her skeptical answer. "I may be your baby sister,
but I know you, Joe. You may be deluding yourself that she doesn't
mean anything to you, but I know better."

"Allison, her husband died two years ago."

"I know that better than you. I met him a few times. I went to
the funeral because I knew you wouldn't. He was a nice man, but if
there was any grand passion between them, I never saw it. They
were comfortable. That's it. In my heart, I always felt she married
him because she couldn't have who she really wanted."

He sat back and considered what his sister had said. "Me?"

Allison rolled her eyes. "Of course, you. Who else? Adonis was
already taken."

He laughed, both at his sister's sarcasm and her supposition that
Cara had still wanted him. As far as he knew, he'd killed any tender
feelings she'd had toward him. That kiss tonight—he had no idea
why she'd allowed it, but he doubted the reason had been pent up
desire from a life spent pining for him.

"Think what you want, brother dear, since you always do. But
ask yourself this: why did she move back here after her husband
died when she had a perfectly nice home in a neighborhood with
better schools, a lower crime rate, and quieter neighbors? The only
benefit to living here is we pay less in taxes. Makes you wonder if
on some subconscious level, she was looking for something she'd
lost."

"Your psychology minor is showing, sis. Maybe she just wanted a
shorter commute."

Sighing, Allison stood. "As I said, think what you want. I'm going to bed. You can bunk up in Corey's room. His father let him watch some monster movie, and he's scared to sleep by himself, anyway." She moved to his chair and placed a sisterly kiss on his forehead. "Tell Cara I say hello the next time you see her."

After Allison left, Joe cleared his place, washed the few dishes he'd used, and climbed the stairs to the small front bedroom his nephew occupied. From the window, he had a clear view of the front of Cara's house, including the roof. The light in the window of her master bedroom was on. He could imagine her stripping off her clothes, readying herself for bed, but immediately tamped down that line of thought in his mind. What he needed to consider was the man who'd approached her in the parking lot earlier.

In all likelihood, that man had nothing to do with the case. The only people who knew about Cara's involvement were a few officers at his precinct. Offhand, he could only think of himself, his lieutenant, and his partner, Caffey, as the ones who knew her name.

The only other way someone else might have known about her involvement was if they'd seen her close that trunk that night in the parking lot or if they'd witnessed officers questioning her the following day when the crime scene investigators showed up. That's why he'd asked her to wait for him inside the school. The presence of the CSI team had brought out onlookers, any one of whom could have been connected to Randazzo's death. He hadn't wanted to paint a big red *X* on her chest by being seen talking or leaving with her.

Even if someone had seen her, and had waited around for her the next day, they probably didn't know her address. The Department of Education was more tight-lipped about employee information than the FBI. Anyone trying to get information out of them would be out of luck.

Still, he worried that something might happen to Cara because he'd somehow miscalculated. He stripped and changed into the pair of sweats he kept at his sister's for just such emergencies. He had a decent change of clothes in Corey's closet as well. He pulled a chair over to the window and propped his feet on the radiator. He could still see Cara's house and observed that the light in her bedroom was now off.

"Sweet dreams," he whispered, knowing that he wouldn't be seeking any of his own tonight. A little sleep deprivation wouldn't kill him. Besides, what he really wanted had plenty to do with beds, but nothing at all to do with sleep.

Cara woke at five o'clock the next morning, a full hour before her alarm was scheduled to go off. She was like that sometimes, when something was on her mind. She'd fall asleep fine but wake up too early. Any attempt at falling back to sleep was useless, so she got up, took a shower, and dressed in the clothes she'd taken out the previous night to wear to work that day.

She combed her hair and put on her make-up, taking as much time as possible. By the time she was finished, she still had an hour before she needed to leave. With nothing else to do, she paced her living room. She turned on the television, but the local news report didn't hold a scintilla of her attention. Her thoughts drifted back to Joe.

She was too old to be playing the kind of game she played with him last night. For a moment, when they were standing at her door, it reminded her of so many nights in their youth when he'd brought her home. They'd stand at the door talking, both of them reluctant to ever let the night end. They could talk for hours about everything and nothing. But sooner or later, he had to go. He'd pull her to him and kiss her good night.

She sighed, reliving both those long-ago nights and the one just past. She should be ashamed of herself for what she'd let happen last night. She'd seen the look that came into his eyes. She'd known what he was going to do and could easily have put a stop to it. She told herself at the time that her only motive for allowing it had been curiosity. She'd wanted to know if he could still affect her the way he used to. She'd known her answer before he laid a lip on her. Something about Joe called to her; there was some silent sensual communication between their bodies.

But it wasn't the kiss that bothered her so much. It was perhaps the only honest communication they'd shared the previous night. No, she took that back. He'd tried to lay the past to rest, but she'd squashed that attempt. To bring up the past would mean having to bare to him her own sorry truths, which she hadn't wanted to do.

But she was a grown woman now, not a teenager. He deserved to know why she'd reacted the way she had, why she'd shut him out. At this late date, it wouldn't change anything, but it would rid her of a burden she'd been carrying around for twenty years. It wasn't a heavy one, but she felt its weight nonetheless.

Hearing a sound outside, she went to the front window to look out. Joe must have spent the night down the street at his sister's house rather than make the long trip back to Brooklyn last night, since he was now getting into his car. Part of her wanted to go after him and explain the truth of what had happened all those years ago. He deserved that much from her. As Joe revved the engine and drove off, she vowed that if she ever got the chance again, she'd tell him.

Four

The first thing Joe did when he got in to the precinct the next morning was to fax Cara's sketch to his friend Gus. It took forty-five minutes for Gus to get back to him.

"I asked around," Gus said after the men greeted each other. "This guy doesn't ring a bell with anyone here. Sorry, buddy."

Joe shrugged. It had been a long shot, anyway. Hopefully, it signaled that Cara's assailant had nothing to do with the Randazzo murder. The last thing any law-abiding citizen needed was to get inadvertently mixed up with the mob.

After he hung up with Gus, Joe called Cara's local precinct and reported the incident to the desk sergeant. The desk sarge requested a fax of the subject and promised to keep an eye out for the guy. Joe had done all he could in regard to the matter. He checked his watch. He still had another couple of hours before he had to make it to Randazzo's autopsy. It was enough time to maybe round up a couple of Randazzo's associates to see if they knew anything or would perhaps implicate themselves. That is, if he could pry Caffey away from one of the civilian assistants, who, at the moment, stood beside Caffey's desk for no good reason other than to flirt. In the last two days, Joe had thought Maya had taken an unwarranted interest in their case, that is, until it occurred to him that his partner interested her more.

Kids! Being that obvious wouldn't do either of their careers much good, but since no one asked him, Joe kept his mouth shut. "Hey, Caffey," he called. "Feel like getting some police work done today?"

Caffey straightened. "What have you got?"

Joe's gaze lifted to Maya, who listened avidly, before settling again on his partner. "I'll tell you on the way."

"Sure," Caffey said, rising. Once they were seated in the car outside, Caffey added, "There's nothing going on."

Joe pretended to focus on adjusting the rearview mirror. Just how gullible did he look? Joe only hoped he'd never made that much of a fool of himself in his youth, but he had. He could think of a few times before Cara went off to college that she'd turned him into a lovesick pup. But never on the job, for Chrissakes. Police family or not, this kid had a lot to learn. "Glad you cleared that up," Joe said, then pulled away from the curb.

By the time Cara got home that afternoon, she was bone-weary and soaked to the skin. It had started to snow around two o'clock, one of those heavy, wet affairs that rarely stuck to the ground but made anyone caught in it miserable. Without an umbrella and wearing a lighter trench coat since the weatherman had predicted unseasonably warm temperatures, she'd been drenched and freezing before she reached her car.

Thankfully, a police car parked at the corner of the school parking lot had prevented any more evening run-ins. Cara had gotten into her car, started the engine and the heater simultaneously, and waited for warmth before driving off.

Once in front of her house, Cara reluctantly turned off the ignition and got out. Immediately, the swirling snow enveloped her, making her dream of a house with a garage with a door that led directly inside. She trudged up her walk. The snow had gotten heavier and was beginning to accumulate despite its wetness. Her body trembled with small shivers, which didn't abate until she'd made it inside, sat on the sofa, and wrapped the afghan on the back of the sofa around herself.

She sat there for a few moments, her head against the back of the sofa, her eyes closed. The house was silent, tomblike, but then it always was when she came home. She'd often considered getting one of those timers that could turn on the TV before she got home, just so that she could hear some noise. She'd never minded being alone. In fact, often she preferred it, especially if the alternative was noisy or boisterous people. Just sometimes . . .

She sighed, mentally filling in the rest of her own thought. Sometimes she was lonely. Sometimes she had been lonely despite Marcus's presence in her life. She hadn't lied to Joe. Marcus had been a good man, and she had loved him. He'd been good to her, but there had never been any grand spark of passion between them. She hadn't been looking for that. Grand passions brought grand troubles, or at least they had for her. If she was honest with herself, she'd only considered marrying Marcus because she knew he was a man she could handle. Now what did that say about her?

She'd often puzzled over that question, never finding an answer. Tonight she was too tired to dwell on it at all. She was too tired even to bother with dinner. Instead, she made herself a cup of cocoa, blending whole milk with rich chocolate syrup in a saucepan until the light liquid was indistinguishable from the dark.

She poured the cocoa into an oversize mug and trudged up the stairs, without shoes but still wearing her trench coat. She'd take it off when she put on her pajamas, as she found an odd comfort in wearing it. Up in her bedroom, she put the cocoa on the night table beside her bed, found a pair of flannel pajamas, and slipped into them. Her trench coat she left draped along the foot of her bed. If she went back downstairs, she'd hang it up, she told herself.

Settling under the warm cocoon of her covers, she debated turning on the television, then decided against it. As much as she craved noise, she needed quiet more. The last few days had been crazy, with some strange man perhaps trying to accost her and with seeing Joe again. Her lack of sleep the previous night didn't help any, either. And now, an odd jittery feeling claimed her, as if her nerves were suddenly and inexplicably on edge. The three cups of coffee she'd consumed during the day in an effort to stay awake were probably catching up with her.

Maybe what she needed most was not cocoa or quiet but a few hours of decent sleep. She turned out the bedside lamp, the only illumination in the room, and settled back against the pillows. Cara yawned. Sleep could easily overtake her if she let it. She shut her eyes, and instantly, she felt herself drifting into the black void.

Suddenly, there was a large gloved hand over her mouth, its fingers biting into the flesh of her cheeks. Her eyes flew open, and her brain scrambled to make sense of the vision standing above her—a man dressed in black, including a black ski mask, which exposed only a pair of dark eyes.

"Don't make a sound," a familiar voice threatened.

For a moment, Cara squeezed her eyes shut. She knew who that voice belonged to. It was the man in the school parking lot. She'd been right. He had intended to harm her. That fact gave her no comfort now, especially since she knew there wouldn't be anybody coming to her rescue, inadvertently or not. Worse, she felt herself trembling, alerting him to the fact that she was afraid.

She opened her eyes and glared back at him, hoping to dispel that effect. She tried to ask him what he wanted, but the hand on her mouth was clamped down too tightly.

"What did you see that night?" he growled.

Nothing, she wanted to say, but the hand on her mouth prevented any communication. Instead, she shook her head.

His grip tightened, which suggested he didn't believe her. "Did you sic that cop on me?"

She shook her head, even though this time her answer was a lie.

There was no point in antagonizing him further. But his gaze drifted from her face to her throat, and for an instant, panic raced through her as she contemplated what his actual intentions might be.

He leaned down so that his face was very close to hers. "Don't worry. I'm not a pig like him. I'm not going to hurt you. I'm just going to kill you."

Then his hands closed around her throat, tight enough to thwart any effort at breathing. Uselessly, she tried to drag air into her lungs, while her fingers clawed at his hands, and her mind whirred. She tried desperately to think of some way to get him off of her. She could barely move, as her body was trapped by the man's weight and the heavy covers. Then she remembered the hot cocoa at her bedside. She groped for the cup, found it, and grasped its handle as best she could. With all her might, she swung it toward her assailant, splashing both him and herself with the scalding liquid. The man screamed and released her. She swung the cup again, this time connecting with the side of the man's head. He fell sideways, away from her.

Breathing erratically, she scrambled from the bed, tripping over something damp and heavy—her trench coat. She grabbed it and ran. Behind her, she heard the man groan, which hastened her footsteps. He might be down, but he wasn't out, and she wasn't taking any chances. She pounded down the stairs and down the hall to the front door. She dashed out the door, leaving it open behind her. Barefoot, she ran down the street to Allison's house and pounded on her door. As she waited for Allison to let her in, she checked the street behind her. The man hadn't followed her. Yet.

When Allison opened the door, Cara pushed her back inside and shut the door behind them.

Allison eyed her with concern. "Cara, what's going on? What happened to you?"

Cara took the first deep breath she'd been able to manage since that man showed up in her room. "I think you'd better call your brother."

Finally on his way home from the job, Joe fastened his seatbelt before pulling out of the precinct parking lot. He was tired and was looking forward to a relatively early dinner and bed. He yawned. His sleeplessness the night before was catching up with him. Aside from that, he'd spent the day chasing down one Ronnie Morales, a man Randazzo had had a beef with, supposedly over some woman. The lead had seemed promising, particularly since the guy fit Cara's general description and more than one witness had identified Morales as the man Cara had drawn.

What Joe still couldn't figure out was the connection with the other end of the city. He'd pulled Morales's jacket, but there was nothing there but some petty bullshit that some public defender had gotten dismissed. Joe would have to go on wondering a little while longer, since the man had proved to be as invisible as a damn ghost. It made Joe wonder what the man was up to. Was he up to some mischief, or had he holed up somewhere, knowing the police were looking for him?

He hoped that didn't mean Morales had made another attempt at roughing up Cara. Joe had seen to it that a squad car was parked out in front of Cara's school around the time she usually went home and had asked her local precinct to beef up the patrol in her neighborhood. Now that he had a name for the man who had harassed Cara, he'd issued an APB for the guy. He'd turn up. Sooner or later Joe would find him.

In the meantime, he dialed Cara's number and got her answering machine. He hoped that simply meant that she had a life outside of teaching and was enjoying it at the moment. Still, his cop's intuition nagged at him. He dialed his sister's number. She might not know where Cara was, but at least she could verify if Cara's car was out front or if any of the lights in her house were on. Allison picked up on the fourth ring, just as her answering machine did.

"Hold on," she said, sounding frazzled and annoyed. A few seconds later, the answering machine message stopped abruptly. "Joe, is that you?"

"Yeah. Do me a favor and check if Cara's car is in front of her house. I want to know if she got home yet."

"I don't have to do that."

"Why not?"

"She's sitting downstairs in my kitchen. Someone tried to hurt her tonight."

Alarm raced along his nerve endings as he contemplated Allison's choice of words—*tried to hurt her.* What the hell had gone on? "How is she?"

"A bit shaken, but okay, I think. She asked for you. I was just about to call you."

"Tell her I'm on my way."

He ended the call and tossed the phone onto the passenger seat. He gunned the engine and got into the fast lane. The glut of rush hour traffic had abated, making his commute to the Bronx a quick one. Still, anxiety churned his belly as he drove. He wouldn't feel right again until he saw for himself that Cara was all right.

It was almost nine o'clock when he pulled in front of his sister's house and parked. Two squad cars sat farther down the street, in front of Cara's house. Lights were on inside, probably turned on by a crime scene team looking for evidence. He wanted to know what they'd found, if anything, but first he needed to see Cara.

His sister pulled open the front door before he'd made it all the way up the walk. "She's still here."

"Where?"

"In the kitchen. A detective from the Forty-seventh Precinct is with her."

Nodding, Joe walked past Allison to enter the house. He wondered whose idea it had been to call the local cops. Despite her brother being one of New York's finest, Allison still wasn't a big fan of the boys in blue.

Joe walked through the house until he reached the kitchen. Cara sat at one end of the kitchen table. The detective, a beefy, dark-haired man, had his back to Joe. He knew the instant Cara realized he was there. Her head turned, and her gaze lifted to his. He could see the residue of fear in her eyes, but he also noted her resolve to keep herself together.

The first words she said were not directed toward him, but to the man beside her. "Detective Morris, this is Detective Joseph Malone. What happened tonight is probably related to a case he's working on."

Morris stood. He was a big guy, at least a couple of inches taller than Joe and broad. Morris enveloped the hand Joe extended in a meaty fist. "Good to meet you."

"Likewise. What happened?" Joe looked at Cara when he asked the question, but it was Morris who answered.

"Ms. Williams came home and was attacked by an intruder inside her house. She's sure it's the same man who last night accosted her in the parking lot where she works. He must have been in her house when she got home and attacked her once she got in bed. She managed to flee and came here."

Joe had the feeling that there was plenty Morris had left out of that brief summary, plenty he intended to find out before Morris got out the door. "Anything else?" he asked.

Morris shook his head. "I'm just about finished here."

Joe surveyed Cara's face. For the moment she seemed to be holding her own. "I'll walk you out," he said to Morris.

Neither man said anything until they reached the front door. "That's one gutsy lady," Morris said with admiration in his voice. "She clocked the guy with a cup of hot cocoa. The perp got away. He came in through the kitchen door. Must have gone out the same way. A crime scene unit is at her house now. We probably won't find anything. She says he was wearing gloves."

"If it's the same man, his name is Ronnie Morales out of Brooklyn. I haven't been able to figure out yet what his connection to your neck of the woods is."

"Maybe you need to get her out of here until you figure that out."

That had been his thought. What remained to be seen was whether Cara would go along with it.

The two men exchanged cards. Morris nodded toward Cara's house. "Looks like they're packing up. I'll make sure they release the scene."

That meant that Cara could get back into her house tonight—if she wanted to. "Thanks."

Morris adjusted his collar against the swirling wind and snowflakes and headed down the street.

Joe watched him for a moment, then closed the door and went back inside. When he got back to the kitchen, Allison had taken the seat Morris had occupied. Again Cara's gaze met his. For the first time he noticed her odd attire—beige, patterned men's pajamas beneath a khaki trench coat. Her feet were bare. She'd been forced to run out in the snow-covered street without her shoes. Anger welled up in him. Ronnie Morales was going to be in deep trouble when Joe caught up with him.

Allison slipped from her seat silently, and he took her spot. "How are you doing, sweetheart?" he asked Cara.

She turned slightly to face him. "I'm fine. Can I go home now?"

He'd never considered Cara anything except a strong woman, but he wasn't seeing strength in her now. He saw the look of a woman functioning on autopilot, not really with it. He couldn't blame her. It wasn't every day a man broke into her house and tried to kill her. "In a little while. Feel up to telling me exactly what happened?"

He listened as she recounted her terror at being attacked by a strange man in her bedroom, the same one who'd met her in the

136

school parking lot. He supposed that took all the guesswork out of determining what the man's intentions had been. While she spoke, anger welled up in him again. If being a cop had taught him anything, it was that people were capable of doing the most despicable things with even less provocation than Cara's assailant had had. She hadn't seen him the night of the murder, even if he thought she had. The most she could possibly attest to was that she'd been approached by him in the school parking lot days after the murder. She wouldn't be able to swear to even that if he hadn't shown his own hand. Well, nobody said criminals were smart.

He looked down at Cara's hand, which he hadn't realized he'd been holding. He noticed a patch of reddened flesh on the back of her hand. He nodded toward it. "Do you need to have that looked at?"

She shook her head. "It looks worse than it is. Allison put some aloe on it." She withdrew her hand and pulled down her sleeve to hide the mark. "There's one more thing. At one point when he looked at me, I would have sworn he wanted to rape me, but he said not to worry since he wasn't a pig like *him*. At the time I got the feeling he was talking about the man who was killed. Does that mean anything?"

Joe exhaled, saying nothing at first. It could mean something. According to all he'd heard, Morales's beef with Randazzo had to do with a woman. It didn't necessarily have to be a territorial dispute, that is, a fight over which man the woman belonged to. Perhaps Randazzo had wronged some woman and Morales sought to avenge her—a mother, a sister, or even his girlfriend as Joe had first assumed. That bore checking into, just as soon as they located Morales.

The doorbell rang. At this time of night, it could only be someone connected with the case. Joe excused himself and went to answer the door. Caffey stood on the other side, looking a bit disheveled. Joe had called Caffey on his way to his sister's, but once he'd seen Cara, he'd forgotten all about his partner.

137

Joe gave him a pointed once-over under the glare of his sister's porch light. "Sorry to drag you away from whatever you were up to. Anybody I know?"

Caffey grinned but said nothing to that. "What's going on?"

Joe was about to let his partner inside when he noticed a uniformed officer jogging up the block toward them. When he reached them, the officer said, "Morris wanted me to let you know they found him, that guy Morales, down by one of the houses on Adee."

Joe exhaled, releasing some of the tension he'd felt. As long as Morales acted alone, Cara was out of danger. "Where is he now?"

"On the way to Einstein Hospital. Fool broke his leg jumping from the balcony and tried to crawl away. He'll be under our watch until they patch him up."

Joe nodded. And then they'd probably take him to the Forty-seventh for booking. The Bronx and Brooklyn would have to fight over who had dibs on the guy, though the Bronx had the stronger claim. Morales was a suspect only in the Randazzo case, but they had him dead to rights for what he did to Cara.

But at the moment, who charged Morales with what wasn't the most important concern on Joe's mind. He went back inside to Cara. She was seated in the same place where he'd left her. Allison had reclaimed her seat. Both women looked at him anxiously, but only Cara stood. "What happened?"

"They found Morales. They're taking him to the hospital."

"Does that mean you have to go?"

"For a little while." If nothing else, he needed to make sure that Morales was the one who'd murdered Randazzo, even though no other scenario explained his involvement. "Will you be all right here with Allison until I get back?"

Cara shot him a droll look. "I'm fine now. But I'm thinking Allison probably wants to go to bed."

"Not on your life," Allison said. "My head is not hitting the pillow till I hear the whole scoop."

Joe turned to look at his sister, who looked about as lively as a wilted petunia. He kissed her cheek. "Thanks, sis."

Allison waved her hand, dismissing him. "Aren't you the one always complaining about how nosy I am?"

He couldn't argue there. He turned back to Cara. She didn't look any more lively, but most of the fear he'd seen in her eyes before was gone. He tucked a strand of her hair behind her ear. "I'll be back as soon as I can."

She offered him a wan smile, but somehow it did his heart good seeing it. "I will." He only hoped that the next time he saw her, he'd be able to tell her the danger was all in the past.

Five

"If you're planning on wearing a hole in my linoleum, I'm going to have to charge you."

Cara stopped pacing and focused on Allison as she entered the kitchen. She'd gone upstairs fifteen minutes before to check on her husband and children. In her absence, Cara had found it impossible to sit still. She exhaled. "Sorry."

Allison patted her shoulder. "No need to be. But I should remind you that my brother is a big boy and can take care of himself. He's not even a colossal pain in the butt like most cops, who think they know everything and are determined to let you know it."

Cara smiled at Allison's assessment. "I know that."

"Then what's your problem?"

Cara sighed. "Damned if I know."

Allison gestured toward the kitchen table. "What do you say we girls have a glass of wine and discuss it?"

The wine sounded heavenly, but she knew Allison. In two seconds she would ferret out every secret she possessed. Maybe that wasn't such a bad thing. Cara hadn't maintained friendships with any of the girls she'd grown up with. She didn't have many more friends besides her colleagues at work. Her mother lived in Florida and was too judgmental for Cara to ever confide in her.

Maybe she did need someone to talk to, to be a sounding board. Or maybe the night had just proved to be more than she could handle.

"Sit," Allison urged, pointing toward the table.

Cara recognized when she was beat. She reclaimed her chair as Allison retrieved a bottle of wine and two glasses and brought them to the table. Cara took the glass Allison offered her and sipped deeply. The warm liquid heated her empty insides, leaving her with a slight buzz.

For a few moments, neither of them said anything, though Cara could feel Allison's gaze on her. Finally, Allison broke the silence. In a quiet voice, she said, "Are you planning on breaking my brother's heart again?"

Cara's gaze flew to Allison's face. "Me? I never broke your brother's heart in the first place."

Allison sighed. "All right, maybe I'm exaggerating a little. And I don't really know what happened between the two of you. What I do know is that he wasn't the same when you were through with him. I don't want to go through that again."

Cara contemplated the contents of her glass. She'd wondered how Joe had taken their breakup, but then she'd always figured he wanted out as much as she did. Thinking back on it now, she remembered the look of anguish on his face when he'd tried to talk to her and she'd refused to listen. Echoing her words that first night they'd spent together, at the Valentine's dance, about letting him know when she was finished with him, she'd said, "There's no point in going through this. I'm done, Joe. I'm done." She'd closed the door in his face and had gone back to college the next morning. By the time she came home for the summer, Joe had gotten an apartment down in the Village, and that was that. Even if she'd had something to say, he wasn't there to hear it. So that indeed was that.

"What makes you think there's anything between us?" Aside from one kiss the night before, there wasn't anything between them.

"A pair of amazingly astute eyes." Allison lifted her glass, apparently thought about it and set it down again. "Look, I realize this is none of my business, but it seems to me the two of you have some unfinished business. Maybe it's time you took care of it one way or another."

Cara bit her lip. She knew Allison was right. She still had feelings for the man, even if she'd spent more than half of her life denying that. Cara downed the remains in her glass. Now all she had to do was wait for Joe to get back.

"Is it me, or is this guy one beer short of a six pack?"

That question came from Morris, as he, Joe, and Caffey stood on the other side of the two-way glass of the interrogation room where Morales took about two seconds to confess to both Randazzo's murder and terrorizing Cara. In Joe's experience, there weren't many reasons why someone would spill their guts that fast: either they had some ulterior motive, like covering for someone else or hiding a worse crime, or they were too stupid to know any better. Morales professed to have acted alone in the murder, after finding out his cousin had been raped by Randazzo. Short of bombing police headquarters, he couldn't be in much more trouble, which made Joe think he was stupid.

But if it was true that Morales acted alone, that would mean he came up with the ideas of making it look like a hit, leaving the car in Mafia territory, and tracking Cara down—not only at her school, but at her home. Joe had asked her if anyone had followed her home. She'd said the streets were empty because of the storm. That meant Morales must have known where Cara lived and most likely waited for her inside her home. He doubted Morales was capable of all that.

"How much do you want to bet this cousin put him up to this?" Joe said finally.

"Mmm," Morris said in agreement.

Joe had done all he could for the moment. In the morning he'd have Cara come in and identify Morales as the man she'd seen in the parking lot, just to wrap her involvement up nice and neat. He said his good nights to the other men and left. Morales was in good hands, and Caffey seemed anxious to get back to whosever arms he'd been in when Joe had called him. Frankly, Joe was feeling a bit envious at the moment. It had been a long time since he'd had anyone waiting anywhere for him.

When he got to his sister's house, there were still two squad cars on the block, one in front of Cara's house and one in front of Allison's. He stopped at Cara's house first, to assess the amount of damage done both by Morales and by the crime scene unit. Aside from a broken bedside lamp and the fact that her sheets had been taken for evidence, not that much looked amiss. Morales had gotten in by jimmying the lock on the kitchen door, so there wasn't any glass to contend with. Cara had gotten off easy in a variety of ways.

He went to his sister's house next. Allison opened the door. Her eyes looked glassy, either from a lack of sleep or something else.

"What have you two been up to?" Joe asked as she let him in.

"Just a little girl talk."

"How much trouble am I in now?"

Allison hit him on the arm. "Don't start none, and there won't be none."

He reached the archway to the kitchen. Cara smiled at him from her place at the table. "It's about time. Can I go home now?"

He knew she was teasing him, since along with relief, he saw humor in her features as well. "If you want to." He extended the bag he held toward her. "I think you'll need these."

She looked at him quizzically, as if she hadn't noticed the bag before and couldn't imagine what lay inside it. She took it from him, and when she looked inside, she laughed. "You think of every-thing." She pulled indoor/outdoor slippers from the bag, put them on her feet, and folded the bag into a neat square.

She went to Allison next and hugged her. "Thanks for every-thing."

There was something about the way she said that last word that made Joe wonder what that everything might encompass.

"Thanks, sis," Joe echoed.

"Please, people. Thank me by going home. I've got to go to work in the morning."

Joe kissed his sister's cheek, then led Cara outside. The howling wind had died down, and the snow had stopped. The little bit of ac-cumulated snow had already evaporated. For February, it was a beautiful night. He didn't know why he did it, but as they walked the short distance to her house, he laced his fingers with hers. Despite the cold, her hand felt warm and soft in his. He glanced over at her to gauge her reaction, but she wasn't looking at him, and there was a faraway expression in her eyes. Since she wasn't looking at him, she probably wasn't thinking about him, either, he thought.

That thought saddened him, though he knew it shouldn't. If no-body had decided to knock off Iggy Randazzo, or if she hadn't bothered to close the trunk of that car, she wouldn't have come back into his life two days ago. They could have gone on carefully avoiding each other for the next twenty years.

But Joe wasn't a big believer in coincidences. Things happened for a reason. Maybe what both of them needed was to finally clear the air between them and be done with it. But as sure as he knew his own name, he knew he wasn't ready to disappear from her life so quickly. He wanted more, though he wasn't sure what that more was. Or maybe he wished they could go back in time and prevent the mistakes of their past from ever being made.

Either way, it seemed that Cara's thoughts were elsewhere, so what he wanted was probably moot.

* * *

Cara pulled her keys from her pocket and opened the front door. The house was dark and quiet. There was no sign that someone had broken into it earlier and tried to kill her. She'd held herself together for hours at Allison's, pushing the terror she'd felt to the back of her mind. Allison's frank conversation about her brother had helped, both by giving Cara something else to focus on and by solidifying her desire to clear the air with Joe. She didn't know exactly what she hoped would come of that. Truthfully, the most prominent memories of him in her mind at that moment were the kiss they'd shared last night and the way he'd held her hand just now.

But before she could get to anything else, she needed a few questions answered for her peace of mind. She hadn't considered it before, but if he'd brought her her slippers, he must have been inside her house. She shrugged out of her coat and hung it on the banister rather than in the closet.

"How did Morales get in here? Was he waiting for me?"

"He jimmied the lock on your kitchen door."

It hadn't occurred to her that someone could get into her house this way, but she figured that an enterprising person could manage to get in. Last night's snowfall would have provided plenty of cover for any number of bad deeds.

"What about upstairs?"

"Other than the coffee cup and one of your bedside lamps, there isn't any damage, though the crime scene unit took your sheets for DNA evidence."

"Why?"

"You really clocked him with that cup. It took four stitches to close the wound over his eyebrow. All in all, I'm guessing right now Morales is wishing he'd stayed home tonight. You clipped him, he broke his leg trying to escape, and we've got all the evidence we need to put him away for both murder and attempted murder. On top of that, he actually confessed to the murder."

She had to laugh at that. She scanned Joe's face, seeing the humor there. It was a handsome face, not a pretty one, and full of character. The urge to reach out and touch it assailed her. She resisted it, fearing he would misinterpret her overture, since she didn't know what spurred it herself.

As if he sensed the change in her mood, he said, "Come on. I'll help you put some clean sheets on the bed so you can get some sleep."

He started up the stairs, and she followed, going to the linen closet and retrieving what she needed.

Within a few minutes, they had the bed remade. Though she was dog tired, she had no desire to get into it. First of all, she didn't think she could close her eyes without imagining a pair of hands closing around her throat, and second, she didn't want Joe to leave when she hadn't leveled with him.

Before they made the bed, Joe had taken off his suit jacket and tie and had rolled up his sleeves. Now that they were done, he set about righting his clothing in preparation, she surmised, to leave. "Have you got a minute before you go?" she asked.

Joe paused in buttoning his sleeve and focused his gaze on her. "Sure, sweetheart. What is it?"

Cara moistened her bottom lip with her tongue.

"You know how you wanted to get something off your chest about the past?"

"As I remember it, you told me to forget about it."

"That's because there was something I didn't want to tell you, and I knew we'd get to it if we started down that path. I should have told you a long time ago."

He scanned her face and saw distress written on her features. It had to be something important for her to have held on to it all these years. "What is it?"

"I told you I didn't blame you. I couldn't blame you, since I was guilty of the same thing myself, maybe more so."

"What do you mean?"

"I met this boy at college. I was lonely. I missed you. Every time I came home, my parents would find some excuse to whisk me away from the house, away from you. We were at a party one night, and we . . ."

She trailed off, but she could tell by the closed expression that came over his face that he understood her meaning. "Why didn't you tell me this then?"

"You were all I had, my best friend as well as my lover. I didn't want you to hate me." She'd been a coward, plain and simple. Rather than tell him what she'd come home to say, she'd grabbed the convenient excuse of finding him with another girl to keep from having to tell him what she'd done.

He shook his head, a rueful gesture. "I wouldn't have hated you for that, but it's easy to say that now. Like you said, we were kids. If we'd had any sense, we probably would have kept our hands off each other in the first place. After you left, it was different. I was different. You were the only person who was ever there for me, just for me. I'm not ashamed to admit that I needed someone here, not thousands of miles away. But I never touched her, Cara, out of respect for you."

Perhaps that's what scared her the most about the whole situation. She had always secretly prided herself on being the stronger of the two of them, at least when it came to emotional self-sufficiency. Being one of the older children in his family, and a boy besides, whatever needs for affection or attention he'd felt had never been answered by his parents. He'd turned to her for that. She'd known that about him, but she'd never recognized her own similar needs until she was without him. She'd needed someone, too, and she didn't like finding that out about herself. She'd kept her secret out of a need to protect her ego, but she'd succeeded in damaging his. "I'm sorry, Joe."

He shook his head again, but this time there was a hint of a smile on his face. "Baby, at this late date, there's nothing to be sorry for." He crooked a finger at her. "Come here."

On unsteady legs, she did as he asked, wondering what he

147

wanted. When she reached him, he pulled her into his arms, with one hand around her waist, the other at her nape. She leaned her cheek against his chest, her fingers gripping his shoulders, while she simply enjoyed being held by him. His fingers tangling in her hair set off tiny shocks of pleasure along her scalp.

"Thank you for telling me."

She lifted her head and looked up at him, into those soulful brown eyes that did wicked things to the pit of her stomach. Their gazes locked, and for a moment she felt herself mesmerized by the intensity she saw there. Then his mouth was on hers, and his tongue plunged into her mouth, seeking hers. Her hands slid around his back, holding him to her as one kiss turned into another and another. His arms closed more tightly around hers, the hand at her nape sliding down to capture her buttocks in his palm.

A tiny moan escaped her lips. Oh, God, she remembered this heat, this passion, which in her memories she always attributed to the fire of youth. She should have known better, since she'd caught a glimpse of it the other night, when he'd kissed her. But something was different now. Maybe because nothing stood between them any longer.

When they finally drew apart, they were both breathing heavily. He rested his forehead on hers. "I should go."

Maybe he should, but that didn't mean she wanted him to go. It might be selfish of her, she thought, but she needed him now, and she wasn't ashamed to admit that. And whatever happened between them, she would find a way to make it so that neither of them walked away with regrets or recriminations this time. She leaned up and placed a single kiss beside his ear. "Don't leave me, Joe."

He leaned back to look at her face. "Is this what you want?"

"Yes." She didn't bother to ask if he wanted her. Even now, his erection pressed against her belly. "Yes," she repeated.

His eyes squeezed shut, as if he was trying to summon his willpower to refuse her. She leaned up and kissed his mouth, and the fire between them roared back to life. His hands roved over her, exciting her, until she moaned her pleasure into his mouth. His hands went to her waist to ease her pajama bottoms over her hips. Then his hands were on her bare flesh, moving up her sides, taking her top with them. He pulled away long enough to lift the material over her head. Before she had a moment to contemplate her nakedness, his hand was at her breast, molding it, positioning it for his mouth. His tongue flicked against her engorged flesh, and she gasped.

"Easy, baby," he whispered against her skin. "We don't want the boys outside rushing in to find out what's going on."

She nodded, understanding, but when his mouth closed around her nipple and his fingers slipped between her thighs, she had to bite her lip to keep from crying out. It didn't take long for her orgasm to claim her, arching her back and threatening to buckle her knees. His mouth covered hers, absorbing the cries she couldn't keep from her lips.

When she finally grew quiet, he lifted her in his arms and carried her to the bed. She wrapped her arms around his neck and buried her face against his neck, raining tiny kisses along his throat. "Are you planning to do something about all those clothes you're wearing?" she whispered.

"That's next on my to do list."

He set her down on the bed, then stepped back to take off his shoes. She watched avidly as he removed the rest of his clothing. His body was heavier than she remembered, a man's body, not a boy's, though still nicely muscled. She opened her arms to him, and he covered her, his mouth finding hers for a kiss more erotic than all the others. She wrapped her legs around his waist, wanting him inside her. When he entered her, she squeezed her eyes shut, loving the feel of him filling her. Slowly, he began to move inside her, withdrawing and thrusting into her with a maddening deliberateness. She let him have his way, reveling in the tension that built steadily inside her. Her legs tightened around him, pulling him deeper, drawing a groan of masculine pleasure from deep in his chest.

She pressed her lips to his damp shoulder, and when she inhaled, she breathed in the scent of their arousal. All the while she felt herself drawing closer and closer to that dark abyss. He thrust into her, deeper this time, and then deeper. His movements became less controlled, more frantic. Her back arched, and she called his name.

"Come for me, baby," he whispered against her ear.

And she did, her head thrown back against the pillows, her legs trembling as they tightened around him. A second later, she felt him jerk, and a loud groan rumbled up through his chest. He sank against her, his big body trembling beneath her fingertips.

For a long while, they lay together, recovering, their labored breathing the only sound in the room. Then he rolled onto his back, taking her with him. She ended up sprawled on his chest, their bodies still locked together. When she could, she lifted her head to look down at him. His face bore a contented smile of male satisfaction. "Come for me, baby? Where on earth did you get that one?"

His smile broadened. "It worked, didn't it?" He lifted his hand to stroke her damp hair from her face. "I didn't think I could hold out much longer." His smile turned to a cocky grin. "I'm not as young as I used to be."

She understood that grin. When they were kids, their lovemaking had been novel, but not quite so explosive. Perhaps that was because they were younger then and less experienced with their bodies. Her mood turned serious. "Do you ever regret that we didn't wait?"

That was probably a stupid question to ask a man, any man. But he answered her question with the same seriousness with which she asked it. "I don't regret anything, Cara. Not then, not tonight." He ran a finger down the bridge of her nose. "Except perhaps not getting any sleep. I have to go to work in the morning."

"Good night, then." Cara smiled against his shoulder, content, for the moment, that all was right with her world.

* * *

The next time Joe opened his eyes, it was light outside. For a moment, his only concern was the woman slumbering in his arms. He leaned down to kiss her forehead. She didn't even stir. After last night he couldn't blame her, though the only reason he'd told her he had to go to sleep was that he'd only had one condom tucked in his wallet, and she didn't have any. He'd never made love to her without protecting her, and he wasn't about to start now.

Yawning, Joe looked at the bedside clock. It wasn't usually this light this early in the morning. Once his eyes focused on the clock, he knew why. The digital display read 7:45. Damn. He was due in at eight.

He extricated himself from Cara and got his cell phone from his belt. He figured he'd call Caffey, who was probably already on the job, to pass on the word he'd be in a little late.

On the fifth ring, Caffey picked up. The first words his partner said were not hello or a chastisement for being late. In a strained voice, Caffey said, "Send an ambulance. That crazy bitch shot me with my own gun."

Six

Twelve minutes later Joe pulled up in front of the address Caffey had given him. Morris was already there, standing by the open ambulance doors. Then again, he'd presumably been up and on the job when the call came in.

Joe double-parked behind one of the squad cars and got out. The EMTs were bringing a stretcher out of the building. As Joe got closer, he saw that Caffey was its occupant.

Joe walked over to where Morris stood. "Any word on what happened in there?"

"They were already bringing your guy down when I got here, so I figured I'd wait out here."

Joe nodded. The only information he'd gotten out of Caffey was his location. He still wasn't sure of the identity of the perpetrator. He had his suspicions, but suspicions weren't proof. He needed to hear it from Caffey.

The EMTs wheeled Caffey to where they stood. "How is he?" Joe asked.

"He'll live. You want a few minutes?"

"Yeah," Joe said while casting a glance at Morris. There weren't that many places on the human body where one could get shot without causing the EMTs to haul ass to the hospital. To Caffey, Joe said, "What happened?"

"I woke up before she did, and I was looking around and found a picture of her with Morales. They did not look like cousins."

"Who's she?"

"Maya. I kinda lied when I said nothing was going on, because of the job, you know."

Joe just shook his head. Since he had never tried to pick up women at work, he neither knew nor cared what the policy was on fraternizing within a precinct. Whatever the rules were, he doubted breaking them would get Caffey in that much hot water. Abject stupidity might.

"Did she tell you anything?"

"She owed Randazzo money from when she lived in Brooklyn, and he was after her. She told Morales he'd raped her so he'd help her get rid of him. She had him leave the car in our precinct so that if any information on the case came in, she'd know about it."

And she'd taken up with Caffey so she could pump him for any information that came in that she might not be privy to. *Damn*. At least he knew how Morales had gotten Cara's address. Maya had brought him her file. If she was still on the loose, Cara was still in danger. "Where is she, Caffey?"

"She had a bus ticket. Albany. Leaving out of Mount Vernon. Nine-thirty."

At least Caffey had done a good job of turning the tables and getting some information out of her.

"We really do need to go," one of the EMTs said.

Joe and Morris stepped back and let the men load Caffey into the ambulance.

Shaking his head, Morris chuckled. "How long do you think it's going to take your boy to figure out he's been played?"

"Longer than I've got." Joe checked his watch. It was already eight-thirty. They'd need to roll if they were going to get in place at the bus station.

153

* * *

The Greyhound station in Mount Vernon was little more than a storefront where folks could gather to wait for their respective buses. Joe sat in an unmarked car across from the station with Morris and another detective. There were two other cars full of plainclothes detectives parked across the street. The plan was to take Maya once she tried to board the bus to Albany. The bus was due in less than five minutes, but in all likelihood, Maya was already in the area, in a store or restaurant. She wouldn't want to show herself too soon, just in case the cops were on to her. She'd come out just in time to get on the bus before it left.

"Everybody get ready," he heard Morris say as the bus rolled into sight. It pulled into its spot and stopped with a whiny screech from the brakes. The driver had already been radioed to stay on the bus and not to let anyone out. The two other passengers waiting to get on had been shepherded into the Greyhound office. A male and female officer waited on line instead.

Out of the periphery of his eye, Joe caught a movement. It was a kid with baggy jeans, a baggy coat, and a knit cap pulled down low on his head. Joe watched him a moment. The kid might have had on the right clothes to look like a guy, but the walk said girl.

Joe nodded in the kid's direction. He looked through the binoculars Morris had provided him and recognized the face. "There she is."

Morris looked in the direction Joe indicated. "You sure?"

"That's her."

Morris relayed this information to the other cops. But suddenly Maya stopped midstride, looking around. "What happened?" Morris asked.

"She's on to us," Joe said. That was the problem with sending cops to catch someone who worked with cops—they could spot one a mile away.

"Go," Morris said into the radio. "Everybody go."

Within seconds, Maya was surrounded by almost twenty cops

with guns drawn. She had already shot one cop, and no one felt in the mood to take any chances. Only a fool would have tried to shoot her way out of the situation. Maya put her hands up and offered no resistance when she was cuffed and put in one of the squad cars. They found Caffey's gun in one of her coat pockets. Caffey would be relieved to hear that.

Later, Joe drove back with Morris to where his car was parked. As Joe was about to get out of the car, Morris turned to him and extended his hand. "It was good working with you."

Joe shook the beefy hand. "Likewise."

"Anytime you want to come up to the Forty-seventh, you let me know. I'll put in a good word for you."

"I'll think about it," Joe said. It would be nice to be closer to his family. Although Allison lived in their parents' house, all his other siblings lived either in the Bronx or lower Westchester. And then there was Cara—waiting at home for him. He had no idea what the future held for them, but at least he knew their past was behind them. He got into his car and drove home.

Once again, Cara scanned the gym cum Valentine's Day dance, looking for Joe. He'd been held up at work and told her to go on to their twentieth reunion dance without him. She didn't know why she agreed to go at all, since the only reason she wanted to be there was to be with him.

They'd been together every night since they'd made love. He'd come to her half-dead after the long trip from Brooklyn, but they'd still eat dinner together, make love, and talk into the wee hours of the night, with no parents to tell Joe to go home. She wondered what Allison thought of this arrangement, but for a change Allison was keeping her opinions to herself. Cara supposed if Joe's sister truly objected, she would have made her opinion known. Not that Cara would let anyone's opinion sway her, but she didn't want Joe getting flack from his family over her.

Still, they agreed to take things slowly this time, whatever that meant. She knew she was falling in love with him again, that is, if she'd ever really stopped loving him. But if the man didn't hurry up and get there soon, she might have to reconsider.

Suddenly, she felt his presence behind her. She swiveled around to face him. "Do you want to dance?" she said, repeating her words from that long-ago night. She stood and took his hand.

But rather than letting her lead him to the floor as he had before, he held fast. "I don't know if I have enough willpower just to dance with you in that dress. I don't know if there is that much will-power."

She'd chosen the dress because it reminded her of the one she'd worn long ago, except both the front and back were cut lower, and rather than having a flared skirt, this one molded perfectly to her hips.

"You like?" she teased.

"You know I like. And if I'd seen you in that dress at home, we'd have never made it out the door."

"Then give me one dance; then I'll let you take me home and take it off."

"You've got a deal."

Out on the dance floor, Joe pulled her into his arms. She rested her cheek on his shoulder. This is where she wanted to be, with him, whatever the future held. But there was one question about the past she'd never asked him. She lifted her head. "That night, why were you coming over to my table?"

"Do you remember Willis Greavy?"

She knew the name but couldn't place a face with it. "Why?"

"He knew we were in Spanish class together, and he wanted me to introduce him to you. He had sort of a crush. He was standing right behind me, but I guess you didn't notice."

"Why didn't you introduce me to him?"

He winked at her. "Because once you took my hand, I forgot Willis existed. He didn't speak to me for months after that."

"Joe, how could you?"

"I don't know, but I don't suppose he's complaining today. He owns a Fortune 1000 company and is married to a supermodel."

"So, if he'd been standing in front of you, I'd have grabbed his hand and I'd be Mrs. Greavy right now?"

"No, baby. I think things happened just the way they were supposed to." He sighed. "Are we done yet?"

She knew he meant were they finished with this dance she'd insisted on. She chose to give his words her own meaning. "No, sweetie. I think we're just beginning."

A Taste of Romance

Celeste O. Norfleet

One

Venus Lovejoy watched carefully as she poured the silky chocolate chiffon mixture into the glass and waited. Seconds later a lush froth rose and enveloped the soufflé, then rose to the rim of the large champagne glass. Then it stopped as if on cue. Venus smiled, then topped the decadent dessert with a raspberry and a mint sprig, smiling with satisfaction. "Perfect." She turned the glass around to show the camera its best angle, then arranged the appetizer, entrée, and wine selection on the small, exquisitely decorated candlelit table for two.

She sat down, looked up at the camera, and smiled as she folded her arms on the table in front of her. Shiny black hair, slightly curled, dusted her back just below her shoulders, and her cinnamon complexion glowed to perfection. "And there you have it, a delicious romantic dinner for two. I'm Venus Lovejoy, and this has been *A Taste of Romance*, coming to you all this week from Romance, Texas, where Valentine's Day is every day." She paused and waited, her smile frozen in place, as the lighting slowly faded and the camera panned back.

". . . And, we're clear," Tracy Dent called out after receiving the final all's well from the show's syndication producer. The feed to the local morning show was perfectly taped and timed and would be ready for the following day. They would catch just the dessert portion of the show; the rest would be scheduled to air within the next few days as special commercial promos on the cable network food channel. "Great promo spots everybody," Tracy added as she applauded and walked over to Venus, who was already surrounded by studio stagehands and the two camera operators, who were diving into her edible banquet. "That was wonderful, Venus."

"Thanks, Tracy," Venus said as she washed her hands and removed her *A Taste of Romance* apron. "Thanks, everybody. There's another entrée in the oven and more dessert in the refrigerator if anyone wants them." The studio houselights went up, and the cleanup crew prepared to begin. Venus gathered her recipe cards from the messy counter and placed them back in her notebook.

"See, it wasn't that bad, was it?" asked Tracy.

"Are you kidding! I barely got here today; that car of mine is on its last leg, and as for this place . . . " Venus grimaced. The dread in her expression was obvious as she looked around the small local television studio. It was a cluttered mess.

The studio was acceptable for the local news, weather, and garden broadcasts, but cluttered and messy, it was completely inadequate for an on-location cooking show. "This place is the worst," Venus continued. "There's no way we can do a cooking demonstration here. The stove barely works, the plumbing is shot, and the counters are more suited for carpentry than food preparation. Has Carter found us a restaurant yet?"

"No, not yet. How many restaurants do you know of that are willing to give up their kitchen for a cooking show the week of an annual festival? Not many. If he happens to find a corner in a fast-food joint, we'd be lucky."

Venus sighed heavily. This was it, her opportunity to make it, to have her own show. She'd been doing the segment food specials on the food cable network for three years. This was her opportunity to prove to the network that she had what it took to have her own show and make it work. But she couldn't do it here, not in the last place on earth she wanted to be.

Venus laid her arm across the counter and shifted a mass of books, pottery, carpentry tools, and paper to the side. "Working here is like parting the Red Sea of clutter every five minutes. I don't see how it's gonna work. We need a restaurant or someplace neater, not to mention, cleaner."

"Well, until Carter finds us some place, you might as well just sit back and enjoy it. You're here now, and for the next week, you get to cook on location in your hometown. How often does someone get to come back home a celebrity?"

"That's just it. I didn't want to come home at all, particularly not now. The week before Valentine's Day is the worst." She looked around the studio.

"Why do you despise Valentine's Day so much?" Tracy asked.

"It's not that I despise it; it's just that I don't buy into it, particularly here, in Romance."

"But you have to admit, this is the perfect venue to promote your new cooking show. Valentine's Day in Romance, Texas, as experienced by its most noted celebrity. It's a sure winner. Carter ate it up when the town council proposed it."

"I bet he did. Good old Carter, making plans without consulting me again. Remind me to thank him one of these days," Venus said dryly, sarcasm dripping off of every word. Carter Baxter, her cooking show's executive producer, was a product of the California surfing world. He lived his life trouble free in a bubble-wrapped perpetual state of euphoria. And, as her ex-boyfriend of three years, he was the man most likely to get on her nerves on a daily basis.

"Well, he'll be here tomorrow. You can thank him then."

"And I'm not Romance's most noted celebrity."

"Oh, that's right," Tracy said as she filled her mouth with a spoonful of the chocolaty dessert. "Avery Palmer, ummm, yummy, now that's a rich dark chocolate slice of heaven I can see myself biting into any day of the week. Tall, dark, built, and too handsome.

Girl, that man is a bona fide feast for the eyes and a serious heart-throb," Tracy gushed.

Venus smiled in spite of herself. That was one thing she remembered too well about Avery. "Wait, you remember Avery Palmer, right?" Tracy continued. "Was he like he is now when you knew him?"

"I have no idea what he's like now," Venus said evasively. "I haven't seen him in years." In fact, the last time she saw him he had turned his back on her and walked away.

"You've seen the news, heard the reports. As venture capitalists go, he's right up there with the biggest. The man bought up companies and property like they were Monopoly board pieces, then bulldozed competitors like child's play. I read somewhere that he made Scrooge look like a wimp. I remember that his company was once ranked tenth on the list of successful African American entrepreneurships. Then it plummeted. He just dropped off the map. Money can change people, and serious money can change people seriously."

"Avery Palmer's family has always had serious money. His parents were divorced and remarried to other people when I knew him, but his father was loaded. Even his paternal grandparents had major money. When they were alive, they owned and operated the hotel you're staying at in town. Now I guess he owns it plus, if I'm not mistaken, half a dozen other properties in town."

"I remember reading that he made some bad investments and lost everything. What do you think?"

"I guess anything's possible," Venus said.

"And the two of you were an item, right?"

"We were neighbors and buddies, but that was a long time ago. We were kids. Now he has his world, and I have mine. We haven't spoken in years. I doubt we ever will; we don't exactly travel in the same circles. He left, I left, and that was the end of that." Tracy opened her mouth to question Venus's last statement but stopped when Venus held up her hand. "End of discussion. I'm here under orders by the network. I'll do my one week, and then I'm gone."

"You make it sound like a prison sentence. This is Romance, Texas, one week before Valentine's Day. How romantic is that?" Venus looked at her with an expression that said *don't get me started.* "Still, you gotta hand it to Carter; this is a perfect publicity device."

"Perfect is not always such a good idea."

"Oh, that's profound," Tracy said dryly. "This place is like heaven. It's a little slice of Americana, with its white picket fences, big old country estates, and apple pie on every corner. How bad can a week in Romance be?"

"Don't ask. You have no idea how bad this place can be, particularly around Valentine's Day. Romance, Texas, is like Valentine central. The people here live, breathe, and exist only for February 14. The festival is only the beginning. There are events and programs day and night, culminating with the annual Valentine Balls. It's madness."

"Well, I'm looking forward to it," Tracy said, looking around as the studio crew continued to clean up. "This is my first Valentine's here, and I can't wait."

"Suit yourself," Venus said as she gathered her coat and purse and prepared to leave.

"Are you going to your grandmother's house now?"

"No, there's a small reception a few blocks away, and I told my grandmother and aunt that I'd meet them there when we wrapped here. I'll see you guys tomorrow."

As soon as Venus stepped outside, a sudden rush of chilled wind hit her face. It was the middle of winter, February 7, and the weather, though usually warm and comfortable, was as balmy as spring in Seattle. Venus looked up at the dark sky. Storm clouds threatened on the horizon but looked far off enough. She got into her car and turned the key. The engine stalled. After four more tries, she got out and decided to walk instead of drive the three blocks to the town hall. Within seconds she fell into an easy cadence as she passed the familiar sights of the place she'd lived in all her life.

Romance, Texas, was a small city, and like most cities, it had one extremely popular festival that brought people in from miles away. New York had Times Square on New Year's Eve, New Orleans had Mardi Gras, and Romance, Texas, had Valentine's Day.

The Valentine's Day festival in Romance, known as the Romance Festival, was a tradition that dated back 150 years. One week a year Romance became the gathering place for singles hoping to find their Mr. or Ms. Right. Romance was where Venus's great-grandmother met her great-grandfather, where her grandmother met her grandfather, where her mother met her father, and even where her aunt, now widowed, met her first husband. Unfortunately, the town was also where her great-grandfather walked off and never came back, her grandfather went off to war and never came back, and her father left and divorced her mother. She had witnessed this phenomenon over and over again and thus had learned her lesson well. Men leave Romance; that's just what they do.

Suddenly, the image of Avery popped into her mind. Her thoughts lingered on his many attributes as she remembered Tracy's all too detailed observations. She was definitely right about one thing: Avery Palmer was truly a feast for the eyes. Even in their youth, he was handsome, and the recent photos she'd seen of him revealed that he'd gotten even more attractive.

Tall and perfectly built, he had smooth chocolaty skin and a dimple on his left cheek that teased when he laughed. He also had short, curly black hair and the sweetest, firmest rear end this side of Texas. "Whoa," Venus said out loud as she walked, "where did that come from?"

She shuddered and shook the thought away like a sudden chill. Apparently, being back in Romance had a bigger effect on her than she realized. "One week," she muttered, "just eight more days."

As soon as she turned the last corner, she saw that the reception had ended and people had already begun leaving the town hall. She walked up and began mingling, speaking and greeting friends and neighbors until she heard the familiar, playful, chastising voice. "Don't even try it, Sweets. You're late, and you know it." Expecting no less, Venus paused, smiled, and turned to face her aunt.

"Welcome home. How are you?" said Cynthia Hamilton, her aunt on her father's side, as she walked up beside Venus and pointed to her watch. A time management specialist with her own consultant firm in town, Cynthia thrived on punctuality. Every second of her life was planned perfectly, and given the opportunity, she would have insisted on planning her niece's life as well.

Venus hugged her warmly. "I'm fine, Aunt Cyn. How are you? And stop calling me Sweets," she insisted jokingly. Sweets was the childhood nickname her aunt and grandmother had given her because of her penchant for eating sweets morning, noon, and night. She stepped back to look at her aunt. "You look wonderful."

"Thanks, so do you," Cynthia said, returning the compliment.

"And for the record," Venus continued, "I'm not late. I told you I'd be here as soon as we wrapped. The promo segments just took longer than we anticipated."

"How did they go?"

"Good. I think both the festival committee and the network will be pleased with the promos. We taped several different ones. One will run tomorrow on the local morning show, and the others will run on the network in the coming days."

"That's wonderful. I could use some good news."

"Have you heard anything new about the house?"

"No, nothing lately," Cynthia said.

"So it's pretty much a done deal?" Venus said.

"Yes, but nothing will take place for another few weeks or so. We still have a little bit of time to clean everything out. The settlement isn't for another month. The new owner has given us a wide berth to get things in order and move out."

"It just seems like such a loss. That house has been in the family for four generations, too long to lose it now."

"I agree. I've already talked to the bank about a loan, but it just wasn't enough. It basically came down to the house or the bakery. And the taxes and upkeep on the house are astronomical. We just can't afford them both anymore. Especially, of course, after Mom fell down the stairs and broke her hip."

"I know," Venus sighed heavily. "I understand; I just wish that there was something more we could do."

"I've tried everything, but so far nothing. The house already has a second and third mortgage on it, and the property rates on the hill have skyrocketed. All of a sudden, Romance is the place to be," Cynthia said.

"So I've noticed. I saw all the new construction going on. This place is really taking off."

"It really is."

"What about Dad? Can he help?"

Cynthia reached out and took Venus's hand. "Sweets, your father hasn't been around in almost ten years. He calls from time to time but—"

"I know, good old dependable Dad, still making promises he has no intention of keeping. Grandmom must be heartbroken."

"My dear brother," Cynthia said, shaking her head. "He's her only son, and he's about as dependable as a hurricane. Comes and goes just as often. Anyway, there's no other choice; we had to sell it."

"Yeah, how is Grandmom?"

"The same. You know your grandmother, up two hours before dawn and off to the bakery. Although she's got a great staff, she still insists on being there in the morning to greet her customers." Cynthia smiled lovingly. "She's not walking with the cane any longer, and her hip replacement seems to be working fine. Her living in the house alone and falling down the steps really took it out of her."

"I know. I'm just glad you are here."

"She's completely moved out of the big house and in with me, so you'll have the place to yourself."

"How is she about selling the house?"

"Oddly enough, she's fine with it."

"Really, I would have thought she'd be devastated."

"No, she's come to terms with the sale and is taking the whole thing in stride."

"Where is she now?" Venus asked.

"She's still inside talking with some of the committee members."

"With all that's happening, she's still helping the committee with the Romance Festival this year?"

"She's a grown woman and just as determined and stubborn as ever. Did you really think she'd not help with the Romance Festival?"

Venus knew better. Her grandmother had participated in the town's festival every year as far back as she could remember. "How was the reception?"

"Good. Now that the festival's Grand Marshall is back in town, we're pretty much all set. Although"—she paused and grinned—"since you haven't been back home for over five years, Mom thought it would be a good idea to get you more involved in the festival."

"I am involved. The town council asked me to do some romance cooking demonstrations. I accepted. That's involved."

"You know what I mean," Cynthia said. "She needs a volunteer to help with the Heart's Ball." She looked at Venus and smiled.

"And?" Venus asked, then paused, seeing her aunt's expression. "Are you kidding me? No way, not me. I have no intention of going to that glorified meat market."

"Actually, just going to the meat market isn't exactly what she had in mind."

Venus looked at her suspiciously. "She already volunteered me, didn't she?" Cynthia smiled her answer. "What about you?"

"She's already given me a dozen jobs to do, including soliciting volunteers and decorating the halls," said Cynthia.

"So why me?"

"Kind of obvious, don't you think." Venus opened her mouth to protest, but Cynthia raised her hand to stop her. "All you have to do is match up couples from the invitation questionnaires they sent in and play hostess."

"I have no experience in playing Cupid or Ms. Matchmaker. How am I supposed to know which singles should be matched up? Don't you need a computer or psychology degree or something for that?"

"It's a fund-raiser. For heaven's sake, Venus, you're not mating people for life. Besides, you'll have help. I was able to get another volunteer to assist you. Come by the office tomorrow around five-thirty, and the two of you can get started."

"I don't want help. I don't want to do it. I don't have time to do it. I have shows to prepare for, not to mention a cookbook to promote and recipes to test. My to do list is three miles long and growing daily."

"You'll have plenty of free time. A few hours in the evening, that's all it'll take, and Mom really needs someone. You're our resident celebrity, and when your name came up, it made perfect sense. Because of the show, yours is a recognizable name both here in town and elsewhere. People know you. They relate to you as the woman who cooks and knows romance."

"Oh, please," Venus said.

"It's all for charity, and it's all in fun. Everyone knows that, so don't take it so seriously. Just think of it. You helping Cupid would be great publicity for your cookbook and for the show. But if it makes you feel any better, there's a commonsense disclaimer written on the questionnaire. And as I said, you won't be doing it alone. I was able to get another volunteer to lend a hand."

Venus looked at her aunt absently. Her lips were moving, and words were coming out of her mouth, but nothing registered. The only thing Venus could hear was a vacuumed void as she looked over Cynthia's left shoulder and saw her grandmother, Regina Lovejoy, smartly dressed in a classic brown-and-white houndstooth suit, coming toward her along with a vision from her past.

"Sweets, here you are," Regina said as she approached her

granddaughter and daughter, smiling happily. She reached out and embraced Venus warmly, kissing her on both cheeks. "I'm glad you could make it."

Cynthia turned. "Oh, here he is now. We were just talking about you. Venus, I'm sure you remember Avery Palmer, Mr. Palmer's grandson from next door to Mom's house."

"Grandmom, you look fantastic," Venus said, trying to focus on Regina's nearly wrinkle-free face.

"I feel fantastic now, thanks to this young man here. What a wonderful reunion this will be."

"Hello, Venus," Avery said, his soft brown eyes immediately connecting with hers and holding her gaze for what seemed like an eternity.

Venus's heart lurched, and a rush of feelings she'd long ago suppressed began surging. Too surprised to speak, she just stood there completely numb. Seeing Avery was like seeing a ghost from her past. As his gaze steadied on her face, she was too stunned to look away. Cynthia and Regina began talking, and Avery joined in. It wasn't until a few moments later that Regina realized that Venus hadn't spoken. "Venus, are you okay? You look a little peaked."

"I'm fine. Just a little tired, I guess," she said. "It was a long drive to get here."

"Well, why don't you go over to the house and get settled. We'll catch up with you tomorrow morning at the bakery."

Venus nodded just as a slight drizzle began to fall. "That's a good idea. Can one of you give me a ride back to the television studio? My car wouldn't start so I walked over here. The car's still in the television studio parking lot."

"I'm going that way," Avery said, volunteering. "I'll be happy to give you a ride."

"No," Venus said too quickly, "that's okay; I wouldn't want to trouble you. I'm sure you're busy."

"No trouble at all. We can catch up on the way. Shall we?" he offered.

Venus, looking from her grandmother's face to her aunt's face, decided that it was best to just go with him. "Thanks." She kissed her grandmother and her aunt and said her good nights.

As her family walked away, she turned to Avery. He smiled pleasantly. "My car's over here," he said and led the way as she followed. When they got to the car, he pushed the button on his key chain, unlocking the car and turning its lights on. He opened the passenger door, but before she got in, Venus paused, turned, and looked at him.

"What are you doing here, Avery?"

"Aren't you going to at least say hello?"

"Hello. What are you doing here?"

He chuckled, then grinned that knee-buckling smile she remembered so well. "Is that any kind of welcome home?" He leaned in and kissed her gently on the lips, lingering just long enough for the spicy scent of his cologne to scrabble her brains into a mush. "You look exactly the same," he said too close, "and still as determined as ever."

"No, not exactly. I've changed a lot." The sternness in her tone made him lean back.

"Yes, you have fame and fortune; you did it."

"I've been blessed," she said, "but I guess I could say the same of you, although rumor has it you dropped from sight."

"Really," he said evasively, "you know better than to believe rumors."

"So why have you come back?" she asked.

"I promised you I'd be back."

"It's been fifteen years; you're a little late."

"A promise is for keeps."

The simple phrase was one she'd said all her life. It was a part of her and a code she had lived by for as long as she could remember. And just now she remembered who first said it to her. Why did he have to still look so good? "I don't need to do this. I'll walk," she said and turned to walk away.

"Venus," Avery called out. "Wait." Avery caught her hand as she moved away. "Yes, you do." She stopped but didn't turn around. "It's starting to rain. Come on. I'll take you to your car. We don't have to talk if you don't want to."

Just then the slight drizzle became a downpour. Venus stood looking at the car as if it were a lion's den and entering it would be the end of her. To most, riding in a one-hundred-fifty-thousand-dollar Bentley Continental GT Coupe would be a dream come true, but to her, it was just the opposite.

"Come on," Avery offered again as he pointed to the open passenger door. "I won't bite, I promise." She got in, and they drove the first block in silence. Memories flooded her mind as the rain poured from the sky. What had been a long, exhausting day was now an impossible night.

"After all this time, why come back now?" she asked in the darkness, starting a conversation she knew she shouldn't.

"I was invited."

"If I'm not mistaken, you've been invited here before and didn't come. Why now?"

"Business brought me here."

"Business, right. What kind of business?" she asked skeptically.

"You sound like you don't believe me."

"Your reputation precedes you. As business goes, I heard that you made Scrooge look like a spendthrift."

Avery chuckled at her choice of euphemism. "Is it still that bad?"

"No, apparently, not since you dropped off the map. But, to the folks in this town, definitely not. They think you're the best thing since sliced bread. I believe the last headline I read went something like 'Romance's bad boy makes it big in acquisitions and becomes local hero'."

He chuckled. "Is that what I am now, a hero?"

"Some people think so."

"I guess it's better than the troublemaker title I used to have. And all I had to do was buy a few pieces of property and make a few bucks. Now I'm the Romance Festival's Grand Marshall and the town hero." He chuckled to himself and shook his head. "I'm even supposed to get the key to the city." He smiled in the darkness. "Funny how things change."

"Some things."

"And what about you, Venus? What do you think?" he asked, pulling into the television studio's parking lot and spotting the only car still there.

"People forget," she said, completely avoiding the deeper question she knew he was asking.

"But you don't," he said, looking directly at her. She didn't answer. He pulled up beside her car and shifted into park but kept the engine running. "Venus, I've changed; I'm not the same person I was fifteen years ago, or even three years ago."

"Neither am I," she said simply. He pivoted to get out, but she stopped him. "No, don't get out; it's not necessary. I'm sure the car will start now. Thanks again for the ride," she said, opening her door quickly.

"Venus," Avery said as he reached out and took her hand before she got out, "I just wanted to tell you that I missed, I missed you so much." His voice was deep and rich and gentle as the promise of sincerity covered every word.

Venus felt his openness, and the sudden thickness in her throat made it difficult for her to respond. She didn't turn to face him. She knew if she did, she'd be heartbroken all over again, and she couldn't handle that. She looked out the front window.

Time had stood still, but her mind raced a mile a minute. Her heart wanted her to tell him that she missed him, too, but her mind knew better. She couldn't open her heart up to hurt again. "Good night, Avery." She slipped her hand from his, got out of the car, and closed the door behind her.

Two

It was the perfect exit, the kind you'd see in the movies. The kind you hoped all your life to achieve, and she'd done it. Then, on less than steady legs, Venus managed to take the two steps needed to get to her car. She got in and sat behind the wheel, with her keys in her hand. Her heart thundered, and her pulse raced as a kaleidoscope of thoughts swirled in her mind. No, she admonished herself firmly. She would not go down that path again. She would not do this to herself.

He'd left her. He'd turned her down.

Seeing Avery after fifteen years was not exactly what she needed in her life right now. Her world was set, or at least as set as it was going to get anytime soon. She had her career, her family, and her friends. So what if she didn't have a man in her life? They were a distraction and the last thing she needed, particularly a man like Avery. Their history together had been long and deep and had ended in heartbreak, and she had been certain that their paths would never cross again.

I missed, I missed you so much. The words he'd said echoed in her head over and over again. As clear as day, she heard his deep, rich voice and felt the warmth of his sincerity. Why did he have to look so good, and why did he have to smell so good? It wasn't fair. Every one of her fantasies of him had always played out the same way.

Of course, she'd seen photos of him in *Ebony* and *Jet* magazines, in *Black Enterprise* magazine, and numerous other business-related publications. He was always perfectly neat and attractive, but somehow she wanted to believe that it was all a lie. Airbrushed and computer-generated, Avery Palmer in reality had become old, ugly, fat, and smelly.

She smiled at her humor, brushing aside the shock of seeing Avery again. Venus refused to be affected. She steeled herself, closed her eyes, and said a silent, hopeful prayer, then turned the key. Much to her relief, her engine started. She looked up in the rearview mirror. Avery had maneuvered his sports car just behind her car and appeared to be waiting for her to drive off. Shifting into gear, she pulled out of the parking space and started toward her grandmother's house. He followed. Each time she glanced up in the mirror, she saw Avery's car right behind her. And each time her heart lurched.

This was ridiculous, she protested mentally. She was a thirty-two-year-old professional woman with a rising career in culinary arts and had become a noted celebrity in her own right. She catered, had her own restaurant, and now she was on the verge of having her own syndicated television show and was just beginning to pen her third cookbook. She'd had men in and out of her life for years. Why should one man affect her so much?

There was nothing incredibly special about Avery. Sure, they had been boyfriend and girlfriend when they were younger, but he had since gone on to conquer the business world. And if reports were to be believed, at thirty-three, he had recently retired after a measurable business loss. He was handsome and women flocked to him like bees to honey, but he was also the man that left her without as much as a good-bye.

Driving on mental automatic, her mind miles away, Venus continued to the outskirts of town, to the place she'd always called her true home, her grandmother's house. As she drove, even in the darkness, she noticed the changes along the way. Several new office buildings had been constructed, and there were numerous new residential communities, one in the beginning stage and the others already completed.

Mixed emotions and a sense of loss filled her. Suddenly, Romance, which had once been the best kept secret of Texas, except on Valentine's Day, was now open to the public, and it appeared, judging by the size and quantity of the new residential communities, that the public had come in droves.

The love-hate relationship she had with her small hometown had raged since childhood. The Romance Festival naïveté of its founders and the absurd festival itself were a total waste of time as far as she was concerned. No, she wasn't a huge fan of Valentine's Day. There was nothing about the day that even remotely thrilled her.

As far as she could remember, it was a day of loss and pain. It was the day her father had walked out and never returned, and three years later it was the day her mother had died in a car accident, two of the worst days of her life. It was also the day Avery promised to return and never did.

The windshield wipers kept a steady cadence as she remembered the first time they'd met. He was twelve and she was eleven. It was late at night, and just like tonight, it had been raining. She'd been waiting all day in vain for her father to come by and get her, but he never did. Frustrated and angry, she had climbed the steps to the giant tree house in her grandmother's yard, seeking solitude.

It was dark, and the shadow of a form startled her. Dressed in a white T-shirt and low-riding blue jeans, he looked like a thug rapper from one of those television videos. His hat was turned backwards, and his dark brown eyes shined bright even in the darkness.

"Who are you?" she'd asked.

He'd looked her up and down, considering his answer, then leaned back against the tree house rail and smiled. "I was waiting for you. I knew you'd come up here."

"Of course, I would. It's mine, and you need to get out of here now before I call my grandmother on you."

"He didn't come, did he?" She glared at him, not answering. "Your father, he didn't come to get you, did he?"

"None of your business. This is my tree house, in my yard, and you're trespassing."

"I've seen you up here before from over there, my bedroom window." He pointed to the big house behind her grandmother's house. It was owned by Mr. and Mrs. Palmer, and she knew that they didn't have any children.

"You're lying. Mr. and Mrs. P don't have any kids in their house. Their son is old and moved away a long time ago."

"That's my pops, and he's not old, and I don't lie. I came to visit my grandparents, and that's where they live."

"Whatever. You need to leave my tree house."

"I wondered what you saw from up here."

"I come up here to be alone."

"Why?"

"It's none of your business."

He shrugged and slowly walked past her, heading for the ladder leading down to the ground. As he passed her, he stopped and looked at her. "By the way, my name is Avery, Avery Palmer."

She crossed her arms over her budding chest and glared at him. Two seconds later he stole a kiss on her mouth and dashed down the ladder in the wake of her yells and threats to strangle him the next time she saw him. That was only the beginning. They'd spent the next six years—each spring, summer, and winter break—as an inseparable pair.

The wiper blades on Venus's car washed away the faded memories almost as soon as they began. Others followed, but they also came and went like the flash of light beneath the street lamps she passed under, each lasting seconds and each filling her with the dread of the coming week. She slammed her fist soundly on the steering wheel. "This is ridiculous; I can get through this," she muttered to the empty car. All she had to do was stop thinking about Avery.

Moments later Venus turned on to her grandmother's street. She pulled into the driveway and waited until she saw Avery's car drive past. It did. She looked up at the huge house through the wet front windshield. The first thing she noticed was the UNDER CONTRACT sign posted in the front yard. Now dark and dreary, this was the place she always called her home.

With its five bedrooms, three baths, a formal living room and dining room, a small kitchen, and a massive basement and attic, it was the perfect place to find the quiet solitude and focus she needed for the coming week.

The house, an old gingerbread, was one of a dozen white elephant homes built on this street in the late nineteenth century. Originally a large carriage house, it was owned by a prominent physician and his wife, who lived in the main house on the square of property. The carriage house was passed to the barren couple's dedicated servant, Mandy Stewart, Venus's great-great-grandmother. For years the physician's will was contested, but eventually the house was hers. It had since been passed down through the generations and finally into her grandmother's hands.

Venus grabbed her umbrella and opened her car door quickly. In one smooth do-or-die motion, she snatched her purse and overnight bag from the passenger seat and made a quick dash to the front porch. The wind immediately caught the umbrella and turned it inside out. She tossed it down as soon as she reached the porch. Her hands, wet from the cold pouring rain, trembled as she inserted the key into the lock. Breathless from the mad dash up the wooden stairs and across the porch, she opened the door with her key, stepped inside, stood with her back to the front door, and waited.

Instead of the quiet stillness she'd expected, the loud rain outside and the distant rumble of thunder surrounded her. Musty, damp, and drafty, the house she remembered so well wasn't as welcoming as she'd hoped. She dropped her bag on the floor beside the door, took off her damp coat, and reached for the light switch. She clicked it up, but nothing happened. She clicked it several times, and still nothing happened.

She moved to the old Tiffany lamp at the base of the stairs. She pulled the chain. Nothing happened. She looked around in the darkness, realizing that a circuit must have been tripped. She headed for the kitchen and then to the basement door. As soon as she opened it, she looked down into the inkwell blackness. There was no way she was going to find the circuit box down there without a light of some kind.

For the next fifteen minutes, she searched in the darkness for a flashlight, candles, or a fireplace match. Finding nothing, she walked to the kitchen door and looked out the window. Through the line of hedges and trees marking the edge of her grandmother's property and beyond the tree house, she could see the lights on at the Palmers, so she put on her coat, grabbed her umbrella, and headed back out into the storm.

Avery had watched as Venus got out of her car and ran up the stairs to the porch. He saw her fumble with the keys, then unlock and open the front door. He drove off as soon as she closed the door behind her. He smiled, not at all distressed by their first meeting after fifteen years. He knew that it would be difficult, but surprisingly, it was far better than he'd expected.

She didn't out-and-out hate him; that much was evident. And even though he couldn't get a true read on her feelings for him, he was sure that he had at least a small chance of winning her back. And that was all he needed. He knew that he had been a fool to leave her years ago, but all he wanted now was one more chance to prove that he loved her and always would.

She'd asked him why he'd come back to town, but he couldn't tell her the truth—that he'd come back to win her heart. He knew that it would scare her away and that first she needed to trust him again. That was the difficult part. But he had a plan, and although some parts of it were questionable, he prayed that in the long run their love would prevail.

Patience, confidence, and time were three things of which he had plenty, and achieving the impossible was something he did every day. He'd made millions playing the odds in the oldest game in the book. Unbeatable at poker, he'd found his niche in the commodities market and in the buying and selling of real estate. But at love, he was a novice, and he hoped that he knew what he was doing.

He drove up into the circular driveway to what had once been his grandparents' home. He looked out at the lettering on the new sign in front. What had once been his summer home had now been refurbished, renovated, and remolded into an eighteen-room bed-and-breakfast with a small restaurant.

He got out of his car and hurried up the front stairs to what was now the Palmer House Inn Bed-and-Breakfast. He went inside, turned on the lights, and looked around approvingly. The transformation was remarkable, impressing even him, though he'd watched every stage. The huge first floor he remembered as a child had been divided into a sitting room, a television room, and a game room, complete with pool table, slot machine, and poker and game table.

The large living room had remained basically the same, with its massive fireplace, columned dividers, and stained glass French doors that led to the enclosed sunroom. He walked through to the dining room, noting that the ten or so tables he'd chosen fit perfectly in the open space, then continued to the kitchen. It was massive and professionally stocked.

Moments later he took the back stairs to the second floor and glanced into the rooms as he passed. Everything was in order. Curious, he went into his old bedroom and looked out the window toward Venus's house. The lights were out. Assuming that she'd gone to bed, he began removing his clothes, knowing that tomorrow was day six. He smiled. Seeing the tree house brought back the memory of their first meeting. He chuckled softly as he thought of Venus, which thrilled his body. His chuckle grew to full laughter as he unbuttoned his shirt and stepped into the bathroom to prepare for bed.

Ten minutes later the doorbell rang.

Three

A very opened the front door, and as if he'd conjured her up by magic, found Venus standing there, drenched to the bone. Her hair was matted to her face, her clothes were soaked, and the umbrella she'd been carrying had turned itself inside out. He smiled at her soaked, waiflike appearance and opened the door wider to allow her inside. But instead, she stayed out on the front step.

"I remember you never liked thunderstorms."

"This has nothing to do with me disliking thunderstorms," she sputtered, her face completely wet. "The lights in the house won't go on. I think the circuit breaker tripped, and I need to borrow a flashlight to check it. I can't find one over there."

"Come in," he said, beckoning to her.

"No, I'm soaked. I just need a flashlight."

"Sure, no problem. Just let me get my jacket."

"There's no need for you to come over. I just need a flashlight," she insisted, calling out louder to his retreating back.

"Venus, it might be something other than just a tripped circuit," he said as he grabbed the flashlight in the hall closet, along with his rain slicker. "You might need help. Come on." Too tired to argue, she followed. "Where's your car?"

"At the house. It wouldn't start so I ran over here."

"Let's go," he said as they quickly dashed down the front stairs to his car. They drove around the corner to her house in silence and pulled up in front. Dodging puddles on the pavement, they ran up the steps to the porch. She was still carrying her inside out umbrella, and he the flashlight. As soon as they got to the porch, she unlocked the front door. She opened it and instinctively tried to switch on the front hall lights. They didn't work. Avery switched on the flashlight, sending a bright, narrow beam through the darkness of the front hall.

"Where's the box?"

"It's downstairs in the basement, through the kitchen."

He nodded and headed for the kitchen; she followed. The wind blew, the rain poured, and the house creaked like in every spooky movie she'd ever seen. Moments later, down in the basement, they found the electric box and checked the main circuit breaker. Avery switched it on, but nothing happened. He tried again, and still nothing happened.

"Was the electricity turned on?"

"Of course," she said, beginning to shiver in the cold dampness.

"It might be a blown fuse or maybe a power outage because of the storm," he suggested after trying a third time.

"But you have electricity," she said after sneezing.

"Bless you. I had the house completely rewired. We're on completely different lines now."

"Oh, okay. Thanks for your help. I'll walk you to the door." She turned to head back up the basement stairs.

"What do you mean, you'll walk me to the door?" he said as he followed her up the stairs. "You have no intention of staying here tonight, do you?"

"Of course, I do. I grew up in this house. I know it like the back of my hand." Then, as fate would have it, she turned and bumped into a kitchen chair, knocking it over. She huffed, mortified by the comedic timing. And refusing to look at Avery as he reached down and picked it up—certain of his "I told you so" expression—she just continued as if nothing had happened. "Just leave the flashlight; I'll be okay."

"You won't be okay, and you can't stay here. There's no electricity, no heat, and more likely than likely, no hot water. You're soaking wet. You need a hot bath, or you'll catch a cold."

"I'll be fine," she insisted, then sneezed twice and sniffled.

"That doesn't sound fine to me."

"Okay, fine. I'll go to my aunt's house."

"She's way on the other side of town. In case you hadn't noticed, there's a major thunderstorm going on out there, with flooded roads, downed power lines, not to mention scattered tree limbs. You might as well stay at the bed-and-breakfast tonight."

"Thanks, but no thanks. I'll drive to my aunt's house."

"Venus, don't be ridiculous. There's plenty of room. You'll be the only person there. The bedrooms are all completely finished. The inn doesn't officially open until this weekend, so you can have your pick."

She paused to consider his offer. She was exhausted from driving four hours to get to Romance, cooking a studio meal, and taping it, and the last thing she felt like doing in the middle of a thunderstorm was driving across town and probably waking her grandmother and aunt up just because she was too proud to accept an offered hand. "Fine, thanks." She picked up her overnight bag, and just as quickly he took it from her.

"Do you have a raincoat or something heavier to wear?" She shook her head. "Okay, take this," he said, and he began shedding his rain slicker.

"No," she protested, "I'm already wet. No sense in you getting wet, too."

Ignoring her protest, he draped the slicker over her shoulders. He waited until she slipped her arms into the sleeves, then raised the hood. "Ready?" he asked as he prepared to open the door to the wind and rain. She nodded. "Let's do it." He grabbed her hand, and together they ran down the paved path, avoiding several downed tree limbs.

By the time they reached the bed-and-breakfast, they were laughing hysterically. They were both completely drenched.

As soon as he opened the front door and she stepped inside, her eyes lit up bright. She was stunned by the incredible change. This wasn't the stuffy, proper Old English–style home with the dated twill wallpaper she remembered from years past; it was a comfortably modernized inn with sofas and lounges and soft lighting.

"Welcome to Palmer House Inn Bed-and-Breakfast."

"Wow, look at this place," she said, admiring her surroundings. "It's incredible."

"Do you like it?"

"Oh yes, it's beautiful." She turned, looking around in wonder. The traditional antique style of the main area had a modernized feel that was welcoming and relaxed.

"Come on in and look around," Avery offered.

She stepped into the living room and walked over to the large fireplace and mantel she remembered so well. Then she turned and continued through the stained glass French doors to the sunroom. Venus was pleasantly surprised to find indoor trees and tropical plants in the cozy enclosure. "This is wonderful."

"I'm glad you like it."

"Are you kidding? I love it. You did an incredible job here. Your grandparents would be delighted to see what you've done."

"I'm just happy you like it."

Venus turned to him as he stood in the doorway. "I do. I really do."

"There are still a few renovations left to complete, and we'll eventually expand outward to include several small cottages on the property."

"I'm impressed," she said. A second later she sneezed.

"Come on. Let's get you upstairs and into a hot shower and some dry clothes." He picked up her overnight bag and waited until she came over.

"Thank you," she said.

"You're very welcome."

Together they went upstairs. She chose a bedroom in the front of the house, and he went back to his old childhood bedroom, which was now double in size and completely redecorated.

An hour later, showered and dressed in jeans and an oversized *A Taste of Romance* T-shirt, Venus came back downstairs. She wandered around the first floor, checking out the smaller reading, television, and game rooms. When she came to the formal dining room, she was amazed at the transformation. She remembered the rooms being large, but not this large.

Hearing soft music, she continued through to where she remembered the kitchen being. She called out Avery's name as she approached. As soon as she entered the kitchen, she stopped, and her mouth dropped open in astonishment.

"Hey," Avery said as he noticed her standing at the kitchen door, "I was just about to send out the marines to find you. Come on in; make yourself comfortable."

Venus stepped farther into the kitchen and walked over to the double stove and pizza oven. She peeked into the huge pantry and admired the refrigerators and freezers. She ended her mini tour by going to the huge center island and running four fingers across the marble. Peering into the inset sink and smaller inset cook stove, she said, "Look at this place."

"It's a bit over the top for an average kitchen, I know, but I'm assured extremely functional for what I have in mind," he said, turning back to the stove and the pan he had cooking there.

"Well, I'm not sure what you have in mind, but this room is"— she paused and sighed, then smiled with total delight—"it's a masterpiece." She looked around some more, closely examining the appliances, gadgets, and hardware. With its two stoves, built-in brick pizza oven, double refrigerator and double freezer, enormous pantry filled with everything imaginable, three sinks, and miles of marble counter space, the kitchen was better equipped than any she had ever seen.

"Then you approve?" he said and smiled, knowing she would.

"Are you kidding? Who wouldn't? Who designed it?"

Avery gave the name, and Venus nodded, recognizing the firm immediately and hoping one day to have them do her kitchen.

"Who's your chef?"

"Therein lies the problem. I don't have one yet. I've interviewed dozens, but I haven't found who I'm searching for. Since the kitchen doesn't open for another three weeks, I still have a bit of time."

"What about your guests this week and next?"

"I've already made acceptable provisions for them."

Venus nodded, then turned her attention to the apron he was wearing, which said "kiss the cook." Avery looked up, saw her expression, and smiled. "I'm cooking omelets. I hope you're hungry."

"Actually, I'm starved. Believe it or not, after all the cooking I do on the air, catering, and at the restaurant, I rarely get a chance to actually eat." She walked over to the center island stove, sat down at the counter, and watched as Avery dropped a pat of butter into a small omelet pan and placed the pan on the stove over a gas burner. He picked up a bowl and began gently whipping eggs with a whisk. Impressed by his ease in the kitchen, she nodded admiringly. "I see you know your way around the kitchen."

"Call it basic cooking 101. I've watched a cooking show or two in my time."

"Really? Anyone I know?" she asked, hoping inwardly that he was referring to her.

"Yeah, someone I used to know very well."

"Need any help?"

"Sure. How about you open the bottle of wine?" He motioned to the chilled bottles in the cooler below the counter and to the glasses hanging on inset pegs above. Venus opened the wine and poured some into glasses, watching as he added the beaten eggs to the pan and began swirling them around. He added a small amount of chopped onion, green pepper, cheese, ham, and mushrooms to the eggs then looked up at her. She nodded.

When the assembly was complete, he lifted the pan and flipped the omelet over and back into the pan. "Okay, now you're just showing off," said Venus.

"I'm trying to impress you." He picked up a warmed plate and gently placed the fluffy omelet on it, adding a small sprig of parsley. Then he sat the plate in front of her, beside her napkin, fork, and knife. "Is it working?"

Venus picked up her fork and cut away a small piece. Avery waited patiently as she put it into her mouth. She smiled as she chewed. "It's perfect. I am duly impressed."

He smiled. It was just what he wanted to hear. Moments later he'd made an omelet for himself, and they sat at the counter, eating and talking comfortably. When they finished, he washed the dishes, and she dried them. Afterwards, they sat back down at the counter, drinking wine and talking about years past.

"Okay, personal information time," he said, adding more wine to her glass.

"What do you want to know?" she asked.

"Did you ever marry?"

"No," she said simply.

"Why not?"

"I don't do that love thing, not anymore. Besides, my Mr. Right is probably on the other side of the world."

"Don't give up on love, Venus."

"I didn't; love gave up on me."

"You mean to tell me that you've never been in love?"

Venus looked up into his dark eyes and whispered, "Once." Thick and lasting, the silence of truth hung in the air like the heavy rain outside. "What about you? Did you ever marry?"

"Yeah, as a matter of fact, I did."

"Did?" she asked, interested.

"Yes, did. It lasted six months. It was a messy divorce, but in truth, the marriage wasn't much better."

"Six months, why only six months?"

"Actually, six months is a stretch. I wasn't even there most of the time. Business had me traveling. It seemed easier to just be away."

"So why'd you get married in the first place? No, I'm sorry; that's none of my business."

He waved her off. "I married because it was time. I'd reached a certain point in my career, and it seemed like the thing to do. It ended badly. We had a prenuptial agreement; she tried to break it. She failed."

"Sounds like it was pretty ugly."

"It was, but oddly enough, after all was said and done, she said that she actually would have stayed with me even with all the compulsive working and traveling, but ultimately she realized that my heart just wasn't in it."

"Was she right?"

"Yeah, she was. She also said that she was tired of competing with the other woman in my heart, the only woman in my heart. She was right about that, too." He paused a second, looking up at her, then continued, changing the subject completely. "We didn't end well, either, did we?"

"No we didn't. It was acrimonious at best, but we were young," she said simply.

"Venus, when you asked me to marry you and I didn't answer, it wasn't because I didn't love you. I panicked."

"That was a long time ago, Avery."

"I didn't know what to do, what to say. So I walked away and left. Later, I thought about what you said, and when I came back, you'd already gone."

"Life continues and time goes on, healing everything in the process."

"But time doesn't heal everything. There was no excuse. I should have stayed, but I just wasn't ready. We should have talked, but I ran, and that hurt you even more."

"We both ran."

"But your feelings were—" he began but was cut off.

"My feelings survived, and so did I."

"I realized that I hurt you, and I'm sorry."

"I know that, Avery."

"But you didn't then."

"No, I didn't, not then," she said.

"So how do we go back?"

"To what?" she asked.

"To what we had back then."

"We don't. That part of us is long over."

He nodded, accepting her reply. "Okay, it's my turn to ask a question." She nodded. "Are you happy now?"

"That question implies that I wasn't happy before."

"I'll rephrase it. Do you ever feel like leaving the craziness behind and coming back here?"

"Back here, to Romance? Are you kidding?"

"It's not so bad, is it?"

"You don't live here; you never really did."

"What do you have against Romance?"

"Romance, this place, this town, is the biggest farce ever contrived. It always was, and it always will be. There are no happily ever after endings here. There's only pain. Every year people come here expecting to find their soul mate, their other half, their one true love, and every year it's a lie. My mother is a perfect example of that. She gave everything to my father, and he took everything from her, from us. When she died, he left me here and just walked off."

"That's one man and one woman; that's not everyone."

"It's enough as far as I'm concerned."

"You can't justify your life alone because of what happened between your parents. Not everyone here ends up alone."

"There's nothing wrong with being alone."

"There's nothing right with being alone, either."

"You don't understand," she protested.

"I understand. Your father left you. But that's not all fathers. They all don't abandon their little girls. And not all men make promises, then walk away."

"You did."

"Venus . . ."

"It's getting late, and I have an early day tomorrow." She slid down from the stool and took a step away, suddenly in need of air. Avery stood as well and moved toward her. She stiffened as their eyes connected and he came closer.

He reached out to her. "Venus . . ."

She took another step back. "Good night," she said softly before she turned and walked out.

Four

The night had ended abruptly—and not exactly as either of them had planned. Venus hurried up the front stairs and went directly to her bedroom. She closed the door behind her and plopped down on the bed and shook her head in wonder. She'd put her pain away a long time ago, but now it seemed as real as ever. But more than that, the feelings she once had for Avery were back and were also just as real.

She lay back on the bed and continued to wonder. Years ago her relationship with Avery had been strictly a platonic friendship; then, later, it was teenage love. Then the night before he left, some fifteen years ago, everything changed. Suddenly, the thought of Avery's lips stirred her. What would it be like to kiss him again, to be with him again? She contemplated the image of their bodies pressed together.

A sudden rush of heat shot through her. She looked up at the ceiling fan and listened to the last remnants of rain pouring outside. Making love to Avery was something she'd thought about over the years. Once, they had almost come together, but only once, and they had been so young. Then, the next day, he walked away and never returned.

She got up, slipped out of her jeans, and went into the bathroom. She stood at the counter and looked at her reflection. Her brown, even complexion and dark eyes seemed brighter somehow. Looking in the mirror, she realized that seeing Avery again, laughing and talking with him had brought back feelings she hadn't allowed herself to dwell on in years. An intimacy she missed and a closeness she turned away from long ago had resurfaced.

She looked away in haste, picked up her brush, and removed the rubber band holding her hair in the ponytail. She brushed vigorously as if to shock herself back to her former self. Wistful, she tried but failed.

The innocence of optimism and hope had long since passed her by. She'd learned to depend on herself and trust only herself. That way she'd never be hurt or disappointed.

For the last fifteen years, she'd put her career first and never allowed herself to become distracted by emotions. Knowing from past experience that they would always end in heartbreak, she'd moved from relationship to relationship, with little feeling and even less attachment. And that suited her just fine—until recently.

Being alone never bothered her. She'd been alone all her life. Growing up an only child, she was devastated when her parents divorced. When her mother died and her father left her with his mother, she was heartbroken. But she had gotten over it. When Avery left her and never returned, she'd gotten over that, too. Thus loneliness had become her friend, and she embraced it welcomingly.

She went back into the bedroom, turned out the light, and crawled beneath the covers. The crisp coolness of the cotton sheets were a welcome relief to her tired body. She snuggled deeper, closed her eyes, and tried to relax, but her mind swirled with images of Avery.

Missed opportunities were never to be regretted, only accepted for what they were. She flung the covers back and got up.

* * *

The room was dimly lit by a lamp on the nearby nightstand, and a fire blazed in the fireplace. Avery stood at the window, watching the rain and looking at the tree house in the yard and remembering too much. He knew that he would have his work cut out for him, but he'd assumed wrong. She wasn't still angry with him or ambivalent about her feelings; she was distant and uncaring. He had no idea what to do next.

The knock on his door grabbed his attention. "Come in," he called out. Venus entered, dressed in the oversized T-shirt she'd worn earlier, but without the jeans. Her shapely legs caught his attention instantly. He smiled at the possibilities as she approached.

Nearly forgetting why she'd come to his cozy, comfortable bedroom, she hesitated as she entered. Seeing him standing at the window, she immediately noticed that his shirt was open, his chest was bare, and he was wearing just the jeans he had on earlier. "Um, I have an early call tomorrow, and just in case I don't see you in the morning or get the chance, I just wanted to say thank you for tonight, for the room."

"You're very welcome."

She nodded. "About what I said earlier—" she began as she approached.

"Venus," Avery said, interrupting her, "I'm sorry."

"For what?"

"For hurting you, for not coming back."

"On the contrary, you saved me. I got over that a long time ago when I realized that I didn't need anyone in my life to complete me. I learned to depend on myself. I don't need anyone else."

"No one?"

"No one," she confirmed.

"But what about love?"

"What about it? Love is for poets and for dreamers. I'm a realist, and love and I parted ways a long time ago. I plan and I prepare. No surprises, not anymore." As she stood by his side, she looked out the window at the tree house below. "This is actually the first time I've ever been in your bedroom. It's nice. Fireplace, huge four-poster bed, hardwood floors. Real nice. I often wondered what the view was from this window."

"This is where I first saw you. I watched you."

"I know, the beginning of voyeurism," she said as she glanced at him, then looked back at the tree house.

"No, the beginning of curiosity," he answered honestly. "I was curious. I'd watched you. I wanted to know who you were, so I went to the tree house and waited for you. I believe you threatened to strangle me."

"I believe you were trespassing."

"If I'm not mistaken, you also threatened to cut off a certain part of my anatomy."

"That was payback. You cut off my doll's hair after I threw you out of my tree house."

"You dressed my G.I. Joe in an evening gown, high heels, and purse."

"He was trespassing, too."

The short, quick quips between them ended with a burst of chuckling as they remembered the sight of his action figure in full drag. With the score slightly even, they smiled at each other, enjoying the moment. Seconds passed as they stood just smiling and re-membering. He turned back to the window.

"That's where I taught you how to whistle with two fingers, play Texas poker, and French-kiss," he said.

"I remember. You read about it in a book; we practiced for hours. You were an excellent teacher."

"You were a quick study," he said as she looked up at him boldly.

The power of their playful seduction exploded. Within seconds his lips dropped down to hers in a consuming kiss that lasted an eternity. She parted her lips, opening to him as he had taught her years ago. He entered full and powerful. Their tongues danced as he inched her body closer to his. She wrapped her arms around him, forming a sensual, unyielding bond of desire. When the kiss ended, they were breathless and hungry. She placed one of her hands on her chest and the other on his chest to keep him back lest their passion consume them again.

"That's also where we almost made love," he said, feeling the pull of his desire for her.

She nodded. "Yes, it is. But almost only counts . . ."

". . . in horseshoes," they said in unison, smiling.

"We didn't have a clue what we were doing back then."

"No, we didn't." He paused. "But we do now," he continued, looking deep into her eyes and still seeing the pain she still felt.

"Yes, I suppose we do." She reached up and stroked his smooth, clean-shaven face tenderly. Strong and firm, it was warm to the touch.

"You're still angry with me. I realize that. You trusted me with your love, and I walked away. For that, I'm sorry."

"That's just it. I'm not angry with you, Avery. I was then, yes, but not anymore."

As if time had stood still, she realized that her feelings for him were unchanged, but just as he'd turned away from her, she needed to turn from him. Not for payback or any such reason, but because her heart couldn't stand to be torn apart by him again. He was always kind and loving to her, but she knew that even in his kindness, and without meaning it, he could hurt her.

The battle between her body, her heart, and her mind raged. Her body wanted him, her heart loved him, but her mind knew better. "I need to go," she said, with a step back. After one last look, she turned toward the door.

"You know, I thought about you a lot over the years, about us."

She stopped but didn't turn around. "Really? I would have thought you had more important things to do, you know, building an empire and all."

Avery smiled modestly. "Yeah, well, there were a few less productive moments over the years, and as I said, I'm living a simpler life now." He walked over to her and turned her around. "If we'd made love that night—"

"But we didn't."

"No, we didn't."

The moment stretched long and slow, and Venus knew that if she didn't leave now, she never would. "I shouldn't be here," she said and turned to go.

"Yes"—he grabbed her hand to hold her—"you should."

They looked into each other's eyes. Their hearts met in unison as the years washed away and the moment returned. A second chance was theirs; all they had to do was take it.

"Years ago, when my parents divorced and married other spouses, I felt like I was kind of left out in the cold. They'd gone on with their lives, but I was still shell-shocked. Shuffling between two families every other month, I was lost. But summers and holidays, coming here, to this house, gave me solace. This was the one place in the world where I felt at home. And I know that's all because of you. You have always grounded me."

Venus smiled. "I didn't know that."

"It's true."

"But you were the one helping me. When my Dad never showed up to get me after he promised and promised, you were the one who helped me," she said.

"And now here we are, back where we started."

"No more broken promises and broken dreams."

"I'm glad you're back in my life," he said. "You are back in my life, aren't you?"

"It looks that way, at least for the next few days."

"Good." He nodded. She nodded.

"I have to go to bed," she said, pointing across the room inadvertently toward his bed. "I mean there, in my room, across the hall, on the other side of the house."

Avery smiled and chuckled lightly at her blushing sweetness.

"Yeah, I got that part. But if you want to . . ." he said, leaving his statement open as he motioned toward his bed.

"Good night, Avery," she said, gathering up the last remnants of her resolve to walk across the room without turning back to him.

"Good night, Venus."

Five

To the relief of all, the jet stream had pulled northward, and the wintry chill, the rain, and the fierce thunderstorm of the night before had blown over, leaving in their wake a beautiful, warm Monday morning. Before dawn Venus showered and changed, then walked back over to her grandmother's house for one last look around before starting her day. At six o'clock she stopped by her grandmother's bakery, knowing that she'd find her and her aunt already elbow deep in flour.

An old tradition she remembered well from childhood, every weekday she'd get up early, go to the bakery, and help out in the kitchen before school. It was where she learned to bake and where she got her love of cooking. She would spend hours in the kitchen with her aunt and grandmother, developing new recipes while improving and testing old ones.

As soon as she walked in and the bell chimed, a flood of memories came back to her. Half café and half bakery, Romance Bakery Eatery was small but quaint. It was the only café with its own bakery in town, and it was busy from sunup to sundown. Cynthia was behind the counter, with two other workers Venus didn't recognize.

"Hey, Sweets, you're late," Cynthia called out to her as she finished with a customer.

"I know, sorry," Venus answered, then headed straight to the kitchen, where she knew her grandmother would be. As soon as she pushed through the swing doors, the sweet, wafting aroma of freshly baked bread, cakes, and sweet pies filled her nostrils. She smiled and inhaled deeper. This was why she became a cook. The creation of something from select ingredients had always awed and amazed her.

"Good morning, Grandmom," Venus said as soon as she entered.

"Good morning, Venus," Regina said, smiling as soon as Venus walked in. "Grab an apron, check the bread in the upper oven, and get started on the pastry shells for the cinnamon apple tarts. We have a lot to do this morning." And so it began. Venus grabbed an apron from the wall hook, washed her hands, and jumped right in. She spent the next three hours in the kitchen, alongside her grandmother and aunt, making pastries, breads, cakes, and pies and enjoying every minute of it.

Venus Lovejoy. A smile spread wide across Avery's face as he dressed and prepared for his busy day. She hadn't changed a bit. She was still pigheaded, determined, and sexy as hell. But now the slight, willful wildcat of his teens had the body of woman, and she was everything he imagined and more.

Soft and feminine, she had a body that was every man's dream, a spirit that was alive and exciting, and a mind that was sharp and determined. Focused and creative, she exuded self-confidence, which made her even sexier to him. Yet he knew that the tough, worldly exterior she exhibited to the world was just a sham. In reality, she was just the old-fashioned Texas girl next door with a heart of gold. When she'd come into his room with just the T-shirt, he'd been surprised, and very few things surprised him.

Avery spent the morning in his home office, in front of the computer and on the phone, as usual. Contrary to public knowledge, his companies and fortune were all pretty much still intact. Yes, he'd taken a hit a few years ago with a bad investment and had sold a few companies, but that wasn't the experience that had changed him. Unbeknownst to most, he'd suffered a minor coronary.

At that terrible moment, he'd realized that not everything in life should be summed up on a spreadsheet or listed in an annual report. Some things were far more important. Work and business, which had once consumed him, were now dealt with as needed. And instead of spending every waking hour in the office, he'd learned to let business take care of itself.

Like Venus, he'd thought that success was everything, and that the time spent on cultivating emotional relationships was a waste. He was wrong. His grandfather had had a heart attack, and his grandmother had slipped into dementia associated with Alzheimer's. His perception of life changed drastically after those events and his own minor coronary.

He quit smoking, drinking, and partying, and after these major adjustments in his lifestyle, he was healthy and completely recovered. Then he took a step back and reexamined his life and his priorities. As soon as he did, he couldn't get Venus out of his mind. He knew then that she was still the one for him.

Love was rare, and time was irreplaceable.

So the companies, properties, and holdings were turned over, to be managed by a select few, and he retired into virtual obscurity, choosing to spend his time in a small town called Romance, the place where he could focus on his sole priority of winning the heart of Venus Lovejoy. Unconsciously, he reached up and stroked his heart. Fragile, yet strong, he hoped to one day make it whole again.

Just as he ended a conference call with his assistant and managers, the doorbell rang. He answered it. Carter Baxter stood on his porch, talking on his cell phone. Avery smiled instantly. Carter was exactly the man he wanted to meet. Once Venus's love interest, he was now the executive producer on her cooking show, and unbeknownst to him, he would be instrumental in Avery's effort to win back her heart.

He had learned a long time ago that when money talks to money, money listens, so he suggested to his old friend that it would be perfect to broadcast Venus's cooking show from Romance for the festival. His friend agreed. So far, everything was proceeding as planned.

Avery opened the front door. Carter immediately closed his cell phone and turned. "Avery, how are you?" He held out his hand to shake.

"Carter, it's a pleasure to finally meet you." Avery motioned for him to enter. "Come in. I know you're a busy man, so let's get started."

"And cut . . ." Tracy called out as the cameraman slowly stepped back in preparation to fade to black. Venus breathed a sigh of relief. After a rough introduction and a questionable start, it was nothing short of a miracle that the segment had gone well in the end. Awkward, clumsy, and uncharismatic, Sebastian Hart, the town's mayor, justice of the peace, local tree trimmer, and the owner of the most popular seafood restaurant in Romance had eventually found his comfort zone. Instead of just answering yes and no to her prompts and questions, he'd finally relaxed and begun joking, enjoying himself and answering questions in full detail, ending her first on-location cooking segment beautifully.

During the last few minutes of the show, they sat at the restaurant's front table, reviewing the show's menu. Venus talked about the ingredients, while Mayor Hart talked about easy preparation. Their chemistry was just right, and the conversation flowed like water. The segment ended with the mayor offering viewers an open invitation to visit Romance. By the time Tracy counted down the seconds to the end of the twenty-two minutes, the show was in the can and was a great success.

Several onlookers applauded as Mayor Hart waved his hand around like the celebrity he was. The only man in town to be in *The Guinness Book of World Records* five times, he had been mayor for three consecutive terms, angling to beat the record of his father, who had been mayor for as long as she could remember. A big man, with handsome features, he smiled easily, displaying his Chiclet-like front teeth below an overly curled and waxed handlebar mustache.

"Thank you, Mayor Hart. You were terrific," Venus said.

"No, thank you," he stated proudly, shaking her hand like he was pumping water from a well. "It was a little bumpy at first, but I think we did okay. I had a great time. I was surprised how easy that was once I got the knack of it," he admitted, hugging her in his usual bear grip.

"You were a natural. I see why all the ladies in town adore you. You're a real charmer."

"Actually, there's only one lady who I charm nowadays. When you see your Aunt Cynthia, give her my best."

The twinkle in his eyes gave his comment a deeper meaning, but Venus decided to reserve the question poised on the tip of her tongue for later. "Yes, I sure will," she said just before Mayor Hart walked away to greet his adoring public.

Venus removed the microphone from her shirt and unhooked the battery pack from behind her. She signed a few cookbooks for customers and answered questions about recipes, kitchen equipment, and gadgets. She chatted easily with the locals she remembered and with a few tourists, but it wasn't until she looked up a second time that she noticed someone was standing across the room, smiling and looking at her.

"Good show," Tracy said as she walked over to Venus.

"Thanks. It was a little hairy in the beginning, but I think it went well overall."

"So," Tracy said as she leaned in closer, "did you see who is here?"

"Carter, yeah. I saw him when he came in."

"No, not Carter, Avery Palmer, *the* Avery Palmer. I can't believe it. We were just talking about him last night, and here he was right here in town the whole time."

"Yeah, I know. I saw him last night," she said as she glanced in his direction, knowing that he'd be looking her way.

"Really?" Tracy asked, drawing out the word as if it were gooey taffy. The look of anticipation on her face showed that she obviously expected Venus to fill in the details. "And . . ." she finally asked when Venus went uncharacteristically quiet.

"And nothing," Venus said, hoping to end the conversation before it began.

"Oh, you see that; you are so wrong. You saw Carter as he entered. Well, I saw Avery Palmer as he entered, and girl, the man nearly ate you up with his eyes. If I didn't know any better . . ." She fanned herself with the clipboard in her hand as she casually turned to check if Avery was still looking at Venus. "Lord, Lord, I do know that if a man looked at me the way that Avery is looking at you, I wouldn't be the sweet church girl we all know I am."

Venus turned to her and was just about to say something when she was interrupted.

"Good morning, good morning, good morning. My two favorite ladies," Carter said as he approached, arms opened wide to gather them, one on each side. "Have I got great news or have I got great news."

The weather, much warmer than the day before, had brought with it a sense of serene calm by the name of Carter Baxter. Always disciplined and in control, Carter was the epitome of Los Angeles cool. Charismatic and charming, he was soft-spoken but had a commanding personality that got things done.

As soon as he had entered the restaurant, a swirl of activity had begun buzzing around him. A master of multitasking, to the point of obsession, he simultaneously talked on the phone, answered questions from the cameraman, conversed with Tracy, and read the outline script as he signed off on the next day's activity.

Carter's eager smile, as long and wide as Texas, froze when he heard his cell phone ring. "Hold that thought." He answered the phone, held his finger up for a moment, then stepped aside.

Tracy looked at Venus, smiled, and nodded knowingly—as if she knew something—before walking over to the cameraman to help with the set breakdown. Venus shook her head, noting the ridiculousness of Tracy's remark about Avery. She was obviously reading something into nothing. Avery didn't look at her in any special way, just as she didn't look at him in any special way.

Venus went into the kitchen to thank the kitchen staff and give them each a copy of one of her cookbooks. When she returned to the front of the restaurant a few minutes later, Tracy, Carter, and Avery were laughing and talking, obviously having a good old time.

"Hello, all," Venus said as she walked up, looking directly at Avery.

"Venus, just the woman I wanted to see," Carter said, obviously excited. He hugged her warmly and kissed her quickly, sending an instant spike a jealousy through Avery. Her eyes on Avery, Venus noticed the intense look instantly.

"That was a great show," Carter continued. "Venus, I was just telling Tracy the good news. I've found a base for you to work at while you're in town. I was just over at the Palmer House Inn Bed-and-Breakfast this morning, and the kitchen is fabulous." Venus looked at Avery. "And Avery here is willing to let us use his kitchen for the next few days free of charge. All we have to do is make sure that we mention the bed-and-breakfast on the show."

"That's not how we usually do things," Venus said.

"Of course, it is. We've had sole show sponsors before. The bed-and-breakfast will just be our sponsor for the remainder of our stay."

"I don't think it's a good idea," Venus said.

"Of course, it is. The network has already signed off on the idea. They love it; I love it. The shows are gonna be fabulous. We'll still do the location segments, but the remainder will be from the kitchen of the bed-and-breakfast instead of from the television studio." As Carter spoke, his phone rang. He excused himself.

When Carter stepped aside, Tracy looked from Venus to Avery and smiled. "Ah, I'm gonna go work on some close-up segment details drop-ins, and other stuff like that," she said, pointing to the kitchen before she hurried off, smiling like a Cheshire cat.

"Good morning, Avery," Venus said, then looked around and watched Carter follow Tracy into the kitchen.

"Good afternoon," Avery said, his eyes smiling. "I saw the taping. You were great. How in the world did you get Mayor Hart to relax?"

"I didn't." She looked over at the mayor as he strut around the restaurant like a peacock in full plumage. "He just relaxed and settled into the moment."

"No, you must have said something. The man was falling apart out there."

"I told him to ignore the camera and just pretend that he was in the kitchen hanging out, talking with his best friend."

"It worked."

"Yeah, I guess it did." Venus took a deep breath and looked around the restaurant. There were several small groups of people talking and sampling the food she'd prepared. "Listen, Avery, about last night . . ." she began, speaking softly as she turned and moved closer to him. "We were on the verge of doing, I mean"—she paused—"I was . . ."

"I know," he said, interrupting as he dipped his head to her. "I was, too."

"It's not that I didn't want to. God knows I did, I do, but it's just that for me the idea of being hurt far outweighs the idea of being loved. And whatever we had fifteen years ago is long over now."

"I know."

"I just needed you to know how I felt."

"Thank you." His smile gave her the peace she needed.

"Also, I'd like to speak with you privately."

Avery's dimple deepened as he smiled broadly, humored by her remark. "You mean there's something more private than the very real possibility of us making love last night?"

She blushed and looked around quickly. "You have to stop doing that."

"Doing what?" he asked innocently.

A moment of silence drifted between them as their eyes met and held, and knowing expressions crossed their faces. The memory of their kiss just hours earlier was still fresh in both their minds. "You know exactly what I'm talking about, looking at me like that. We need to talk," whispered Venus. Their coy smiles and knowing grins were obvious.

"Yes, privately, got it. Go ahead. What is it?"

"No, not here. Later possibly?"

"Sure, any time."

"Avery, I'm glad you're still here," Carter said as he walked up, unnoticed, beside them. He handed Avery a large envelope. "Here's all the paperwork signed and delivered back to you." He reached out his hand, and they shook. "Thanks again, Avery. It was a pleasure meeting you."

"It was my pleasure," Avery said. "Let me know if you need anything else."

Carter nodded, winked at Venus, then dashed off to speak with Mayor Hart outside.

Alone again, Venus frowned at Avery, then nodded toward the envelope in his hands. "Thanks for the heads-up. Why didn't you tell me this last night?"

"It wasn't set until this morning. I made the offer when I learned that your show had agreed to come to town. I knew you needed a place to do the demonstration, and since the Palmer House kitchen was available, I offered. Of course, the offer was pending your and

Carter's approval. So, if the whole deal had fallen through, there'd be nothing to tell. Therefore I decided to wait. And since you loved the kitchen, and Carter loved the kitchen, everything worked out fine."

"Not quite. Anything else I should know? Any other plans you have for my life that I might be interested in knowing?"

"Dozens, but I'll let you know when the time comes." She smiled. "Now, about that private conversation you want to have with me, is any time in particular good for you?"

"Any chance we can talk tomorrow evening?" she asked, noting the overly interested, smiling faces around them.

"Sure."

"Could you come over to the house?"

"I'd love to."

"Hopefully, I'll have the electricity on by then. I'll cook dinner, and we can talk."

"Even better."

"See you later," she said, holding her hand out to shake. He nodded as he gently squeezed her hand and left.

As soon as Avery walked away, Tracy came over with a new idea for the next segment at the bed-and-breakfast. Venus half-listened as she watched Carter walk Avery out of the restaurant. Avery turned just as the door opened, and he and Venus shared a brief glance and a half-smile just before he walked out, an exchange that elicited a raised brow from Tracy.

"Neighbors, buddies, right," Tracy said, laughing as she grabbed her briefcase and walked away. Venus tossed a towel at her, just missing. Tracy's sledgehammer subtlety was getting out of hand.

Six

After a quick stop at the electric company, which resolved nothing, then a disillusioned chat with the family's attorney, a disappointed Venus drove to her aunt's office just to see a friendly face. She walked in and looked around. A small comfortable waiting room, with bright colors and soft wood tints, greeted her. Neat and tidy, it was exactly what she imagined a time management specialist's office to look like.

Venus looked at her watch. It wasn't that late, yet the reception's desk was neatly cleared and empty. She walked over to the next door and peeked inside. Cynthia sat at a large desk, typing on her keyboard.

Venus knocked, then opened the door wider. "Got a minute," she said, poking her head through the open door.

Cynthia looked up from her computer monitor. "Hey, Sweets, sure. I was just about to call you. Come on in; have a seat." Venus walked in and sat in the chair opposite the desk. "Where've you been all day?"

"I had the shoot this morning and afternoon, and then I needed to go to the electric company to figure out what is wrong with the lights at the house."

"What do you mean what is wrong with the lights at the house? There's nothing wrong with the lights at the house."

"I couldn't get them to work last night. There was something wrong with the wires. I guess the storm knocked something out."

"Did you check the fuse box in the basement?"

"Avery did. It wasn't that. But his lights were on."

"They're on a different line now, after the renovations to the Palmer House Inn."

"Anyway, they said they'd check it out and will probably have everything working by this evening."

"So last night you stayed there in the cold and the dark. Why didn't you just come over to the house?"

Venus paused, knowing that what she was about to say would probably be misconstrued. "I stayed at the Palmer House Inn with Avery."

"Oh, right, the new bed-and-breakfast. I didn't realize it was open yet."

"It's not."

"So it was just you and Avery there alone? Of course, a raging thunderstorm outside sounds cozy." She smiled slyly.

"Don't start. It's not what you think."

"Of course, not," Cynthia confirmed, but her broad smile belied her innocent words.

"Last night was perfectly innocent, mostly."

Cynthia held her hands up. "I'm sure it was."

Venus began explaining the night before, but each explanation seemed to lead to more explanations and to imply exactly what she was trying to denounce. Eventually, she decided to just give up. "Oh, forget it. Can we drop this subject please?"

"Anything you say, Sweets," Cynthia said, noticing the red blush of embarrassment on Venus's cheeks, "but he is sexy. If I were twenty years younger . . ."

"Aunt Cyn," Venus blurted out, shocked by her aunt's admission.

"Oh, come on. Don't play innocent with me. You two were suited for each other fifteen years ago, and as far as I know, nothing happened then. But you're both consenting adults now, and there are no grandparents to stand in the way.

"The man obviously still has a thing for you. And you"—she held up her hand to rebut what she knew Venus was about to say—"still have a thing for him. Don't make the same mistake again. Treasure what you have now. Don't wait. Time is precious." Venus looked away. Her aunt's words rang too close to the truth. "That said, what else did you do today?"

"I went to the real estate office. I was curious as to who was buying the house and property."

"T. H. Real Estate," they said in unison.

"You already knew?"

"Of course," said Cynthia.

"They're out of Houston, but I've never seen them. The name does sound familiar. The agent seems to think that it's one of several companies owned by a larger company. She also told me that the contract process can still be voided if we want."

"Venus, I told you we can't. I know how much you love the house. I do, too, but there's nothing we can do. The house is just too expensive, and we just don't have that kind of collateral, not to mention cash, to make it livable again. We just can't raise that amount of cash. It's impossible."

"Maybe we can borrow it."

"I already tried; we don't have enough collateral."

"No, maybe we can borrow it from someone who has it."

"You mean someone like Avery," Cynthia guessed correctly.

Venus nodded. "He's coming over to the house tonight. I can ask him then."

"I doubt he has it. Remember he took a major loss a few years back. Rumor has it that he was wiped out. They say that's why he came back here and opened the bed-and-breakfast, because he's tapped out."

Venus looked dejected. "So it's true." Cynthia nodded. "I just hate to give up. That house means so much to us."

"I know, Sweets. It's where your grandmother was born. It's a part of our history, our legacy. Over the years we've turned down dozens of very aggressive offers to purchase it, most of them coming from Mr. and Mrs. Palmer next door. They were desperate to buy the house, but Mom never wanted to sell. But this time we have no choice. There's nothing anyone can do."

"I didn't know that. But they were always so friendly toward me."

"Of course, business is never personal; it's just business. They wanted the property and offered all kinds of money to buy it." She smiled at the irony. "Now it looks like neither one of the families will have it."

Venus frowned. She never knew that the Palmers wanted to buy her grandmother's house. They were always pleasant enough toward her, and she never had the slightest inkling that there was dissention between the two families.

"We just have to accept that it's out of our hands. T. H. Real Estate will own the property in a few weeks."

"I'd like to know more about them."

"Who?"

"T. H. Real Estate."

Cynthia stood and walked over to one of her filing cabinets. "They're out of Houston, and they've been buying up property around here for years. They bought and renovated the town hall, plus half the property on Main Street. I have the letter they sent right here." She pulled out a file and gave it to Venus, who opened it and quickly read through the document, then shook her head miserably. "I should never have left. I should have stayed and helped you."

"Don't ever second-guess your dreams. You needed to leave to make them come true. I'm glad you did. We're all so very proud of you."

"Thank you. But you should have seen me this morning. I was floundering like a newbie on the air."

"Speaking of which, how was Mayor Hart?"

Venus smiled knowingly. "Great. He did really well. A little shaky at first, but after a while, he was a natural. He's still exactly the same. The man's got charm and charisma oozing out of every pore, and he's a serious hunk." Venus noticed Cynthia blush as she looked away. "As a matter of fact, he told me to give you his best."

"Did he now?" Cynthia said, smiling too much.

"He sure did, and with a twinkle in his eyes, no less," Venus said, unable to help smiling from ear to ear. "So give. What's all that about? Is there something I should know?"

"Get out of my business."

"Don't even try it. You were in my business a minute ago. What was that about not waiting too long and making the same mistakes, about time being precious? Treasure what you have. . . ." Venus opened her mouth, then clamped it shut, then murmured, "You and Sebastian." She nodded knowingly.

Cynthia blushed, then cleared her throat and straightened up in the chair. "There's nothing seedy. Mayor Hart and I have gone out from time to time. You know, to the movies, to dinner."

"Really? How long has this been going on?"

"Since the Romance Festival—"

"Really?" Venus said, impressed.

". . . eighteen years ago."

"What?"

"He left town, then returned a few years back."

"Oh, really?" Venus said, even more impressed.

"Don't sound so smug. We enjoy each other's company. I like him, he likes me, and he makes me laugh."

Venus stood and walked over to her aunt and wrapped her arms around her shoulders and hugged her close. "I'm so happy for you," Venus said lovingly, "you deserve someone special in your life, and Sebastian is a wonderful man."

"Speaking of someone special, you and Avery are getting together at the house again tonight?"

"Business, strictly business. I want to talk to him about the house. He was in real estate; maybe he can give us a few ideas."

"Sounds good. In the meantime, I'd better get you started on the Heart's Ball questionnaires. The box is right over there by the file cabinet." Cynthia walked over, picked up the box, and carried it over to the desk.

Venus stood and began shuffling through the cards. There were no names or personal data, but each one noted interests, hobbies, and basic likes and dislikes. "How exactly does this work?"

"Simple," a deep voice said behind her. "Anyone interested in attending was asked to fill out a questionnaire card and send it in. We have to match the common answers and give each pair a number so that the night of the ball, they'll find each other."

Venus turned to find Avery standing in the doorway, smiling at her. "Avery, what are you doing here?"

"Volunteering," he said.

"Perfect timing. Come on in," Cynthia said.

Venus turned back to her aunt, who walked over to Avery. "You're right on time as usual," said Cynthia. They hugged warmly, eliciting an interested stare from Venus.

"Right on time for what?" Venus asked.

"Didn't I tell you that Avery volunteered to help you with the Heart's Ball matchups?"

"No, you didn't tell me."

Cynthia smiled guiltily. "Of course, I did. I distinctly remember telling you last night, right before Mom walked up with Avery."

Avery walked over and stood beside Venus. He picked up a card, read it, and nodded. "Anything else we need to know?"

"No, it's pretty straightforward, really."

"Okay, we'd better get started," Avery said, then turned to Venus. "Ready to go?"

"Go where?" Venus looked at Cynthia, who had returned to her desk. "Aren't you helping, too?"

"Sorry. I have an appointment in"—she paused and looked at

her watch—"six and a half minutes. I'm sure you two will do fine. If you need me for anything, I'll be here."

Venus, stunned by the turn of events, walked out with Avery behind her carrying the box. As soon as they got to his car, she turned to him. "If I didn't know any better, I'd say I was set up."

"But you know better."

"Yeah." She looked at him suspiciously. "Where exactly are we going?"

"The library, town hall, your place, my place, it doesn't really matter. Anywhere where we can sit for a while and go through the cards."

The list didn't sound at all appealing. Venus looked down the main street, noticing the quaint ice cream parlor at the end of the block. Seeing it still there, she smiled. "How about over there?"

"Let's go."

While Avery purchased a milk shake at the counter, Venus sat at a small wrought iron table in the back of the parlor and began stacking the cards into two piles, male and female. She read through a few and noticed similarities and differences right away. She chose a card and began sifting through to find a mate. She came up with one after scrutinizing fifteen cards in one of the piles.

Avery came back and placed an extra large, extra thick strawberry milk shake with whipped cream and a cherry in front of Venus. She looked at it in wonder. "You've got to be kidding. I haven't had one of these in years. There's no way I can drink all this."

Avery smiled and produced two red-and-white striped straws. He looked at the two piles on the table and the two cards in her hand. "Looks like you already have a match."

She handed him the two cards as he sat down, then opened her straw and stuck it into the thick milky drink. She took a deep drag of the straw, and ice-cold strawberry-flavored cream eased down her throat. A sharp sensation shot straight to the back of her head. She coughed and grimaced at the brain freeze, then, a glutton for punishment, immediately took another drag.

"These two sound good together." She agreed. He looked at the two piles she'd made on the table and at the remaining cards in the box. "All we have is about 198 more to do."

"Guess we'd better get started."

With the milk shake long since finished, an hour later they still sat at the table in the back, laughing and talking more about their youth than about the cards in front of them. With a little more than three-quarters of the cards done, they decided to finish the rest the following afternoon.

"It's still early. Got any plans for the rest of the evening?" he asked as he placed the rest of the cards back into the box.

"Yeah, work." She looked at him questioningly. "What about you?"

"I still have a few things on the burner."

"Avery, what happened, with the business I mean?" she asked. The solemn tone of her voice made her question clear.

Avery smiled, knowing exactly to what she referred. "The money, the power, the companies, the life?"

"Yeah."

"One Tuesday morning, after a particularly long night, I got a serious wake-up call. After a few months, I realized that everything I had was superficial and meaningless, and that just wasn't enough, not anymore."

"What do you mean? What more could you want? You had it all."

"That's just it; I didn't have it all. I had nothing and didn't even realize it."

"So it's true? It's all gone?"

"I have the Inn, and that keeps me busy enough."

"So now you're an innkeeper like your grandfather?"

"Let's just say that I've chosen a simpler life. I've had success, and I've made money, lots of money, and I've lost money as well. I'm taking life easy now."

"Good for you. There are a lot of people on the verge of massive heart attacks and strokes who need to come to that realization. But most times it's too late for them." Venus saw Avery tense and changed the subject, realizing that it must still be painful to talk about his failed businesses. "Oh man, I can't believe we drank that whole thing," she said, reaching up to play with the straws in the empty glass.

"Years ago we would have had one each," Avery said.

"Were we ever that young?" she questioned rhetorically.

"Younger. You worked at the bakery, and I worked here."

"That's right. You got me free ice cream," she said.

"And you got me free cookies and cake," he said.

Introspective, she paused, then said, "Sometimes I miss those days, having you as a friend, talking all hours of the night about our plans and our dreams. Things were a lot simpler then."

"I know what you mean." He placed his hand on hers. "I missed you. I missed being with you and talking to you like we used to for hours in the tree house, remember?"

Venus nodded, then cleared her throat. This conversation needed to end, now. "Well," she said, slipping her hand away to look at her watch, "it's getting late." She dotted her lips with her napkin and tossed it on the table. "I need to get back to work."

"Do you have another segment this evening?"

"No, not tonight. The next one is tomorrow morning and afternoon at the carnival. We'll be doing local color shots for the show's introduction, and the carnival should be the perfect backdrop." She stood.

He stood. "Sounds like fun."

"It should be." She looked down at the box of cards.

"Don't worry about these. I'll take the box with me. We'll do the rest later."

She nodded. "Okay." She paused for no other reason than just to look at him. "See you later."

"Later," he said, then watched her leave. A smile curled his lips as he stood there, his eyes riveted on her.

She stopped and turned around to him. "Oh yeah, one more thing, do you know anything about, or have you ever heard of, a company named T. H. Real Estate?"

He paused almost reluctantly. "Yes, I've heard of it," he said. "Why do you ask?"

"I'm just curious. See ya."

Venus turned and quickly walked across the tiled floor of the ice cream parlor. She opened the door and stepped outside, then turned around before closing it behind her. The sight of Avery standing there watching her go warmed her. Knowing that he was the only man to capture her heart, she realized that she was falling in love with him all over again.

She walked back to her car and quickly drove off. As she passed through the town, a sense of loss filled her. In five days she'd be gone again, back to her life and back to her world, leaving Avery behind a second time.

Seven

Late Tuesday afternoon Venus stood behind the makeshift counter, with her *Taste of Romance* apron on, and passed out neatly cut square samples of her favorite brownie recipe and mini crepes topped with a cherry glaze sauce. With great pleasure, she signed a few autographs and waved at the passersby. All in all, she had a much better time than she expected.

The carnival, festive and celebratory, featured the typical rides and the typical attractions. Kids of all ages paraded back and forth, seeking the best and most outrageous entertainment as they ate and laughed and played. Boisterous venders hawked balloons and cotton candy nonstop, and by evening Venus was nearly insane.

With the carnival now hot, humid, crowded, and loud, Venus was ready to call it a day. She'd been there for six hours already, and that had been five hours and fifty-five minutes too long. She helped the cleanup crew pack away her crepe pan and dispose of her foil brownie pans, and then she stacked the unused paper plates and napkins to the side for the next vender who took the booth.

"Excuse me, Miss, is this the kissing booth?"

Venus looked up and laughed so hard, tears moistened her eyes.

Shaking her head slowly and sadly, she said, "What are you doing here?"

"I'm looking for the kissing booth."

"Yeah, I got that part. Why are you dressed like that?" She erupted in another bout of laughter.

"I'm incognito," he said quietly, a large, white, gloved finger to his lips.

"Hardly. You stand out like an elephant in a bikini in a kiddy pool. Kinda hard to miss, but funny as hell."

"That's ridiculous."

"Which is about how you look." Avery frowned, then straightened his red-and-orange top hat, moving the big yellow daisy on top away from his ear. It instantly drooped again. He adjusted his gigantic purple-and-yellow bow tie; then he pulled out a bright green handkerchief the size of a bed sheet and blew his big, red, round nose into it, making a horrendous sound with his mouth. And finally, he straightened his posture.

"Better?" he asked in all seriousness.

"Oh yeah," she chuckled again, "much, much better."

He nodded with sober satisfaction. "So is this the kissing booth?"

"No, this isn't the kissing booth. Try two stalls down on your left," she said. Knowing that it was Mayor Hart's booth, she chuckled as he leaned back to see.

Avery glanced down the row and saw Sebastian Hart in a mile-high white chef's hat, a bright red kerchief, a fake bald head, puffy green sideburns, and enormous blue eyeglasses. He was laughing it up with a few customers as he handed out samples of his barbeque ribs and chicken.

"I think I'll pass," Avery said as he turned back to her. "So what time do you get off?" he asked, seeing the cleanup crew removing the last of the equipment.

"About twenty minutes ago."

"Care to take a stroll around the carnival with me? No clowning around, I promise." He raised two gloved fingers in a boy scout promise.

"Awe," she said, sounding extremely disappointed. "I was looking forward to that part." She turned, said thank you to her crew, then walked around to the front of the booth. Avery held his arm out, and she slipped her hand through. "You realize that this is a small town, Ms. Lovejoy. People will gossip."

"Yeah, a cook and a clown, who would have guessed."

They made a quick stop to wash up, and Avery took the opportunity to remove the clown face and costume. Then arm in arm, for the next two hours, as the sun slowly set, Venus and Avery strolled around the fairgrounds, enjoying the carnival like a couple of reform school kids. Hooting and whistling, eating everything in sight, they completely enjoyed themselves.

"That was fun," Venus said, then looked at Avery. His expression was quite the opposite. "Oh, come on! How can a grown man not like a merry-go-round?"

"Going up and down on a wooden horse while spinning around in a circle, going nowhere, is just a waste of time," Avery declared. "There's got to be something more interesting to ride."

"What? You used to love these rides."

"I was thirteen."

"Okay. There's the Ferris wheel. Come on; let's go."

"No way. I'm not going up there."

"It's not that high. Come on, or are you chicken?"

"No," Avery said. Venus began clucking, making other chicken sounds, and flapping her arms. "That's a good look for you."

"Come on," she whined. Avery looked up at the Ferris wheel as it spun around. He shook his head. "Come on, please."

"All right," he said, finally relenting. "Just stop with that chicken thing; people are starting to stare."

They waited in line for ten minutes as Avery anxiously looked up each time the Ferris wheel circled and stopped. It was finally their turn. The machine operator stopped the Ferris wheel to open an available seat. Venus climbed in, and Avery reluctantly followed.

The Ferris wheel slowly ascended as more couples got on. When it was full, the operator shifted it into full motion. It spun slowly. Each time they went up, Avery grimaced and closed his eyes. "You're afraid of heights," she surmised quickly.

"No."

"Yes, you are. Look at you. You're afraid of heights. How is that possible with all the travel you did in business?"

"Airplanes I can handle. There's something unnatural about sitting on a swinging metal bench held together by a few nuts and bolts, and going three stories high just to spin in a circle and come back to where you started."

"But look at the view. It's spectacular." Venus looked out as the Ferris wheel spun higher. The colorful lights of the carnival shined brightly against the now darkening sky. The stars glistened up above, and hundreds of people mingled down below. "Come on. Look at the view."

"No, thanks."

"Don't worry"—she cuddle closer—"I'll protect you."

"Promise?"

"A promise is for keeps."

After a few more spins, they were the first to get off. Avery seemed to relax instantly. As they climbed down off the Ferris wheel, Venus laughed heartily. Barely holding Avery up as they walked—he on shaky legs—she sputtered through chuckles, "Are you okay?" Her concern was obviously overshadowed by her mirth.

Avery glared at her. "Is there anything here that doesn't spin horizontally or vertically?"

"Yeah, this way," Venus said and led him away from the carnival toward Hearts Lake. Serine and calm, the dark water of the lake glittered beneath the stars and surrounding lights. They walked hand in hand along the banks and talked. "Thanks. I really had a good time tonight."

"My pleasure," Avery said, stopping and pulling her into his arms. She fell into his embrace with comfortable ease. They rocked and held each other, looking out at the idealic scenery. He stroked her back lovingly as she snuggled closer. "Do you realize that this is the first time you and I have actually been out together?"

"No. Really?"

"Um hum," he said as he kissed her forehead and squeezed her even closer. "I could get used to this."

She looked up at him. "Me, too."

Their eyes met as he leaned down, and they kissed, not the sweet, loving peck of dear friends, but the passionate hunger of a man wanting a woman and a woman wanting a man. When the kiss ended, Venus stepped back, gathered her arms around her body, and turned toward the lake.

"That's been happening a lot lately."

Avery stood by her side but didn't reply. Instead, he took her hand. "Come on. We have one more stop before I see you home. I think it's time we get married."

"What!" she exclaimed just before he broke into a run, pulling her behind him.

They returned to the festivities and went directly to a woman seated in a chair, with a drawing pad. Ten minutes later, posed and positioned, Avery and Venus were immortalized as a caricaturist's cavewoman bride and caveman groom. Afterward, each time Venus looked at the drawing, she chuckled. His seriousness made her laugh harder.

Later that evening Venus kicked her shoes off and headed for the shower in one smooth motion. Tired but exhilarated, she giggled as she dried off. It was just like old times. She'd forgotten the fun they used to have together. She dressed in a T-shirt and jeans and padded barefoot downstairs.

An hour later she was in the kitchen, pounding down the first rising of her bread dough while listening to the radio. As she put the two bowls of dough in the refrigerator and danced around the kitchen, singing along, she thought about her afternoon with Avery at the carnival. Giggles bubbled up all over again.

Avery looked up at the back of the Lovejoy house as he climbed the rear stairs. The lights were on in the kitchen and on the back porch. He looked at his watch; it was nearly twelve midnight. He knocked on the window of the pantry door and waited.

Drawing back the lace curtain on the door, Venus looked out. She unlocked the latch and stood in the doorway, with her hand on her hip. "What, are you stalking me now?" she asked.

"Is that any way to talk to your favorite clown?"

"What do you do? Sit out back and wait for the lights in the kitchen to go on?"

"Mostly."

"You need a hobby; you're a very sick man."

"I was, but not anymore."

"So what are you doing here?"

"You wanted to talk privately, and I'm starved."

"Are you kidding? You ate enough cotton candy, candy apples, and hot dogs to fill a barn."

He lowered his head and made a sad face, turning his lower lip out like a two-year-old. "Please," he said, holding up a bottle of wine, candy, and a large bag of buttered popcorn.

"Is this your idea of temptation?"

"Nah"—he smiled, making her knees weak all over again—"that comes later."

Venus shook her head and opened the door wider to let him come in. "You're lucky you brought the popcorn and Mike and Ike candies, or you'd still be standing on the back porch."

"Some things never change." He chuckled as he stepped inside. "Actually I was out walking and saw your lights on."

"And you thought you'd stop by for a visit."

"Yeah, something like that." As soon as he walked through the pantry into the kitchen, the aroma of cooking made his mouth water. He put the wine, popcorn, and candy on the table, noticing the books and cards scattered about.

He immediately went to the stove. Several pots and pans were simmering, and the grill was heating up. There were chopped vegetables, sliced fruit, and a dish of seafood.

"Wow, look at this spread."

"Don't get too excited. I'm testing recipes for my next cookbook and the upcoming season of the show."

"And I'm your test subject."

"As I said, don't get too excited. This is only my second run through. Like anything else, creating recipes is a test, a process of trial and error. The measurements and ingredients are only still approximates."

"So the tastes might be completely off."

"Not completely, but noticeably." She walked over to the stove and lowered the flame beneath a saucepan.

"What can I do to help?"

"Taste this." She picked up a teaspoon, dipped it into the sauce she'd been preparing, then held it out to him. He tasted the sauce and smiled.

"That's good. A little salty maybe, but very tasty."

She nodded and made a notation on a small card on the counter. She repeated the action with a second pot, then with a third pot. Each time Avery gave his opinion, and Venus wrote it down on the note card.

They ate and tested and ate more. Afterwards, they sat talking.

Venus walked over to the refrigerator, pulled out a large bowl, then came back to the table. "Avery, what happened last night and tonight, the kiss—"

"Was last night and tonight, Venus. I didn't come over for a repeat performance. What happened between us was special. I know that. I just came over to hang out. You mentioned the other day that you wanted to talk to me privately, so here I am."

"Actually we already did."

"Really? Refresh my memory. We talked about a lot of things, none of which I would consider particularly private."

"When I asked you about your businesses."

"Oh, that?" She smiled and looked at him oddly. "What?"

"I have to admit, you've taken the whole thing in stride. I was—" She looked away quickly.

"What?"

"I was devastated when my restaurant failed."

"You had a restaurant that failed?"

"I partnered with a businessman, a silent partner who wasn't particularly silent, and who was more interested in a tax break than a successful business. The tax write-off was fine for a while, but when the restaurant started making money, and push came to shove, he pulled out his investment and walked off."

"Men leave you a lot, don't they?" he chuckled.

She chuckled with him. "Yeah, I've noticed that, too."

As their laughter faded, Avery relaxed, sinking back in the kitchen chair. The fact that Venus could now laugh about her loss made him smile. It meant that the hurt had passed, and she had not only recovered but had learned something, and was stronger for it. "Is that why the cooking show is so important to you?"

She nodded. "It's my second chance; I don't want to blow it. I really want this."

"I know what you mean; second chances are all we have some-times." He paused, seeing a glint of hope in her eyes.

"Okay, speaking of promises. Food, I promised you dinner, right?" She stood, grabbed two jelly jar glasses from the cabinet, and sat them in front of him. As he opened the wine, she opened the candy and popcorn. Moments later they were munching on popcorn and candy while drinking wine and going through her files, choosing recipes for her next book.

"Umm, this one sounds good," Avery said, handing her a cake recipe card.

Venus took the card and read the ingredients. "Sweet bread," she said, smiling brightly. "This is one of my great-grandmother's recipes. I remember my grandmother used to make it for me when I was a kid. She'd have the whole kitchen smelling like heaven when she pulled one of these out of the oven."

"It sounds perfect for the cookbook."

"No. Somehow I never could quite get it right. Besides, it's too special to me. It's one of those family heirloom recipes that you pass down to your children."

"Children?" he asked. "You want to have children?"

"Sure, why not?" Venus said as she stood and walked over to the refrigerator. She pulled out one of the large bowls of dough she'd been kneading earlier. The dough had risen and doubled in size again.

"What happened to the whole alone theory?"

"That doesn't apply to children," she said as she dipped her hand in flour and spread it out on the marble surface. She dumped out the dough, which plopped with a thud. She began kneading it slowly, folding it over onto itself as she went.

"What exactly are you doing?" Avery asked as he came up behind her and observed from over her shoulder.

"Kneading dough. I'm making pepperoni bread for tomorrow."

Avery smiled, interested in the physical action of kneading. "Can I help?"

"Sure, flour down and grab the other bowl of dough from the refrigerator."

He washed his hands, then grabbed the second bowl and began kneading, repeating the action he'd seen her perform. However, instead of actually kneading the dough, he smashed it with his fist. "Like this?" he asked.

"Not quite. You have to be a bit gentler. Come here." He stood behind her. "See, slow and easy. Now you try it." Following her instructions, he reached around her with both hands and mimicked her actions. Soon they were both kneading her dough, and the slow, pulsating motion took on a sensuous tone.

He leaned in to her, his lips just inches from her ear. Then his whole body was right behind her, pressing her gently against the counter. He brushed his lips against her neck. Her legs weakened. He licked one of her earlobes, and her stomach fluttered.

She arched her hips back against his lower body. The dough and everything else was soon forgotten as she pivoted within his arms and threw her floured hands around his neck. They kissed with passion and purpose, sealing every promise made, and making a single one in return.

They kissed and kissed and kissed some more but went no further, letting their mouths, lips, and tongues explore the depths of their passion. Moments later Avery rested his forehead against hers, then stepped back. Breathless and hungry, they reveled in the swell and intensity of their desire, which begged to be satisfied. "If I don't go now, I'm never going to want to leave your side," he whispered.

She nodded, not trusting her voice to speak. He grabbed a towel and wiped the remainder of the flour from his hands. "Good night." She nodded and watched as he slipped out the door.

Venus walked over to the pantry window and watched him walk across the path leading to Palmer House Inn. When he disappeared around a large tree, she turned back to the kitchen. The marble counter was a doughy, floury mess, and by the looks of her T-shirt and jeans, she didn't look much better. After cleaning up, she went back to the pantry door and looked up at the shadowy figure standing at a window across the way. *So much for making bread.* She turned the light out, and a few minutes later, across the path, another light went out.

Eight

The next morning Venus arrived at the Palmer House Inn bright and early to prepare for the cooking segment that evening. As she drove up the driveway, she noticed several cars already parked in the small lot next to the house. When she did not recognize Avery's car among them, a curious expression crossed her face.

Anxious to see him again, she hurried from her car. As soon as she climbed the steps to the porch, a pleasant-looking young woman opened the front door for her. "Good morning," she said brightly.

"Good morning," Venus answered curiously.

"Venus Lovejoy?" the woman asked. Venus nodded. "Great, I've been waiting for you. It's good to finally meet you. I'm a big fan of yours."

"Really? And you are?" Venus asked, her curiosity turning to confusion.

"Oh, sorry, my name's Regina Mills, but everyone calls me Reggie. I'll be assisting you today. Whatever you need, just let me know, and I'll get it for you," she said as she reached out to take the grocery bags Venus carried. "I'll take these for you," she continued as they walked into the house.

Venus followed, noting a number of new people walking around.

They each smiled or greeted her as she followed Reggie to the kitchen. "Is Carter here yet?" Venus asked.

"Carter, no, not to my knowledge. You're the first, as far as I know. But I've been prepping the kitchen most of the morning, so I'll ask at the front desk to make sure."

As soon as Venus walked into the kitchen, she noticed the difference. The cavernous space of just a few nights ago had been transformed into a working mini studio. A stationary camera had been set up, along with several handheld cameras and an overhead sound mike. All were neatly situated to one side of the counter, giving as much space as possible for a walkway.

Venus moved over to the small, elegantly set table in the corner and fingered the fresh flower centerpiece. "You did all this?"

"Yes, but actually just this part. The rest was just a matter of requisitioning equipment and making sure that the suppliers delivered on time, left room for you to work, and didn't clutter the place too much."

"It looks great."

"Thanks. Where would you like these to go?"

"On the counter is fine."

"Actually, I'll be happy to do the shopping for you in the future. Just give me a list the day before, and I'll make sure that everything is prepped and set."

"That's okay. I stopped yesterday morning at the local grocery store and gourmet shop in town to get a few of the items. The rest of the ingredients should be arriving soon."

"They're already here. I put them in the refrigerator. Oh, and by the way, I ordered a few sets of pots and pans. I noted which you prefer when watching your show. They arrived yesterday. Although I suggest you use the Palmer House Inn dishware for promotional reasons." She held up a large dinner plate for display. "The designed crest should make a nice addition to the plated food, and since we're promoting the Inn, it would seem to make sense."

"Yes, that's fine with me. Thank you, Reggie," Venus said, walking over to the refrigerator. Reggie nodded and smiled as she continued emptying the grocery bags. "I made both tea and coffee this morning; I didn't know which you preferred. They're in the thermoses in the pantry. I also stopped at the bakery in town and picked up some morning snacks. That place is divine."

"Wow, perfect," Venus said, looking in the refrigerator, impressed by Reggie's enthusiasm and arrangements. "I must say, the network did a wonderful job when they hired you to assist me. You're an angel."

"Thanks, but the network didn't hire me," Reggie said.

"Good morning, good morning, good morning," Carter said as he walked into the kitchen. He turned around completely and clapped his hands and nodded his head approvingly. "This place looks fabulous. Good job."

"Thanks. Hi. I'm Reggie Mills. I'll be assisting Ms. Lovejoy today."

"Carter Baxter."

"Wait. You two don't know each other?"

"No," they said in unison.

"But I thought you hired Reggie," Venus said, looking at Carter as he shook his head, then headed to the pantry, seeing the Danish on the tray and smelling the freshly brewed coffee.

Before Reggie could reply, Tracy arrived, carrying several bags of groceries. "Good morning," Tracy said as she walked in, then stopped in her tracks. "Wow, look at this place! Talk about a studio setup. It looks incredible."

"Thanks. Hi. Reggie Mills, Ms. Lovejoy's assistant."

"Tracy Dent, the show's director," she said, introducing herself and following Carter to the Danish.

"Hold it," Venus said. "Reggie, if neither Carter nor the network hired you, who did?"

"Good morning, everybody. Welcome to Palmer House Inn," Avery said as he entered the room.

"Good morning," they all said. Reggie walked over and handed

Avery a small pile of letters, several manila and Express Mail envelopes, and a large mailing tube. "You'll have a second delivery this afternoon. And there's a fax on your desk that needs your attention."

"I already got it, thanks," Avery said.

"Would you check with the new linen service? I think there's a problem with the next delivery."

"Sure," Reggie said, and with that, she immediately disappeared through the dining room's swing doors.

"You hired Reggie to assist me?" Venus asked.

"Yes. Well, actually, Reggie works for me. I'm just lending her out to the show for the time being. I thought it might make your job easier. She'll be like a liaison between you and the house staff."

"Bravo. Whoever made the coffee, it's perfect," Carter said as he and Tracy came back into the kitchen.

"Thank you. That was really sweet of you," Venus said to Avery.

"Don't mention it," he said.

Carter and Tracy exchanged knowing glances and sly smiles. There was obviously something going on between Venus and Avery.

"Well, I'd better let you get started with your day. I'm gonna borrow Reggie for a few minutes. If you need her or me, just call the house or office numbers. They're on the corkboard in the pantry."

All three looked at the corkboard on the wall in the pantry, then nodded. Then Tracy went to the refrigerator to put away the groceries she'd purchased, and Carter stepped away to answer his ringing phone. Avery turned and walked away.

"Avery," Venus called out in the empty dining room. Avery stopped and turned. "Thank you for Reggie and everything."

He reached down, took her hand, and kissed it. "You're very welcome." He released her hand and continued to the front of the house. Venus, smiling, watched him go.

When she returned to the kitchen, Tracy was already detailing the recipes for the evening's show and checking ingredients and cookware essentials.

"Let's get started," Venus said, and for the next four hours, they prepped and prepared dishes as mouthwatering aromas wafted from the kitchen. By the time the network's hired cameramen arrived, that evening's initial set was complete, and they were ready for the first walk-through. After a quick run-through and a timed rehearsal, they took a break to set up for the show's taping.

Avery poked his head in just as the cameramen were stepping out back. "Hey, how's it going?" he asked as he held the door open.

Venus, leaning on the counter, with her back to the door, turned upon hearing his voice. He stood in the doorway, with a smile that sent a hot flash into her. It had nothing to do with the fact that the oven was still on. "Great," she said, clearing her throat. "Couldn't be better. This kitchen is a dream. I wish we could use it all the time."

"That could most definitely be arranged," Avery said playfully. "Where is everybody?" he asked, seeing her alone in the room.

"They're out back, taking a much deserved break."

Avery walked farther into the kitchen and peered out the back window, seeing Tracy and the two cameramen sitting on the lounge chairs by the swimming pool and chatting, and Carter standing off to the side, on the phone. "Have you been working them too hard?"

"Not at all," Venus said, her eyes still admiring his business-like attire. It was the first time she'd seen him dressed in anything but a polo shirt and jeans.

He walked over to the larger oven and peeked inside. She followed. Three gently browned and bubbling entrées were warming. "Is this the final?"

"Yes," she said as he leaned closer to the oven's glass window. "Careful. It's a bit messy over there."

Holding his silk tie against his chest, he continued to lean in. "Umm, yum, that looks incredible."

"It's a little something I came up with a few months ago," she offered.

"We were wondering what smelled so delicious all day."

"I met a few members of your staff earlier."

"I hope they didn't disturb you."

"Not at all, anything but. As a matter of fact, they were very helpful and seemed really excited that the Inn would be opening this weekend. Do you already have reservations set up?"

"We'll have a full house this weekend."

"That's great."

"Actually, the Inn's been completely booked for the past three months and will be full for the next six."

"Wow, congratulations. You must be really proud."

"I'm more proud of the staff. They did an incredible job pulling it together and getting this place ready. Everyone had a say in what they thought might fit well, so it was really a group effort to finish the job. Of particular interest was the equipping of the gym and the game rooms."

"I bet. I saw the pool table in there."

"But it came together well in the end." The oven alarm sounded, signaling that the entrées were ready to come out. Avery paused, then said, "I'd better let you finish your show."

"Okay," Venus said, not really wanting their conversation to end. "Will you be around later tonight?"

"Actually, I'm on my way out for the evening, but I should be back in a few hours. The doors lock automatically when closed, and don't worry about the alarm system. I'll take care of it when I get back." He turned and headed to the dining room doors.

"Uh, Avery," she called out louder than she wanted.

He turned. She smiled awkwardly. "Thanks again."

"No problem. Good night. Enjoy."

"Thanks."

As soon as he disappeared through the swing doors, Venus felt a sense of disappointment. He looked good. The obviously bespoken business suit fit him perfectly. She wondered where he might be going. Perhaps he was headed to a business meeting, one of the many events or parties in town, or possibly even out on a date. A sudden sense of regret gripped her. The thought of Avery on a date with another woman sent a sharp pain into her heart, and sadness clouded her mind.

If it was indeed a date, he had every right, she thought. A few kisses do not a commitment make. It wasn't like she encouraged him. As a matter of fact, she did everything but literally push him away. The disappointment she felt deepened as she realized that she wanted Avery in her life again. But she feared that she was too late. There was no way any woman in her right mind wouldn't give her eyeteeth to be with him. He was funny, charming, and sexy as hell.

The clatter of the crew coming back inside startled her, and she returned her attention to the business at hand. She needed to put together a television segment, and she needed it to be the best she'd ever done.

Two hours later they finished the thirty-minute show. The kitchen was perfectly cleaned, and everything was back in order. Carter and the cameramen went on their way, leaving Venus and Tracy sitting in the kitchen, discussing the live cooking demonstration, which was two days away.

Tracy stood, stretched, and yawned. "I'm beat. Thank goodness, we have the day off tomorrow. I'm gonna sleep late, then check out more of the town. There were several interesting faces in the lobby of the hotel this morning. I think the Romance Festival just might be starting early." She stood, gathering her things.

Venus smiled as she remained seated.

"Aren't you leaving?"

"Yeah, in a minute. I'd like to finish a few things before I go."

"Okay. Get some rest. The cooking demo is the day after tomorrow," Tracy said as she gathered her purse on her shoulder. "If I don't see you tomorrow, have a good one."

Moments later Venus walked to the front of the house and sat down in what used to be the Palmers' parlor. She smiled, remembering the fun she and Avery had years ago. Then, for no particular reason, she stood and walked upstairs. Heading for Avery's bedroom, she noticed that the door was open, so she went inside. A dim light was on beside the bed. She looked around, admiring the décor, which was functional yet elegant. It was a man's bedroom, with its dark wood and heavy furniture.

She walked over to the cozy seating area in the corner and sat down on one of the two upholstered chairs. She reached over and turned on a small light, illuminating the area. Her mind continued to wander as she absently fingered the rolled-up blueprints on the desk in front of her.

Moments later she stood and crossed the room to stand by the window. She glanced out over the yard and across the path to her grandmother's much smaller house. A small, patient voice inside her told her what she really wanted. She wanted Avery, to be with Avery. She knew that if she was with him, then maybe he would finally be out of her system for good.

"Venus, is that you?" She didn't answer. "Venus?" Avery repeated, tossing his jacket on a side chair and loosening his tie as he walked across the room.

The silhouette of her body was a beacon, and he obeyed willingly. No longer in the jeans and shirt she'd had on earlier that morning, she wore a sleeveless, formfitting dress. Her hair fell just below her shoulders. His fingers tingled, itching to touch her and unzip the single hindrance to her body.

"You once told me that you were curious," she said, standing at his window in the dimness of the room. He remained silent as he walked over to her. She turned to him as he approached. "Tell me something. Are you still curious?" she asked.

Knowing exactly to what she was referring, he nodded slowly

with unquestionable certainty. "Me, too," she said. She reached around, caressed the back of his neck, then pulled him toward her as she removed his tie. It flew across the room, instantly forgotten. "Kiss me," she whispered. He leaned down and kissed her sweetly, lovingly, holding back the smoldering passion that had burned inside of him for the past fifteen years. When the kiss ended, their lips parted slowly. She opened her eyes, knowing that after fifteen years she was still in love with him.

"That was nice."

"Yes, it was," he said.

She smiled, seeing the fire in his eyes. A rush of excitement passed through her as the sincerity of the moment shot to her heart. The kiss belied the swelling turmoil she saw, and its gentle chasteness only tempted her to want more. "Do you want to make love, Avery?" she asked.

The words she spoke were music to his ears. For months he'd dreamed of them making love, and now she was there in his arms, asking him the question to which there was only one answer. "Yes." He nodded. "Hell, yes! I thought you'd never ask."

She smiled at his exuberance. "Me, too."

The spark from memories of their past ignited a fire in them, and an instant later their mouths connected in an explosive passion born long ago. This kiss—this time anything but chaste—had the ardent fervor of passion. Her arms were wrapped around his neck, and his encircled her waist as the embrace deepened even further.

Taking her with him, he pressed back against the frame of the window, then kissed her with single-minded focus and wrapped his arms around her body, drawing her closer, molding her to fit against him. She went willingly, pulling his hard body to hers. Feeling him, leaning against him, it was like heaven.

Her mind whirled and spun in a million different directions. Her heart beat wildly, and her breath caught as every nerve ending in her body tingled and her stomach fluttered uncontrollably. His kisses were like a searing flame, scorching her. It was too hot. She was too hot, on fire for him. This moment had been a long time coming, and she wanted it. She wanted him.

Then, breathless, she pulled away from his embrace, took his hand, and led him to the large bed in the center of the room. She turned and released his hand, then reached up and touched his face, letting her hands roam down his jaw to his neck. Then, with deliberate ease, she unbuttoned his shirt and flung it back over his broad shoulders. The sweet dark chocolate of his skin made her smile with anticipation. She licked her dry lips, leaned in and kissed his neck, then nibbled tenderly at his bare chest and shoulders, releasing the shirt to the floor.

A deep, low primal groan of satisfaction escaped his throat, prompting her to explore his body further. She ran her open palms over his broad shoulders and across his chest. She felt the stubble of a slight scar over his heart. "What's that?" she asked.

Avery looked down at his chest and then into her eyes. "That's where you mended my broken heart."

The poetic sweetness of his words made her smile. She ran her fingers gently over the scar, then continued down his tight, firm, muscled arms to the flat of his stomach. She kissed his chest; he moaned; she smiled. She kissed his scar; he groaned; she smiled. She enjoyed the power she wielded. The passion of his yearning fed into her desire, prompting her to boldness.

His body was magnificent, and she intended to enjoy every inch of it. Touching and caressing, she felt the slightly separated six-pack that was his abdomen muscles. Then she slowly felt her way down to the waistband of his suit pants. She undid his belt buckle and slid it through the loops. Afterwards, she unsnapped and unzipped his pants, allowing them to fall to the floor.

She eased around to the back and felt the tight, sweet rear she remembered so well. Holding him close, she pressed her body into his, feeling the hardness of his desire against her stomach. She stepped back and looked down the length of him. He was ready, and his body was reaching out to her in earnest. She touched him, held him, and stroked him. But before she could continue her ardent pursuit, he stopped her.

His hands clamped on her wrists. He'd waited a lifetime to have her in his arms. There was no way he was going to rush through this now. "My turn," he said huskily as his eyes pierced hers. He brought her hands to his lips and kissed her fingers, then her wrists, then her arms, and then her shoulders. Then he returned to her mouth.

He kissed her firmly and passionately, and she opened to him, parting her lips to welcome him freely. He entered and tasted the sweet richness of her mouth. Their tongues became intertwined and moved in delicious, soul-pleasing perfection. Savoring the succulent sensuousness of the kiss, he pulled her closer.

His hands moved to her breasts, finding them full, firm, and soft. He kneaded, massaged, and gently caressed them through the fabric of her dress, feeling the taut, pebbled nipples as they begged for freedom. He slipped his hands behind her and unzipped her dress, letting it fall.

The soft silkiness of her bra and panties were little hindrance to his pursuit, yet he needed to see her and feel the bare essence of her body. As if reading his mind, Venus reached back and unsnapped her bra. She shrugged it from her shoulders. The bra slipped down, and she pulled it off, freeing her breasts to him. Then she reached down and slowly, purposefully, removed her panties. She stood before him, proud and perfectly comfortable in her complete nakedness.

Avery looked down the length of her body in adoring reverence. His breath caught in his throat. He knew she'd be beautiful, but he had no idea that she would be as breathtaking as she was. She was the perfectly sculpted form of womanhood. Round and taut, she was voluptuously endowed with the perfection God intended. He exhaled, breathing for the first time in what seemed like decades.

She was too beautiful for words. Seeing her bare and exposed before him was his undoing. In an instant, a wave of passion erupted, and he grabbed her up into his arms and kissed her over and over again. Reckless and rapturous, he showered her face, neck, arms, and shoulders with hungry kisses, unrestrained in their passion and fervor. Then he slowed down, kissing her leisurely as he laid her down on the bed.

Relaxed and yet filled with anticipation, he removed his briefs, then lay down beside her and ran his hands over her body. She closed her eyes and relaxed, enjoying the feel of his hands caressing her. A swelling passion overwhelmed her. She opened her eyes and reached up to him. "Come inside."

"Not yet." He leaned in, and his tongue licked and teased her earlobe as he planted nibbled kisses on her neck and shoulders. He hovered over her, lowering the kisses to her breasts. As he massaged one, he suckled the other, with tender pulls and teasing kisses. Moments later the kisses roved to the flatness of her stomach and her thighs.

The madness of his torturous mouth sent a blast of rapture through her, and her body burned for him. He'd started a fire in her, and it burned uncontrollably. As his mouth wreaked havoc, his hands touched her in places, bringing her to the point of pleasure she never knew existed. "Now, Avery, come inside."

"Not yet." He reached over to the nightstand, opened a drawer, and pulled out a condom. He opened it. She took it from him and slowly rolled it up the hardness of his manhood. A wave of desire shot through him instantly. With her task completed, she lay back and reached out to him. He came to her and slowly eased into her moist tightness, filling her completely.

She encircled him with her legs, and the dance began. Rocking his hips and holding her tight to his body, he moved with slow deliberateness, increasing his intensity gradually. As an ancient rhythm moved their bodies together over and over, again the cadence increased. Faster and faster, thrusting and pulsating, their desire surged and swelled, climbing to the point of their release. Finally, they yielded to ecstasy, and it took them over the edge, exploding with climactic spasms. Pouring every ounce of his being into her they exploded with the same passion that brought them together. Then, wrapped in each other's arms, they collapsed, closed their eyes, and slept soundly in the serenity of their love.

In the early morning hours, Avery, still half asleep awoke and smiled. His thoughts immediately focused on the night before. Their passion had consumed them, and they'd made love twice before finally falling asleep again. The memory of their night lingered in his mind. He reached out across the sheets. The bed was empty. He sat up and looked around the bedroom, knowing that she was already gone.

Nine

"What a beautiful day," Tracy said cheerfully as she walked into the kitchen, yawning, with an extra large Styrofoam cup of coffee in her hand. "You're here awfully early."

"My grandmother's house is right next door."

"That's convenient."

"Yeah, it is." *Too convenient*, she thought to herself.

"Are you okay? You seem a little off. Did something happen with the show?"

"No. Everything's fine. I'm just a little tired this morning, that's all."

"Well, you'd better snap out of it. We have a segment to do this afternoon and a live cooking demonstration this evening."

Venus slid onto one of the stools at the counter and rested her head on her crossed arms. "I know. I will. Just give me a few minutes."

"How was you day off?" Tracy asked, busying herself.

"Okay. I drove back home for a few hours. Yours?"

"Well, I had a blast. I don't care what you say. Romance, Texas, is my new home away from home. I love this place. There are more attractive single men around here than anyplace on earth. I swear, if you'd move the show here, I'd be in heaven."

"With that said, I presume you had a good time."

"The best. I went to the carnival, to a singles' mixer, and then out to dinner with this handsome man from Dallas. He's staying at the hotel, too. Where do you want me to put these?" Tracy asked of the vegetables in the sink.

Venus looked up, then around the kitchen. "Over there, on the counter," she said, pointing to the long empty space against the far wall. She picked up her recipe cards and began flipping through, with disjointed thoughts. Tracy continued talking, but Venus couldn't focus on what she was saying. Her thoughts centered on Avery. They'd made love two nights ago. Then she'd left without a word.

She'd panicked.

Suddenly, the reality of their actions and the realness of her feelings had rushed over her, and she'd run from his bed. Like a thief in the night, she'd jumped into her car and had driven until she reached her condo in Houston, four hours away.

She'd come back late the night before, knowing that Avery must have called and come by looking for her. But what could she say? She realized that she had to say something. She was in his kitchen, and the chances of not running into him for the remainder of her stay in Romance were slim to nil.

"Good morning, ladies," Avery said as he entered the kitchen, with a cup in his hand and a stack of mail under his arm. Both Venus and Tracy looked up. "You got a few deliveries yesterday. They're either in the pantry or in the refrigerator."

Dressed in another stylish business suit, Avery was straight out of *GQ* magazine. Venus's heart stopped beating for a second when she saw him. She opened her mouth to speak, but nothing came out. So she just stared and couldn't stop, even when Avery glanced at her and half-smiled.

"Good morning," Tracy said brightly, with a singsong tone in her voice, as she admired his attire. "What a beautiful day."

"Yes, it is. Tracy, Reggie's looking for you. I believe she's still at the front desk."

Tracy dried her wet hands on a towel. "Thanks, Avery. Don't you look gorgeous this morning? Got a hot date?"

Venus frowned at Tracy and was just about to respond when she hurried out, heading to the front desk. "Good morning, Venus," Avery said as he walked over to the sink and rinsed the cup he'd been carrying. "Um, something smells good already."

"I put coffee on and picked up some bagels, muffins, and Danish from the bakery this morning. Help yourself."

Avery dried his hands on a paper towel, tossed it in the trash, and smiled at her. "No, thanks." He turned and headed for the door.

"Avery," Venus called out before he left, "can we talk a minute?"

"Sure. Is it important?" She nodded. He walked back into the kitchen. "Go ahead."

"About the other night and yesterday, the reason I left was . . ." she began softly, looking around the empty kitchen.

"Regrets?" he asked even softer.

She smiled in spite of herself. "No, no regrets."

"Good. I'm glad to hear that."

"You?" she questioned.

"No, never."

She looked around again. "I just wanted you to know that I didn't plan on what happened happening. I mean, even though I was in your room, I didn't—"

"Neither did I, but I'm glad it did. It was a long time coming." He kept eye contact, forcing her to see the sincerity in his expression.

"Also—" she began but was interrupted by the ring of his cell phone.

Avery pulled it out of his jacket pocket and glanced at the phone number. "I'm expecting this call. Excuse me." He stepped aside to answer.

Relieved for the slight reprieve, Venus turned away. Her mind whirled, and her heart beat wildly. When she heard the click of his phone, she turned back to him. "As I was saying—"

"I can't do this now, Venus," he said, stopping her in midsentence. "We'll have to continue this later." He looked at his watch for confirmation. "I have an appointment, and I'm already running late."

"Okay," she nodded. "Later then."

He walked out without another word. Venus frowned mentally, questioning what had just happened. But before she could analyze their conversation, Tracy returned with Carter and the two souschefs he'd hired for the day. The moment passed, and the day began in a rush of activity and excitement. Four hours later the segment was taped and in the can, ready for broadcast.

The first half of the day had dragged on for Venus. As preparations began for the live cooking demonstration, everyone seemed nervous and eager except her. She was calm and composed, more anxious about her upcoming conversation with Avery than the event that evening.

How do you tell a man that you're in love with him after walking away from him fifteen years ago and after making love the night before?

"Are you all set to get started?" Tracy asked.

Venus nodded. "Yes, I'm ready. Let's do it."

When Venus walked into the kitchen, she was stunned by the transformation. The dining room sliding wall had been removed, and one massive cook area had been arranged. "Good evening, all," she called out as she reentered the main kitchen area.

Boisterous applause sounded, and Venus waved to the small assembly. She immediately saw her grandmother and aunt sitting at the front table, and then she caught sight of Sebastian Hart, who was seated next to Cynthia. Venus walked over, kissed and hugged all three, and then addressed her audience. "Okay, are we ready to get started?" she asked. The crowd clapped loudly.

"Okay, great. Let's go over a few basic rules for taping this segment, a live cooking demonstration." As she talked, she scanned the audience for Avery, but he was nowhere in sight. By the time she finished, the cameramen had completed their final checks, and the small audience excitedly waited for the demonstration to begin.

Venus stepped back behind the island counter, adjusted her apron, and checked the counter for her initial supplies. She and Carter spoke briefly, and Tracy walked up, nodding her readiness.

"We're gonna get started in a minute," Venus told the audience. "Anybody have any questions before we begin?" A few people asked questions, and she answered them until Carter gave her the okay signal. "Okay, we're just about ready. But fair warning; don't get too excited about the meal this evening," Venus said jokingly. "Most of the cooking is literally half-baked, with a lot of camera magic to surmount time constraints."

"Don't pay Venus any mind. The food's gonna be fantastic. Trust me," Tracy said. Everyone laughed as Tracy walked over to the main camera, held her hand up, and counted down, "four, three, two . . ." She motioned for the audience members to applaud. They did, and the live segment was well on its way to a resounding success.

After the segment was over, Venus spent the rest of the evening thanking her guests and accepting well-deserved accolades. As she stood at the door of the Palmer House Inn, she hugged and kissed her grandmother good night, then turned to her aunt.

"Venus," Cynthia said as she hugged her niece warmly, "thank you so much for everything. The taping was fascinating, and the meal you prepared was incredible." She rubbed her stomach. "I don't think I ate so much at one sitting in my life. Girl, you seriously have talent, and you really worked the audience. You're a pro up there, funny and quick, and a joy to watch. I'm so proud of you."

"Thanks, Aunt Cyn."

"I hate to be a wet blanket but the Heart's Ball is tomorrow night, and I'm going to need those cards finished by tomorrow afternoon."

"Now that everything is pretty much done, I was going to work on them a little later this evening."

"Alone?"

"Yes."

"I thought you and Avery—"

"No," Venus said, "he's not here this evening."

"Of course, he is. I saw him just before the taping started. Then again, right after dinner was served."

Venus frowned. She'd searched the audience several times before the taping began and she was sure that Avery wasn't there. "You must be mistaken. He left early this morning; I haven't seen him since."

"Well he's here. Not only did I see him, but I spoke with him. He was on the way to his office upstairs last I saw. Anyway, it's getting late. We're gonna take Mom home."

"We?"

"Sebastian and I."

"Good idea," Venus said, winking.

"Great idea," Cynthia said, winking back.

"Good night," Venus said one last time, waving from the porch. She went back inside and gathered her purse and briefcase. Carter and Tracy were leaving, while Reggie was staying on to see the kitchen staff out.

Just as Venus was gathering her things and preparing to leave, she decided to look for Avery. She went behind the front desk and entered the back office of the inn. The door was open and the light was on so she walked inside. No one was there. As she turned to leave, she noticed the T. H. Real Estate logo. This time it was on a mechanical blueprint that showed the dissection and perimeters of the Palmer property.

A wave of curiosity hit her. Whoever T.H. was, he had gobbled up most of the acquisitions in Romance. As Venus exited the back office, Reggie was coming around the desk.

"Oh," Reggie said, slightly startled at seeing Venus still there. "I thought everyone had gone."

"I was just about to leave, but I wanted to thank Avery again for his hospitality this evening and over the past few days."

"I believe he's in his office still."

"No, I checked. There's no one in there." Venus said, motioning to the office behind the front desk.

"No," Reggie said, "not the inn's office, his office upstairs."

"Oh, I didn't realize."

"I'll be happy to take you up to the office; I was just on my way."

"No, don't bother. I'll catch up with him later," Venus said, getting cold feet. She picked up her purse and briefcase to leave, deciding that a quick exit would be best.

"Reggie," Avery called out as he approached.

"Over here," Reggie said, much to Venus's dread. "I'm just saying good night to Ms. Lovejoy." She walked over to Avery and handed him several envelopes. "These need your attention," she said to him as she walked to the front door. He followed.

Venus noticed a familiar logo on one of the envelopes. It was the same one she'd seen on the letterhead in her aunt's office. As Reggie and Avery continued talking Venus's mind clicked away. T. H. Real Estate, the name was still too familiar. She was sure that she knew that name, but she couldn't figure out where.

"Good night," Reggie said as she left.

Avery turned to Venus.

"Hi," she said awkwardly as she walked over to him.

"Hi back," he said, turning and meeting her halfway.

"I see you're working with T. H. Real Estate."

Avery looked down at the package she'd pointed to in his hand. "Yes, in a manner of speaking."

Venus looked at him questioningly. His cryptic answer made her even more curious. "I hope you're not already thinking of selling this place."

"No, I'm not selling."

"I don't know if you heard, but they're the company buying my grandmother's house."

"I see," he said. He could see that she was still curious, so he quickly changed the subject. "You were incredible in there, and the show was fantastic. I've seen you on television, but to see you in person was a real treat."

"Thanks, although I didn't see you earlier. I thought you'd missed it."

"I came in a few minutes before the taping started."

"Did you get anything to eat?"

"No, I wasn't very hungry."

"Are you hungry now? Can I fix you something?"

"No, thanks. You must be tired."

"I am, a little."

"So I'll say good night to you." He turned and began walking to the front door. She followed.

"Avery"—Venus paused in the doorway—"about what happened the other night, or rather yesterday morning."

"What about it?"

"I left."

"I noticed," he said tightly.

"You're not gonna make this easy, are you?"

"We make love all night, and then you get up and leave before dawn, without a single word, then pull a twenty-four hour disappearing act."

"It wasn't like that. I just needed space. I needed to think, so I went home."

"I went over; I called. You didn't answer."

"No, not to my grandmother's house. I went home to my place in Houston."

"And?" he asked. "What did you think about?"

"You."

"And what did you come up with?" She shook her head. "Why are you here, Venus? Why did you stay?"

"I don't know."

"Yes, you do. The crew's gone, Carter's gone, even Reggie and Tracy are gone, but you stayed. Why?"

Venus swallowed hard as her throat suddenly went dry. "Look, Avery, this isn't what I'm looking for in my life right now. I don't have time for some grand . . . I mean, my life is set. I have my career and my show, and it's pretty full. So anything else, like a . . ." She paused, searching for the word.

"Romance, a love affair, a committed relationship, a future," he offered.

"I just want you to know that we had our moment, a wonderful moment, but that has to be it for us."

"I understand," he said smoothly.

A part of her sank when he acquiesced so easily, and a dizzying flow of emotions overtook her mind. "Wait a minute," she said as if hit by a bolt of lightning. "T. H. Real Estate," she said as she stood there in the doorway. "Tree House Real Estate?" The fire in her eyes said it all. She knew.

Avery nodded his head. "Yes."

"I presume that you just answered my question." He remained silent. She glared at him a moment; then, too filled with anger, she turned on her heels to leave. She took a few steps, then turned back around to him. "Why?"

"Years ago I came back two days later, but you'd gone."

"So this is payback?"

"No," he insisted. "It is my way of getting you back."

"Don't you mean getting back at me?"

"No. That was never my intention. I did it for you."

"You stood right here and lied to me, twice."

"No. The first time you asked me if I'd ever heard of T. H. Real Estate, I answered truthfully. I'd heard of them."

"I just asked you about them."

"You asked if I was working with them. I told you the truth."

"That's just splitting hairs. Damn it, Avery, you own the company, don't you?"

"Yes."

His straight, single-word answer went straight to her heart. Suddenly, her aunt's revelation about their grandparents' mutual enmity made sense. "You finally got my grandmother's house for your grandparents, didn't you?"

Avery didn't answer, but he knew precisely what she was saying. While not exactly the Hatfields and the McCoys, his grandparents and her grandmother had engaged in a long and bitter feud over the small house and property. The Palmers wanted the entire plot of land belonging to her grandmother and her grandmother's refusal to sell ruined their plans.

"No. It was our plan. We devised it fifteen years ago. Tree House Real Estate, remember?"

"You son of a—" He turned and walked away before she finished. "Don't you dare walk away from me," she yelled, following him through the house. "You steal my grandmother's house, then turn your back on me and just walk away. I don't think so."

Avery went upstairs to a room she was unfamiliar with. As he opened the door, Venus could see that it was the office that Reggie had mentioned earlier. Avery crossed the room to his desk and opened the top drawer. He pulled out an envelope with her name on it and handed it to her.

"What is this?" she asked.

"Open it."

"My aunt told me the other day that business is never personal; it's just business. So just answer me one thing: all this week, the past few days, what was it, business?"

He didn't answer. She nodded, taking his silence as an affirmation. "I guess we don't change as much as we think we do. The coldhearted Scrooge lives on."

"Venus, it's not what you think."

"You're right. It's exactly what I think. I'm going to go home."

"Maybe that's a good idea."

"Yeah, maybe we need to rethink this."

"Is that what you want?"

She sat the envelope on his desk and in silence walked out.

Ten

Going home was the furthest thing from her mind. Venus went directly to her aunt's house. She needed to talk; she needed answers. As soon as she climbed the stairs to Cynthia's front door, tears began to fall. When she got to the screened door, the front door opened, and her grandmother stood there smiling.

"Hi, Grandmom."

"Sweets, come in. What's wrong?"

Venus entered the house, sat down in the living room, and waited as her grandmother went to the kitchen to get her a cup of tea. When Regina returned, she sat down next to Venus and placed her hand on her knee. "Okay, tell me."

Venus began, and within minutes the entire story had poured out of her. She told Regina that she'd just found out who owned T. H. Real Estate, and that she'd come to talk her out of selling. There was no way the Palmer family would ever get the house.

"Sweets, calm down," her grandmother said. "First of all, tell me about Avery. I've heard quite a bit of scuttlebutt about the two of you."

"Don't believe everything you hear, Grandmom."

"That's why I'm asking you."

Venus gave her grandmother a very abridged version of her current relationship with Avery, including the fact that he'd offered his kitchen for filming and that on occasion they'd been seen in public.

"And what about romantically?"

Venus looked away, wondering how she was going to answer the question. Then she heard her grandmother chuckle and say, "I guess that in itself answers my question. Of course, it was none of my business in the first place."

Venus smiled, then seconds later smiled broader. "Grandmom, I was thinking on the way over here. I'll get a business loan, and instead of having the show taped in Houston, we can tape it right here in Romance. I'm sure I can talk Carter into the idea, and he'll take it to the network. We can turn the house into a studio and film from there. If we did it at the Palmer House Inn, I'm sure we can do it at the house. It's the perfect solution. That way you don't have to sell to Avery or anyone else."

"Sweets," Regina said calmly, "the house is already sold. I signed the papers yesterday."

"And Avery was there?"

"Yes."

"So you knew that he owned T. H. Real Estate?"

"Yes, he told me a while ago. He and I have had some very interesting and informative conversations over the years."

"Over the years?" Venus repeated with surprise.

"Yes, he said that the initials stood for Tree House, something the two of you came up with years ago."

"What else did he tell you?"

"He told me that three years ago you saved his life."

"Really," she said, more than a little skeptical. "And how'd I do that when we haven't been in contact for fifteen years and just saw each other five days ago?"

"Three years ago Avery came back to town. He'd just suffered a heart attack."

"What?" Venus gasped as her heart lurched and panic sliced through her. "Is he okay?"

"Oh, he's fine now. After a few major changes in his lifestyle, he's as good as new."

"I had no idea."

"Few people do; that's how he wanted it. To most of the business world, he suffered a financial loss and just slipped away. Of course, he still has considerable wealth; he's just not suffering the day-to-day trials and stress of maintaining it. He's hired others for that."

The ever proficient Reggie Mills instantly came to Venus's mind. "And he came back here to Romance?"

"Yes, he decided that this was the perfect place to recuperate and regain his strength."

"But why? With his kind of money, he could have recuperated anywhere in the world."

"He said that Romance was the only place he really felt at home. So he stepped away from the intense business world and made Romance and the Palmer House Inn his permanent residence." She smiled, remembering. "He and I have spent many an afternoon sitting on the back porch, talking."

"Talking? About what?"

"Oh, nothing much, just this and that. One day I told him about the tax and property problems I was having, and he offered to help."

"By taking your house away from you," Venus said.

"No, by giving me relief and peace of mind," Regina said. "As small as it was in comparison to the Palmer place, the property had just gotten too big for me to take care of alone."

"Why didn't you tell me? I could have helped."

"No, you were making your way in the world. And your aunt was finally happy again after the terrible grief of losing her husband. She'd opened her business and was finally getting her life back on track. As a matter of fact, I suspect she'll be residing in the mayor's mansion in the very near future. There was no way I was going to bring you into my troubles."

"But that's what families are for, to help each other out."

"Yes, that's true. And this was my way of helping you both out. Avery stepped up just when I needed him."

"But for him, it was all for personal gain. Aunt Cyn told me about how his grandparents always wanted the property."

"Avery is not his grandparents. What he offered was the perfect solution."

"This makes no sense," Venus muttered. "Okay, so what does this have to do with me supposedly saving his life?"

"As he recuperated, he watched you on television. The more he watched, the more he wanted to change. He finally decided to do something about his lifestyle."

"I don't cook lifestyle cuisine."

"It wasn't your cooking that changed his life."

Venus sat shaking her head in amazement. The day, tumultuous at best, had been nothing compared to the stark revelations of this evening. "Grandmom, this whole thing comes down to one bottom line: Avery now owns your house."

"No, he doesn't."

"Of course, he does. Tree House Real Estate owns it, and he owns Tree House. Therefore, he owns the house," Venus said, finding herself even more confused.

"Go and talk to him. He'll explain everything."

"I just came from there."

"Did he give you anything?"

"Yes, an envelope. I left it there. What was it?"

"The deed to the house—paid in full, taxes, mortgages and all—including a very nice equity account from which to draw."

"I don't understand. He gave the house back to you?"

"No, he gave it to you. Go talk to him."

"But, Grandmom," she insisted.

"Go." Regina stood and picked up her tea cup. "Tomorrow's Valentine's Day, and I need my beauty rest. I have a feeling that it's gonna be a very memorable day."

Eleven

Sixty minutes later Venus showered, changed, and went outside to sit on the back porch swing, her mind a swirl of questions. She looked up at the Palmer House Inn. All the lights were out except for the main security lights on the property. She stood and looked in the direction of Avery's bedroom window, but a tree obstructed her view.

She went down the back steps and walked across the dark yard to get a better view. As she walked, she noticed the tree house, where she'd spent so much time. She was overcome by a stray, wayward impulse to climb up.

Steady and balanced, she climbed the wooden ladder and eased through the opening in the tree house floor. Nearly seven feet by seven feet, the tree house was larger and sturdier than most. It had been rebuilt and reinforced over the years to last the lifetime of the tree. Once inside, Venus stood at the side rail and looked around. A myriad of memories surfaced as she looked up at the starry night and listened to the crickets and night birds around her.

She looked out at nothing in particular as random thoughts intruded on the tranquility of the moment. The tree house had always been the perfect retreat for her, a place to run and hide from the world, where trouble never came, and life's drama never reached the top step.

But tonight it was her place to think and reflect. The day had been perfect, but the evening had been a complete shambles. So many things had happened, and so many mistakes had been made. She'd thought the worst of Avery and he'd done nothing but give her everything she ever wanted. He'd offered her a place to do her show and a solution to save her family home, and most importantly, he'd offered her his heart.

But each time she'd distrustfully turned away from him.

If he indeed had bought the house just to turn it back over to her family, then she had done him a terrible wrong in accusing him of treachery. Now, knowing all the facts, she felt terribly ashamed. And she felt lost.

She had no idea how to make it right. There was no way he would give her another chance. The realization that she'd lost him but would always love him burrowed deep into her breaking heart. Then she looked up and saw a light go on in the kitchen across the way. "Avery," she whispered in the night.

She hurried down the tree house ladder and raced across the lawn to the inn. She ran up the back steps and knocked on the pantry door. There was no answer. She ran around the side of the house to the front door. She rang the bell and knocked repeatedly, but to no avail. He wasn't there. She slowly walked back to her house.

The solemnness of her mood sent her back out onto the back porch. She slowly walked to the tree house again and climbed up for the second time that night. Cocooned in the moment, she stood watching the stars above and praying that fate would give her another chance.

"Knock, knock." She turned quickly, not expecting anyone to see her, let alone climb up behind her. "Want some company?"

"Avery, hi. Yeah, sure, of course, join me, please," she said eagerly as Avery climbed through the opening and stood across from her.

"Hiding from the world again?" he asked.

"No, not this time, not anymore. I think I'm done running away and hiding out for a while, a long while."

"Really? Why is that?"

"Running and hiding don't solve anything, and I can't run forever."

"What were you running from now?"

"You."

"Me?" he asked. She nodded. "Why?"

"I spoke to my grandmother tonight." Avery looked away. "She told me about your heart attack and—"

"It was a minor obstruction, more like a wake-up call than anything else."

"Whatever it was, I'm glad you're better."

"Yeah, me, too. What else did she tell you?"

"The arrangement the two of you made regarding her house."

"I see."

She sighed heavily. "I realize that years ago, when I asked you to marry me and you didn't say anything, I ran more from myself than from you. Then when you left town without a word, I decided that I would never let anyone into my heart again. I was afraid of getting hurt."

"Venus—"

"Wait. Let me finish; I need to say this. Ever since I came back to Romance, I've been fighting against my feelings for you all over again. We made love, but even before that, I realized that my feelings for you will just never change. The thing is, I know that I never got over you. I still haven't."

"Venus . . ." Avery closed the space between them in three steps. He reached up and stroked the softness of her cheek. "I've compared every woman in my life to you, and they've all come up short. When I lost you, I lost my center. I lost my heart. I've been floundering ever since. There is a lot of truth to the whole Scrooge thing. You're the best thing to ever happen to me."

"And you just realized this?" she joked.

"No. I've known it all along. I guess that I just forgot and needed that wake-up call to remind me. I promised you that I'd come back, and I came back here only for you. I love you. I always have; I always will. Know that."

"Avery," she said wistfully.

"You want me, you have me. Here I am." He kissed her.

The happiness she felt in his words brought tears to her eyes. He reached up and gently brushed the tears away. "This is a good thing. Don't cry."

"I can't help it." She wrapped her arms around his body and hugged him close. "We waited so long. We missed so much."

He tipped her chin up. "Nothing we can't recapture now." She nodded, smiling from ear to ear. "You know, I just realized that I've never technically asked you out on a date." She chuckled. "Would you go to the Heart's Ball with me?"

"Yes, I'd love to." She reached up and kissed him. "Oh no, I almost forgot," she said, breaking the kiss instantly, "we have a few cards to finish matching up."

"They're already done."

"You finished them already?"

"There were only a few left to do."

"Thank you." She kissed him on the cheek.

"Is that all I get for all the hard work I did?"

She kissed him on the other cheek.

Avery laughed heartily. "Hey," he said as he looked at his watch, "it's one minute after midnight and officially Valentine's Day." He reached out and wrapped his arms around her. "Happy Valentine's Day."

"Happy Valentine's Day," Venus said, and for the first time she could remember, she actually meant it.

Twelve

Venus yawned as she curled up next to Avery in the back of the limousine as it cruised beneath the red balloon arches that extended the length of Romance's Main Street. She closed her eyes and rested in the knowledge that this was the best Valentine's Day she'd ever had. Gone was the pain of her father's abandonment and her mother's death. And thanks to Avery, the troubles of her grandmother's house had been resolved when he formally presented her with the deed to the property and full partnership in Tree House Real Estate earlier that morning.

She opened her eyes and smiled at the memory of the night, then looked dreamily out of the window into the darkness and watched the crowded street and Valentine revelers walking from party to party. "That was by far the best Valentine's Day I ever had," she mused aloud.

"It's not over yet."

"Really? What else do you have in mind?" She yawned a second time.

"Tired?" Avery asked.

"Yes, but in a good way. I had so much fun today. The parade this morning, the picnics this afternoon, and finally the balls this evening. I don't think I've ever laughed, talked, or danced so much in one night. I still can't believe that we visited all ten of the balls."

"It was my duty as the Grand Marshall. I'm just happy you were with me. I can't imagine doing all that alone."

"My favorite ball was definitely the Heart's Ball. Being there to witness Sebastian's marriage proposal to Aunt Cynthia was definitely the highlight."

Avery smiled in the darkness of the car. "Yes, it was," he agreed. "I also think we did a pretty good job with the matchups. A few of the couples seemed to really hit it off."

"Yes, they did," she said as she ran her hand over the soft leather seats of the car. "I could seriously get used to this."

"My intentions exactly," he said.

"But isn't this a bit extravagant? I mean with the business loss and all."

"Believe me. I'm fine."

Venus looked at him skeptically. "Exactly how much did you lose in the financial deal a few years ago that ruined you?"

"Actually, it was a poker game, and I lost my shirt."

"Oh, Avery, I'm so sorry. But don't worry. I have a great idea about my new show. I already spoke with Carter, and he's excited. We're gonna film right here in Romance, in my grandmother's house."

"You, in Romance, permanently?"

"Yep, that's Valentine's Day and every day. As a matter of fact, I already have some great ideas about my next romantic Valentine's Day special. So with the show's draw, you'll have guests at the Palmer House Inn all year round. And you'll be back on you feet in no time."

"About that"—he cleared his throat and chuckled—"when I said I lost my shirt, it wasn't a euphemism. I mean it literally. The bet was my shirt, and I lost it."

"So you're not broke?"

"No, far from it."

"Why am I not surprised?" she said, shaking her head and snuggling closer. "Thank you," she added.

"For what?"

"For making this Valentine's Day the best I've ever had. Valentine's was always a day of heartache for me, but thanks to you, it won't be anymore."

"As I said, it's not over yet."

"I don't think I could go to another ball this evening."

"Just one more," Avery insisted.

Venus yawned and nodded as she closed her eyes again. "Okay, but just one more, then back home."

"I promise." Avery smiled as the limo drove out of town, leaving the revelers to continue the Romance tradition.

"Did I tell you that you look spectacular this evening?" Avery said.

"Yes, several times. Did I tell you that you look dashing this evening?"

"Yes."

"By the way, where exactly are we going? The balls are usually all within easy walking distance of each other."

"Be patient. You'll see."

Venus looked out the dark, tinted windows and noticed that they were approaching the Palmer House Inn. "We're at the Inn?"

"Yes."

"I thought we had one more ball to attend?"

"We do."

"Where is it? In the tree house?" she asked jokingly.

"Yes, as a matter of fact, it is."

The limo pulled to a stop in front the Inn, and Avery opened the door. "Shall we?" he asked, extending his elbow to her.

Venus slid her arm into the bend of his elbow, and together they walked to the top of the porch steps. He opened the front door, and she dropped her purse and wrap on the foyer table.

"For you," Avery said, giving her several dozen long-stem red roses and a heart-shaped box of chocolates.

"Thank you. They're absolutely beautiful."

He continued to the kitchen. She followed, carrying the flowers and candy. "What exactly are you up to?" she asked as he opened the pantry door and went back out into the night.

Venus stopped at the back door and looked in wonder at the tiny tea candles lighting the path to the tree house. "It's beautiful! When did you do all this?"

"Come on," he said, waiting for her.

Venus hurried to his side, and they walked hand in hand to the tree house. They climbed up the tree house ladder in the darkness. Avery pressed a nearby switch, and tiny miniature lights came on, illuminating the tree house. It was a fairy tale come true.

Venus gasped when she caught sight of chilled champagne and two glasses sitting on a small, white wrought iron table flanked by two chairs. "This is too much."

"It's only the beginning," Avery said, and he pulled a chair out for her to sit down.

"I love it," she said, looking around, then up into the tree house canopy, which was decorated with colorful lanterns and red and white balloons.

"I love you," he said, bending down on a knee.

Venus turned to him and placed her hand on his cheek. "I love you."

"Venus, years ago you asked me a question that I never answered. I'd like to ask you that same question now. Will you marry me?"

"Yes, yes, yes," she said. She wrapped her arms around him and showered him with kisses, as she exclaimed yes a dozen more times.

Moments later they sipped champagne and gazed out into the night. "This is the most beautiful proposal I've every seen." She picked up her box of candy and opened the lid.

"It's not over yet."

She gasped upon finding the box filled with Mike and Ike candies and a small ring box. "Oh, Avery." She opened the small velvet box and beheld a perfect square diamond set in a platinum ring. "It's beautiful."

He placed the ring on her finger. They kissed beneath the stars, beneath the lights in the tree house, where it had all begun and was sure to continue for many Valentine's Days to follow.